HIGH TREASON

High Treason

A novel
by

ALBERTO AMBARD
and
AMELIA MONDRAGÓN

Adelaide Books
New York / Lisbon
2020

HIGH TREASON
A novel
By Alberto Ambard and Amelia Mondragón

Copyright © by Alberto Ambard and Amelia Mondragón
Cover design © 2020 Adelaide Books

Published by Adelaide Books, New York / Lisbon
adelaidebooks.org

Editor-in-Chief
Stevan V. Nikolic

For any information, please address Adelaide Books
at info@adelaidebooks.org

or write to:

Adelaide Books
244 Fifth Ave. Suite D27
New York, NY, 10001

ISBN: 978-1-951214-07-4

Printed in the United States of America

To the young generations of Venezuelans.
To Leo and Victor with all the love in the world.

Contents

High Treason

I do not love my country.
Its abstract glory is beyond my grasp
But (although it may sound bad)
I would give my life for ten of its places
And for some of its people,
Its ports, woods, deserts, fortresses,
A city of ruins, grey and monstrous,
Several figures in its history
Its mountains,
And three or four rivers

José Emilio Pacheco.
From "Don't Ask Me How Time Goes By" [1]
1964-1968.

---

[1] Translated from the original version in *"No me preguntes cómo pasa el tiempo"*

Preface
(2020)

High Treason was born in 2008 as a reaction against what was developing in Venezuela back then. As Venezuelans living abroad, we felt as voiceless witnesses of the profound transformation that our country was experiencing at all levels. The novel was a way to express ourselves and be part of a process that belonged to us, even though we no longer lived in Venezuela.

Once the novel was completed in 2012, we wrote a preface to offer our non-Venezuelan readers a historical context. We limit ourselves to the facts, avoiding much reflection, making an effort to remain objective. In a tone even academic, we concluded that "the consequences of chavismo could not be entirely measured." Yet, we thought the country would recover from the dictatorship.

Even today in 2019, we can't entirely measure the consequences of chavismo, but we believe that if Venezuela ever recovers, it would be in a very remote future. Not even the most ingenious of the writers who experimented with magical realism could have imagined the damage caused by the 21th Century Socialist Plan created by Hugo Chávez and continued by his successor. The vulgar levels of corruption—even considering Venezuelan corruption standards; the progressive collapse of the infrastructure and natural resources, the total annihilation of democratic institutions, the rise of extreme violence, the systematic polarization of society, and the machination between chavismo and the Cuban government to deplete the country's riches are now part of an unquestionable argument against a failed regime.

Who could have imagined that inside the South American Pearl that was Venezuela, we were going to see children eating from garbage, and dying in hospitals due to lack of basic medical supplies? The humanitarian crisis that is occurring in Venezuela is something no Venezuelan imagined back in 2012.

High Treason is a historical novel because it registers historical events that occurred in Venezuela from 1998, during the beginning of chavismo, until 2008, with Hugo Chávez in full power. It is also historical because it registers the innocence of Venezuelans back in 2012—including us, as writers.

Preface

Until the beginning of the '80s, Venezuelans experienced life as one long celebration where the only controversy was whether Caracas or Magallanes would win the baseball league.

However, in 1981, the illusory and paternalistic effect of the oil dollars began to fade away. As oil prices dropped, administrative corruption surfaced as well as marked social economic contrast, which had been brewing since the first government of Carlos Andrés Pérez (1974-1979).

In 1989, Venezuelan people showed their contempt for the rise in the cost of public transport in the "Caracazo," perhaps the most violent protest ever in Venezuelan history, which resulted in three thousand deaths and the looting of dozens of small businesses. Three years later, two successive coup attempts marked the end of Venezuela's political stability that up to that point had been the envy of other countries in the region.

However, even when the distance between social classes became more and more pronounced, there was no imaginary collective demanding the total rejection and consequent annihilation of the country's powerful elite.

Without exception, the democratic governments that came to power after the fall of dictator Marcos Pérez Jiménez in 1958 were characterized by their extraordinary ability to incorporate leaders from all echelons of society into their ranks. It was this efficiency which enabled the heterogeneous governing groups to mediate between the interests of the big capitalists, their own ambitions of power, and the interests of the more vulnerable of Venezuela's citizens, who lived off promises to eradicate hardship which never came to fruition.

In this way, the patrimonial structure of the governments, although threatened by the dashed hopes of the Venezuelan people, was able to keep the country united even throughout the '90s. *Somehow, the celebration continued.*

In 1998, Hugo Chávez—leader of the first coup of 1992— suddenly emerged as a political figure and was elected president after defeating both of Venezuela's main political parties: *Acción Democrática* and COPEI. Such a triumph was due in large measure to his radical and belligerent speech, which spoke of the need to emancipate the masses from their exploiters. This soon triggered a profound and violently irrational polarization within Venezuelan society.

Those who shared the ideology of Chávez raised their voices to make demands while blaming their hardships on all those who remained skeptical of the President's revolutionary political ideology. The skeptics in turn could foresee the isolation that awaited them if they did not publicly side with the Chavistas, even at the expense of their deepest convictions.

Many events took place in this climate of ideological tension but, without doubt, the first of its kind was the Vargas tragedy, which occurred at the same time as the constitutional referendum that eroded the country's democratic foundation. This incident was the decisive factor in leading those who had voted for Chávez into a deep tunnel of disappointment.

In December 1999, about fifty thousand people died following mudslides in the coastal mountains of La Guaira, in the state of Vargas. Although warnings had been issued since December 10, instead of evacuating the danger zone, Chávez's government used the media to exhort citizens to vote in the referendum that was set for December 15, just as the tragedy occurred.

On this rainy December day, ignoring the deaths caused by the mudslides and in spite of a meager 45% turnout, Chávez won the right to reconstruct what he insisted on calling "the dying Venezuelan constitution." The new law soon dissolved congress and transferred to the president the powers and instruments necessary to develop his 21st century revolutionary socialist plan.

After just a year in government, Chávez began to face harsh criticism from the civil opposition, and this grew in strength over the following two years. Amid these growing tensions, Venezuelans turned out en masse to demonstrate in public against the government. Social polarization became much more pronounced and provoked acts of violence.

The first of these was the Puente Llaguno tragedy. On April 11 2002, several of those opposed to the regime died during a demonstration, when Chávez supporters opened fire on the protesters. The next day there followed a failed coup against Chávez. After yielding to public pressure to step down, Chávez returned to the presidency three days later thanks to the support of a considerable proportion of the Venezuelan populace and the failed vision of his political opponents.

With Chávez in power again, tensions continued to mount until they exploded in the Altamira square tragedy. At the end of 2002, and after several weeks of an opposition group gathering in the same square to demonstrate peacefully, Joao De Gouveia, a follower of Chávez, opened fire on the demonstrators, killing three people. *The celebration had surely ended in Venezuela.*

Since 2003, due to the extreme increase in oil prices, history has repeated itself and the illusion of oil money has helped Chávez to regain his popularity, consolidate power, and radicalize his socialist policies even more, provoking violent demonstrations that have led to a number of tragedies over the years, and which continue into the present.

Supporters of Chávez claim that his government is fairer than those that have gone before because he serves those who were neglected by previous administrations, and that Chávez has sought to tackle poverty, illiteracy, and the inequities of the healthcare system.

On the other hand, his opponents argue that poverty continues to increase while Chávez uses the nation's assets to develop his political agenda overseas and to strengthen his position within the country through a new social class, the "Chavistas." In the same way that many people became rich by working the ruling parties in previous decades, those who now support Chávez accrue more wealth and power with each day of his tenure.

With the new bureaucracy, Chávez has created a centralist system that has eroded individual initiative and has acquired privately held assets, despite the Venezuelans rejecting this approach in a referendum called by Chávez himself on December 2, 2007.

In this atmosphere, those who oppose him perceive not only their own personal fragility in the new regime, but also the violent and anti-constitutional nature of his government administration, in which the opposition continuously accuses Chávez of participating in terrorist activity and inability to curb the never-ending crime which plagues the country. Caracas, a city with 7 million inhabitants, is one of the most violent cities in the world today.

The quality of life has fallen to such a degree that Venezuela—a country that until 1982 had traditionally welcome immigration—has lost at least 1.5 million Venezuelans, mostly professionals who have now settled in the USA and Europe since Chávez took power. To date, no information is available on the number of illegal emigrants, so this figure could be higher.

The consequences of the so-called Chávez revolution cannot be completely measured yet. However, there is no doubt that this regime has changed Venezuela dramatically, not only politically and economically, but also psychologically. Venezuela is now a deeply divided nation, and the psychological fault lines are so enormous they threaten the sense of nationhood that has existed in the country since Independence.

While one sector of society keeps hoping for and imagining a better future, others express resignation and bitterness in the face of an onslaught of violence and intolerance.

The novel begins during the festive climate of 1998 and ends in 2007. Although the characters are fictitious, almost all the situations they are involved in belong to Venezuela's recent history, to its drastic changes and the emotions borne from these changes.

Introduction
(2007)

Newsflash! A bomb exploded this morning at the headquarters of Banco del Tesoro in Porlamar where President Chávez was attending the bank's opening ceremony. Several people were injured, including a camera operator from the national Venezuelan television channel who was adjusting the spotlights close to where the bomb went off.

The person responsible for the attack was shot dead after police located him in Bella Vista. The man in question, 38-year old Maikel Salgado, worked for the government on Margarita Island. It's believed that Salgado acted alone using a defective homemade bomb that failed to fully detonate. Officials and agents who worked with Salgado have confirmed that he had experience with explosives.

Through television and radio, the first report of the incident reached homes around the country. It also reached market places and supermarkets, cafes and bars, stores and stands, offices, factories, beaches, mountains, and plains. The news even travelled to the jungle, and after being edited and translated, it was transmitted to homes in other countries. These reports sent out by satellite lacked, however, the sense of urgency that could be heard in the voice of the Caracas newscaster, who seemed to know how extremely powerful the event made him sound as he read out the news with a mixture of arrogance andmistrust.

His words took all of Venezuela by surprise, from Caracas to La Guajira in the west, to Santa Elena de Uairen in the south and eastwards to Curiapo. However, the newscaster had no idea of the effects of the attack or whether any of the nation's twenty- eight million inhabitants felt anger or fear, sadness or joy. You never know how people are going to react until they react, he thought.

It was four in the morning at the police headquarters in Porlamar, Margarita Island. A police officer was looking for the latest baseball results when he decided to switch on the radio. He was alone at that moment, with the newspaper spread out on the lone rickety desk in the room. Hearing a local folk song playing on the dilapidated radio, he started humming along, drumming the dirty nails of his left hand on the porous wood.

Two electric bulbs dangling more than a foot from the ceiling on peeled wires cast a welcome light on the police officer, who sat with his ample belly protruding from his unbuttoned trousers as he leafed through the newspaper in search of the boxing news.

Hanging high on the wall behind him, a picture of the national hero Simón Bolívar, prisoner of old writings and in something of a trance, contemplated the almost empty room and its yellow walls. However, Bolívar could not smell the odor of rancid butter that emanated from these walls, nor could he see, due to the slight angle of his head, the passage where three cells joined.

The three small cells with rusty bars and no more ventilation than the little they shared with the passage were almost entirely cast in shadow. Like the other two, the darkest compartment farthest away from the police officer was covered in a layer of grime consisting of urine, vomit, and dried blood. Amid this pile of filth, that had been accumulating since time began, lay Rodrigo, more disgusted with himself than with what lay around him.

The police officer's radio began to blare out the news of the day. It was one of those radios that looked like an unbreakable toy. Out of the yellow box rose an antenna, bent in several places by wear and tear. Rodrigo tried to listen to the broadcast but due to the numbness of his brain, the pitiful sound quality of the radio, and the distance that separated him from the guard, he could hardly hear a thing. However, when he made out Maikel's name, a shudder ran through his body and he began to vomit, leaving on the pestilent floor a fresh record of his stay in the cell.

When the nausea had passed, he sat with his legs bent, leaning his elbows on them to support his head with both hands. The radio repeated the news like a scratched record and Rodrigo was finally able to catch what they were saying about Maikel and Chávez.

Inert and trembling, he tensed his face muscles before finally giving way to a broken, dry sob.

When he was able to compose himself, he heard the buzzing of a fly and looked at the ground, searching for it in the puddle of fresh vomit. The fragile rays of light coming into the cell from the weak bulb in the passage helped him to find it, fluorescent green and scrutinizing the feast that lay before it. Restless and greedy, it began to fly around the room, trying to land on Rodrigo's head and chest. That was when he realized that at some point during the previous night he had been sick down the front of his t-shirt. Another more prolonged fit of inconsolable crying immediatelyfollowed.

The fly ended up making do with the vomit on the floor and did not bother him again. Trying to ride out the fresh wave of nausea, Rodrigo stayed still, letting the events that had led him to this Porlamar cell swirl around his head like a swarm of vomit-hungry green flies.

PART ONE.
THE CELEBRATION
(1988 – 1997)

CHAPTER 1

My name is Rodrigo Fernandez and I'm a Spanish language and literature teacher. My friends and neighbors usually call me affectionately but mistakenly "Gallego," due to my Spanish descent, thinking everything that comes out of Spain must come from Galicia.

My father Emiliano was born in Asturias, where my mother also grew up, although she and her family are from Navarre. They met in Caracas and got married when he was just a bricklayer, and she a seamstress in a children's clothing factory. He soon became a master builder and she left the factory, but she continued to sew. Now, she works from home, making dresses for the elegant and not-so-elegant ladies in the east of Caracas. I also have a younger sister, Raquel.

At the time I'm telling you about, my adolescence, we lived in an apartment which looked out over Francisco de Miranda avenue, in a neighborhood called Bello Campo, which although it belongs to the wealthier east, is an area mainly inhabited by the middle class, a species now extinct in Venezuela.

Before that, we lived in La Candelaria, a neighborhood notable for nothing apart from the concentration of Spanish and Portuguese immigrants there. The people are versatile, noisy, and unpredictable. Our family upped and left for the east when a professional motorcycle racer who lived in our neighborhood decided to practice in our block and began to serenade us with revving engines and exhaust fumes every ten minutes in the early hours of the morning.

Papa would say that he wanted to flee to the middle of nowhere, giving the impression that he would have been happy if he could have moved to the easternmost edge of the city. Here amid the deep vegetation of the coastal mountain range he would still be able to enjoy the simplicity of the small villages, which at that time bordered on Caracas without wanting to belong to the city. Nevertheless, due to his work and above all the job of my mother, who did not drive and so could not get to her customers' houses, we had to make do with Bello Campo.

My sister and I were brought up within the strictest Iberian conventions: all privileges were for me, the prince, and all the household chores (cooking, cleaning, washing, and ironing) for my poor sister, whose only fault was having been born a girl. As if that was not bad enough, from the time of her eighteenth birthday, Raquel was a victim of my mother's sage advice about getting married, something a woman should do while young and preferably to a Spaniard with whom she could bear happy, healthy children. "But how can I do that?" my sister would wonder, when our father had converted our apartment into an inaccessible fortress which deterred those brave enough to imagine my old man as father-in-law.

I often felt sorry for my sister, for her well-kept virginity and the future that my mother had mapped out for her. However, my pity was not of a militant kind, like Don Quixote's, because I knew from a very early age that despite her tenderness, my mother was a like a windmill, a force to be reckoned with and I did not feel like playing the hero in a story where the only possible outcome was defeat.

I remember that Thursday when I mentioned the matter to Manuel and Alfredo. We were at the beach having a beer, and I decided to use the word "dichotomy" instead of "contradiction" to explain to them my parents' behavior.

"Dichotomy? What the hell is that? Did you hear, Manuel? A typical word the Gallego pulls out of his sleeve to sound intelligent, ha ha ha!"

With his teasing, Alfredo could conceal the kind intentions that always motivated him when he was faced with my worries.

"Just because I like reading, unlike others I could mention. Sorry, but for a second there I forgot that you wouldn't know the meaning of the word. Let me explain: reading is basically what you do with porn, except I look at thewords"

"What, Rodrigo? Do the words turn you on?"

Alfredo and I laughed at Manuel, who for a few seconds shot me an astonished look as if he was taking me seriously.

That is how it always was. We enjoyed going to the beach, spending hours talking until the afternoon chill took us by surprise, encouraging us to head back to Caracas.

After we had graduated from high school and were waiting to start university, we had a simple routine based on never-ending drinking and the same old jokes, which, though they were mostly harmless, could sometimes be darkly humorous and quite caustic. Anyone who saw us engrossed in this activity would think that we hated each other, when really we were just three supposedly virile young guys, trying to express the immense fondness that kept us together.

We first met at the Don Bosco School in Altamira. Although in those days, public education was not bad in Caracas, my parents had agreed to send me to a Catholic school so that with one lucky shot, Mom could fulfill her Christian duty to educate her son as God required and at the same get a free rein from my father to entertain one of his favorite beliefs: it is not what you know in Venezuela, but who you know that counts.

My father was so satisfied with this agreement that he forgot the ten-hour days he spent on building sites, and my mother forgot the few back-breaking hours she spent sewing. For them the sacrifice was worthwhile. They did not mind working longer hours because they believed that life should be hard—that was what life was for. They had always lived in Venezuela with this belief, differentiating themselves from most native Venezuelans, who treated life like a perpetual party.

My father enjoyed giving me long lectures on what he viewed as the pathological weaknesses of these people. He proclaimed for example that our indigenous people had never had to work like Europeans. He imagined them before the conquest, playing with themselves in the jungle, with mangos, which they would eat later, falling on their heads.

My father's argument was usually extensive and occasionally metaphysical, digging deep into the country's history, and usually concluded with the assertion that the last straw was Venezuela's new oil. Wealth had weakened the Venezuelan character, my father argued, as nothing good comes from an easy life. Without the immigrants from Spain, Italy, and Portugal who began arriving at La Guaira port at the beginning of the fifties, Venezuela would have been a jungle full of onanists of no great consequence.

The Thursday of the aforementioned conversation about dichotomy, while I was settling into bed with a belly full of beer, Papa burst into my room. I saw in his eyes that he was furious about my little alcohol-fuelled vacation to the beach, and without hesitation, he told me he was not putting up with layabouts in his house. I should get a job until university classes began.

He tried to force me into selling insurance for a friend of his who was an agent, but being a son of my country like none other, I had a better idea. During his exhausting litany and shower of saliva, I thought I would get myself a job more suited to a true Venezuelan.

CHAPTER 2

July 20, 1988

Three religions coexist in Venezuela: Catholicism, baseball, and beer. The latter worships one god alone, like the Catholic religion, or should I say one goddess, La Polar, which dominates 95% of the unsophisticated Venezuelan market. However, although its followers claim that Polar is the only real beer, it's a plural concept known by many names: "the Little Pot," "Blondie," and "the Bear" among others.

The night that my father and I discussed my work situation, I called Alfredo to tell him about our discussion, and ask for his advice. He recommended that I contact his cousin, a successful PR agent who employed young lads like me who had just graduated from school, and who were eager to find easy, well-paid work.

Alfredo's cousin's ambitious campaign strove to change the beer culture of the Venezuelans drastically, in its effort to overthrow the dominance of Polar forever. As part of this strategy, dozens of youngsters somewhat lacking in the sense department were sent to the restaurants and bars of Caracas with some cash. Their mission was to give the proprietor five hundred bolivars each time they offered their customers the beer in the campaign. Whenever for some reason the proprietors ignored their instructions, our graduates would give them a lecture and, as an afterthought, a ballpoint pen as a souvenir of the money they could haveearned.

Therefore, at the age of 18, my first job consisted of going to bars with the mission of spying on proprietors, drinking a few free Polars, giving a sermon or two, and doling out money.

Unfortunately, the great strategy hatched by Giovanni, Alfredo's aforementioned cousin, went unnoticed. At that time, the people of Caracas were more worried about the growing crime wave. Each weekend, an average of twenty people lost their lives. The causes were different and at times absurd. How can you kill somebody to steal their shoes for example? That is how it was. Insecurity seemed to have reached its peak, and from there things could only get better.

We were wrong however. Only a few weeks ago, my mother was reminiscing about "those glorious days" as she called them, sighing with immense nostalgia, of finding yourself shoeless and bruised in the middle of Francisco Solano avenue, because after Chávez became president, the weekly number of deaths began to multiply in a remarkable way.

With the body count growing daily, some wary citizens began to wonder if we were secretly or unconsciously competing with the Iraq war. If so, the statistics showed that we had nothing to fear—we were way out in front. Caracas had the second highest instance of death from violence in the world; double that of Baghdad, a city in a state of war.[2]

Several days after the argument with Papa, and several Polars later, I was walking through the center of Caracas, happily thinking about how I had already been in my nice new spy job

---

[2] According to a study performed by the 'Consejo Ciudadano para la Seguridad Pública', Mexico, 2008

for a week when a short guy with a scarred face approached me and said:

"Don't stop, you rich piece of shit, just carry on walking. When I say so, give me your money. You do anything, motherfucker, I'm going to kill you."

Out of the corner of my eye, I noticed that the thug was hiding his hands in his nylon jacket. Thinking that he was taking out a knife, I decided to push him and run for it.

"He has a knife! He has a knife!" I yelled at the top of my voice. As I was running, I knew, just as gazelles do, that you don't need eyes to see you're defeated, because without looking, I knew he was going to catch me.

The only thing I remember is the coldness that penetrated the back of my ribs, and the immense pain that began to paralyze me while I tried not to fall over. That day I decided that my father was talking sense, and that hard work was my destiny. The last few strides of the chase became my first steps to reality.

CHAPTER 3

July 21, 1988

I woke up in an extremely clean and well-lit single room of a private medical center, and saw my mother sitting on one of the two chairs for visitors by the large window. On the small table between the two chairs was a vase of white lilies. For an instant, I focused on them, trying to decide whether they were real or plastic, but my vision was blurred. I tried to move but the pain in my ribs paralyzed me. Since I was feeling cold, the first sound that came out of my mouth was a mumbled request for a blanket.

"Darling, what a scare you gave us! How are you feeling, honey?" asked my mother closing her *Hola!* magazine, to which she had always been addicted. She leaned over to attend to me.

I repeated that I was cold but as she still did not seem to understand, I decided to change the message. Gathering all the energy in my belly, I managed to emit a kind of gurgle that sounded something like "water."

"Rodrigo, how can you ask for water when you haven't eaten for twenty-four hours?! Look at you; you're like a scarecrow, my poor dear! Here's some fruit salad I made for you last night when I couldn't sleep. I also made you some squid with onions that you're having as soon as you come home... Let's see, let's give our little boy a bit of pineapple and orange so that he gets well and strong again!"

I opened my mouth with the sole purpose of rejecting her offer and a spoonful of chopped fruit was rammed into my mouth, making me shiver. Resigned to my mother's stubborn insistence, I had no choice but to endure the torture.

"You were lucky, kid," a doctor who had just entered the room announced in an incredibly powerful voice. "The stab only fractured a rib. We're going to keep you in for observation for a couple of days. Then if everything is ok, you can go home on Friday."

When I saw him, I forgot all my suffering, as the doctor was so amazingly short that he had to look up to see my mother, who was small herself and walked with a stoop due to the sewing. He checked my wound, and since the hospital bed was higher than usual, he looked like a greyhound busily sniffing out a bone it had lost the night before.

Removing his face from my shoulder, he shot over to the door at the speed of light, which astonished me as much as his size and similarly distracted me from my pain. He seemed to me a diminutive Hermes, the Greek god with winged feet.

Before leaving, he stopped dead and, without noticing the touching devotion with which my mother attended to me, said to her in a brusque voice that resonated like heavenly thunder:

"Ma'am, please don't hassle the boy too much while he's still feeling the effects of the anesthesia. Give him a few sips of water."

That same afternoon, my room was transformed into something like a Spanish tavern. I was on display like a leg of Serrano ham at the bar, bruised and being ripped open again, this time psychologically although no less deeply, as my school friends who came to see me joked and teased me about how I looked. Taking advantage of the party atmosphere, the nurses, who were almost all young, began to come in at random intervals on some pretext or other: a juice, the thermometer, the drip, urine… humiliated, I listened to my friends' jokes, applauded by their youthful paramedical audience.

"What happened, Rodrigo? Did you stick your foot in your helmet?"

It was Vicente. He was talking about that embarrassing episode in my short baseball career when I was running to second base and my helmet fell off and got wedged on my foot, forcing me to dive ridiculously to the ground.

I bore the sarcasm like a hero, as I did the throbbing from my wound, which was getting stronger and stronger, as if the anxiety that had gone in with the knife was still inside, trapped by the stitches. At night, the pain was unbearable, so the doctor prescribed me intravenous morphine, which I could self-inject by pressing a trigger.

The nurse on shift, much larger than the ones on day duty and with the face of a sergeant, showed me how to use the lever that dispensed the painkiller.

"When you feel pain, press here, and if you need anything, press this other button and I'll come right away," she said, pointing to the controls.

Ironically, I concluded that in the field of medical services, you could get anything you wanted by pulling a trigger, whether you had an automatic prefilled syringe full of drugs in your hand like in my case, or a pistol, like when we decided to spend Easter Week at the beach near Cata Bay, where my father had rented a house.

My sister, around six at the time, used to suffer quite severe asthma attacks. The night before the trip, she had slept badly, but my father was not in the least bit worried, being convinced that sea air cures everything. Although it was quite late when we got to the beach, Raquel and I went for a swim and chased each around on the sand for ages.

Perhaps because of the excitement and God knows what else, my sister had a strong asthma attack. At midnight, Papa got us all in the car and in ten minutes, we were at the local first aid clinic, run by the state. It was nothing more than a small gloomy shed with a waiting room furnished with old chairs. Not a soul was around.

Holding Raquel in his arms, my father begged the male nurse to help each time he came to tell us that the doctor was coming. Papa's pleas and the rasping breath of my sister mingled with thuds of domino pieces and roars of laughter coming from the back of the hut.

After half an hour, Raquel began to turn purple and my father, after giving her to my mother, got up very slowly, went out of the clinic toward the car, and came back in even more slowly, if that were possible, with hardly a glance at us. The passageway, which led to the back of the hut almost swallowed him up. After barely a minute, there was a deep silence. We heard his voice, which was so hoarse we barely recognized it.

"If the kid dies, then you die too, you son of a bitch"

At that moment, the doctor appeared in the waiting room followed by my father, who was pointing a gun at him, his eyes looking bloodshot. The imposing stature of the doctor contrasted with his young face, fearful and dim-witted.

Until then, I did not even know that my father owned a gun. I've never seen it since, despite inventing excuses to stay at home alone and go through the cupboards. And I've never seen that look on my father's face, darkened by hatred and despair, since that day.

CHAPTER 4

My convalescence days were very quiet. Alfredo, Manuel and I kept ourselves amused by hanging out at Manuel's house or playing dominoes. We knew that once classes started at university, our lives would change forever, and even though we looked ahead thinking that the future would bring good times, we were not in a rush to be separated. Even if we could carry on meeting each other, the careers that we had chosen would involve different rules and ambitions. So, along with a sense of worry about this new world that we would be inhabiting in a few weeks' time, there was also a feeling of deep nostalgia for the old world we were leaving behind.

We preferred meeting at Manuel's house because he had a pool, tennis court, and games room where the previous owners had installed a great billiard table, two dartboards, and a multi-functional table with roulette to boot. Dazzled by the luxury, Alfredo and I, and sometimes even Manuel, who couldn't but have noticed our unceasing awe at the house's fixtures and fittings, all tried to make light of the great fortune of the Sánchez family, who seemed to have amassed immense wealth in the last few years.

"Shit, Rodrigo, I can't sleep," joked Manuel only a few weeks after moving to his new house. "I'm used to hearing shots, car brakes, and sirens and now all I can hear is the frogs croaking." And he was laughing because the croaking of the frogs gave him the chance to show us his incredible repertoire of onomatopoeic words, which made us think that instead of sleeping, Manuel would happily spend the whole night learning to imitate grasshoppers, birds, toads, and cats in heat, just to impress us.

Before moving to the mansion in upscale Las Lomas de Prados del Este, Manuel Sánchez lived with his parents in Mariipérez, a quite centrally located neighborhood that had been built up in the seventies. The Sánchez family apartment was comfortable, although rather basic, and was in keeping with every other building that went up in Caracas during that decade.

The families that lived there were also similar. They were mostly young professionals with small children and great aspirations, especially where climbing the social ladder was concerned. Theirs had been the first Venezuelan generation that had benefitted from the expansion of the universities, and now they worked for national and international corporations, for the government, or in one of the many industries that, in those days, were turning Caracas into a real metropolis. Too happy due to the oil bonanza, this burgeoning class did not realize that they were dependent on jobs, fixed salaries, bonds and bonuses that could all suddenly disappear if the country went into economic decline.

Alternatively, perhaps some, like Mr. and Mrs. Sánchez, felt that everything comes to an end. Manuel's mother was a lawyer and his father was an accountant at Jeep Venezuela. When they married, he was a car salesman, something he was probably born to do, as he was a genius at convincing people to buy things they did not need. However, after a few years Mrs.

Sánchez thought her husband should build himself a more solid career, and so he started studying at night to leave his vocation behind.

In 1984, when Jaime Lusinchi became president, Mrs. Sánchez, who in those days worked for herself as a notary in a tiny office on Baralt avenue, landed an important job with the county of Baruta. Four years later, Mr. and Mrs. Sánchez moved to the mansion in Lomas de Prados del Este. In addition to extraordinary luxuries, they also had a chauffeur and a security guard, two new cars, three servants, and made many trips abroad.

Their good fortune disappeared when money was embezzled from Jeep and all heads turned toward one of the bosses and Manuel's father. Forced to retire, Mr. Sánchez was never able to get a decent job again, and gradually and discreetly began to fall to pieces, as he was an introverted man, or at least, as Manuel would tell us, he had become that way over the years.

I always thought that the strange nature of Mr. Sánchez had a lot to do with his wife. He always looked at her as if he was seeing her for the first time, although not in a pleasant way, but rather with frightened and sometimes terrified eyes, like someone lost in the forest who suddenly sees a wolf. Thinking back now, I'm not sure whether the real corrupt one was Mr. Sánchez, quiet and discreet, or his wife, a plump woman who pretended to be sophisticated, but who would gossip like a fishwife all the time, only taking a breath to crush the ice in her Cuba Libre with her teeth. One of those afternoons as we were sunbathing at the swimming pool, Mrs. Sánchez shouted to us:

"Manuel, Rodrigo, Alfrredo, come over here a second and help me with this!" "Jesus, my mom is a pain in the ass. Turn a blind eye and maybe she'll shut up."

"Manuel! Boys!" Her bothersome chattering got the better of us. "We're coming!" cried Alfredo.

When we reached the garage, we saw a huge truck filled to the brim with boxes of anisette, sugar cane liquor, and cheap rum. There must have been at least three hundred boxes. The security guard and the chauffeur were already busy unloading them.

"But Mom, are you crazy? Rodrigo's still screwed up with his injury and there are like a million boxes of liquor here. Why the hell did you buy this junk?"

"First of all, show your mother some respect," said Miriam Sánchez with a stern face. "Second, these boxes are from the mayor's office. We're organizing the rally of the century. I don't know what will happen in the rest of Caracas, but I'm telling you that in Baruta the vote will go to *Acción Democrática* no matter what! Carlos Andrés Pérez for the people! AD will make our day!"

The debate went on. Meanwhile I had to laugh at the ignorance of Miriam Sánchez. The *Acción Democrática* had no chance! When it came to corruption, Lusinchi could only be outdone by the head of their clan, Carlos Andrés Pérez, who Venezuelans had already seen in power filling his pockets with large sums of money. Surely, they would not re-elect the *Acción Democrática's* most notorious thief. However, in December of 1989, history smiled down once more on populism and rum.

CHAPTER 5

July 28, 1988

It was one of those many nights that I slept over at Manuel's house. We used to switch off the light and chat for a while. Sometimes we got deep into "heavy" conversations and would talk into the early hours without sleeping a wink.

More than just chitchat, the heavy conversations were a kind of ritual for us, as we would cautiously circle around topics before finally homing in on the one that preoccupied us most, and that usually ended up provoking uncomfortable memories and confessions that over the years cemented our friendship. Quite often, these conversations involved the three of us, but that evening Alfredo had gone to the movies with his girlfriend, Maria Fernanda.

Although Manuel's bark was frequent and tough, he did not bite. On the contrary, he was the most gentle and sentimental of the three of us. With the transparency that I had often envied, and not without making a joke of it first, he expressed his want of a vocation and his ineptitude to me:

"I don't have a frigging clue what to do, Gallego. The problem is I just don't know what I wanna do. Look at you, dude. You pretty much got lucky with your literature thing. And Alfredo…, well he's a genius. He'll graduate and become a brain surgeon for NASA… But me, pana[3], to tell the truth, I don't give a shit. This lawyer disguise is just like, something to do…"

Manuel was about to start a law degree at Universidad Santa María, a private university that required little for candidates to be accepted. He had enrolled without thinking it through, encouraged by the idea that the professors there did not bore their students with philosophical stuff: law was law; you just had to memorize it parrot-fashion and learn a couple of clever tricks to apply it.

At least that was what Manuel's mom, who had also studied at Santa Maria, said about her teachers, or rather what she quoted them as saying, imitating them in a pompous way, as if she was talking at the Roman Forum. I can still remember her puffing up her chest and putting on tame animal eyes to pronounce the word "subtleties" in a stage whisper without the final "s", perhaps with the intention of simplifying the question of law evenmore.

Miriam was delighted that her son had chosen to follow in her footsteps, but no one had approached his father about it. Since Mr. Sánchez had no option but to retire, Manuel seldom mentioned him, and I think that father and son hardly spoke. Manuel felt sorrow for Mr. Sánchez rather than animosity, watching him deteriorate day by day.

As I was listening to Manuel in the total darkness of the room, I imagined the resignation etched on his face and my heart skipped a beat. My friend was not a dramatic type; on the contrary, his true talent consisted in his ability to laugh at his own misfortunes. At the most difficult times of my high

---

[3] 'Pana' and 'chamo' are both colloquial Venezuelan expressions, meaning 'friend' or 'buddy'.

school life, I always went to Manuel, not so that he could solve my problems, as he was never any good at that, but to hear him laugh and to understand the simple way he looked at things.

Right then, I did not even have the heart to tell him about the sense of uneasiness I was also feeling, which might have helped him to overcome his own discomfort. Deep down, and in an egoistic way, that night I was hoping he would rise from his own ashes as he had done on other occasions, spontaneously and without even noticing his own miraculous rebirth. He did not let me down, as after a few minutes I heard him say casually:

"My life is the country, pana. I'm telling you, just give me a hammock, a beer, a couple of kids messing around, my wife, and the country. Easy life."

His frankness was a ray of sunshine that invited me to tell him about myself.

Nevertheless, I did not feel able to talk to him about my vulnerabilities, not out of pride, but because I did not want to tarnish the image he had of me. Of course I liked literature, but not as much as my friends thought; I wouldn't lose my sanity if I had to leave it behind. In addition, the idea of writing did not appeal to me in the slightest, as not many could keep hunger at bay with a few poems or books. For me, studying literature was just as comfortable and necessary an option as law was for Manuel. I would be a teacher with a half-decent salary and, above all, my studies wouldn't put financial pressure on my father. What he had to pay for my high school had been enough, and for that reason I had decided to study at Universidad Central de Venezuela, completely funded by the government.

The word "vocation" did not mean any more to me then, when I had just turned eighteen. While others saw studying at university as a kind of lucky charm that would help them to satisfy monetary or personal goals or both, I had just made a short-list of the degrees I could easily study for, without denting the family budget and without going crazy learning about things that did not interest me and that I did not understand. As far as university degrees went, the verb "to choose" was a breathless bird with nowhere to fly.

However, instead of reaching out to Manuel and telling him exactly how his words revealed so much of myself to me and how similar we were, even when he was surely the brave one and I the coward, I wrapped myself up in the absolute silence and total darkness of the bedroom while he went on talking:

"Yeah pana, I just don't want to complicate things. I know I have to do something; I wouldn't be very good at being poor. But hell, pana, medicine, literature, no thanks. Keep it simple, pana. My thing is some simple business that pays enough to keep me happy, without the horrible stress that people create for themselves."

CHAPTER 6

August 8, 1988

It was one o'clock in the afternoon. I went to the Foreign Office to renew my passport as Alfredo, Manuel, and I were planning to go to a rock concert in Miami. I woke up really early and got there at 6:30 in the morning, thinking I would be first in line and could leave that bureaucratic hellhole soon after.

Unfortunately, I did not know about "the numbers". Basically, you take a number and it goes in a lottery. So no matter what time you arrived, you could be the first or the last on the list. As the first office clerk arrived at eight, the numbers did not go into the lottery until 9:30. I got number twenty-three. They told us not to even consider leaving the building: If they call you and you're not there, you miss your turn. If a stamp is missing, you miss your turn. If you don't have the right number of photos, you miss your turn. And they always tell you off, no matter what.

Years later, I discovered with surprise and shame how absurd it was to travel abroad just to see a rock concert. Where I was going, to the richest country in the world, education, and retirement meant huge expenses for the average citizen, so that for them, leaving the United States was a luxury, just like many of the habits that some of us Venezuelans had adopted at that time, thanks to the oil dollars.

"Twenty-three!" They called my number.

As I approached the window, sticky with sweat and having wasted three precious hours, I felt angry when I thought that Manuel and Alfredo had renewed their passports the common Creole way. That is, from home and under the table, fattening up the squalid salary of some foreign office official. There I was, condemned to the tyranny of the lottery tickets for supposedly being a good person.

"They're off! They all get away cleanly except for Caravaggio whose jockey had to ..."

The horse race began just as I was handing my documents to the official at counter number ten, a thin nervous man who, loyal to the national sport of our people, pressed his ear against the portable radio and ordered me to wait.

"Seventy-two seconds, coming up to the sixth furlong and "I Love You Baby" is still in front!"

With crazed eyes and with regular thumps on the counter, the man yelled at his radio. "C'mon, dammit, C'mon!"

I took advantage of the moment to glance discreetly at his horseracing magazine and prayed to all the saints in heaven that his favorite "Trojan" would win the race.

That was my lucky day.

CHAPTER 7

August 22, 1988

In the middle of August, Manuel, Alfredo and I went to Miami to see The Cure in concert, a rock group we worshipped. We had planned the trip for months thinking it would be the cherry on top of the cake of this part of our lives. Indeed it was. None of the Miami nightclubs that friends had recommended to us let us down, possibly because we were drunk, although we always had the good sense to reserve a bit of sobriety to get to the concert and back to our hotel in onepiece.

We did not even see the beaches on Miami Beach, at least not during the day, so we returned to Caracas no more sun-tanned than when we had left. We also did no sightseeing. My friends were not interested since they had been to Miami several times and had already seen the sights. Even though it was the first time I had set foot on Miami soil, I had no interest in crocodile parks or rainbow parrotfish. I only wanted to savor the delights of living without my father's early morning alarm call and my mother's soups.

I experienced pure joy, or possibly something close to nirvana as I realized that no one cared if I did not shower or if I wore the same t-shirt day after day. Or if I sat at a kiosk, or on the beach or just on some street eating hamburgers full of mayo and ketchup. For me, much more than for Alfredo or even Manuel, the trip to Miami was the craziest and most pleasurable send-off that anyone could ever possibly give to their adolescence.

Out of the three of us, Alfredo had been the most prone to living in the future. While Manuel and I did stupid things, Alfredo swayed like a sail in the wind, leaning toward common sense or brashness depending on the moment, without giving himself completely to anyone.

Even at the airport, when we were about to board the plane for Miami, a maturity alarm went off in his head and he surreptitiously went to a public telephone booth to call his girlfriend, to whom he'd promised to report every day. He was trying to stay loyal to his word, as keeping Maria Fernanda happy must have been so important to him that he patiently put up with the teasing that Manuel and I inflicted upon him.

Our sniggering started as soon as Alfredo turned his back and spoke into the receiver in a sweet, hoarse whisper, searching for impossible privacy against the wall. That sunny day, full of expectations of what we would find in Miami, neither Manuel nor I understood a thing about commitment, as neither of us had ever had a girlfriend. Calling Maria Fernanda, to whom Alfredo had only said goodbye the night before, seemed ridiculous if not totally pathetic.

Alfredo was the most methodical and focused of the three of us. He belonged to a well-known family in Caracas. His father, Roberto Piruggi, of Italian descent, had studied architecture at the Universidad Central in Caracas and had finished his studies in Italy.

On his return, he married Isabel, Alfredo's mother, a pleasant woman from a good Caracas family. She had recently graduated as a dentist and now shared her time between teaching and looking after the teeth of her very prosperous patients.

Despite his success as an architect and his exalted social position, Roberto exuded popular virtues. Among other things, he religiously attended a shady domino game every Friday, about which questions were strictly forbidden. No one knew a thing about the contestants, not even which part of town they came from. Whether it was his character, or what he had learned in his mysterious exploits, Roberto also had an extraordinary ability to come to the level of the person he was talking to, regardless of their social status, beliefs and habits. For the colorful crowd of people that he did business with daily, Roberto was the "soul brother" and the gutsiest of his group of friends.

With him lived his father, "Nonno," who had emigrated from the south of Italy with his wife Nina in the forties. When he had been widowed twenty-three years before, he had no desire to his native village of Casoria near Naples. He did not feel homesick for his native country and never talked about his youth. The only thing he said about his father, Alfredo's great-grandfather, was that he had died young in a hunting accident.

Sometimes Nonno was heard talking about his mother and younger brother, who had looked after her with great care in her old age until she no longer wanted to go on. When he talked about them, Nonno had the same cryptic tone that Roberto used when talking about his domino games.

Strapping and energetic for his seventy years, Nonno was no Joe Schmoe. He had made his fortune in Venezuela importing wine and cheese, a pioneer rather than an immigrant, who effectively was ahead of the whole Italian community in immigrating a few years later. This helped him to stand out from his fellow citizens and establish himself in the country. Some people still remembered his generosity back in those days, but Nonno was not one to sit down and be flattered or to reminisce about old times. He was satisfied with himself and his family, and submitted to the ailments of old age with more patience than he did visits from his fellow citizens.

Despite the annoyance caused by those speaking his language, the grandfather oozed with pride in his native Italian countryside, its wine, language and Neapolitan songs. He was racist in an eccentric and impulsive way, as his era was one of "supermen" who, for better or for worse, overcame with the fist, like Mussolini. He proclaimed left, right, and center that men should not only be classified according to their color and nationality, but also by their courage and intelligence. If a man was intelligent and had "balls," he had the right to any skin color he chose. He did not put women into any category, apart from those who loved gossip and intrigue. These he classed as witches and would never call them by their first names, even though he may have known them for fifty years. Instead, he addressed them as "madam," so that the witches never had an inkling of his disdain for them. He did not want to offend them in any way, although for him they were not realwomen.

"Women are like flowers," he used to say. "Each one gives off a different and marvelous perfume. God gave men who are unable to smell them a crooked nose and a miserable existence. What's the point of life without the fragrance exuded by women?" That is what he would tell Manuel and me, smiling wickedly with a glint in his eye. We, mere kids at the time, were in awe of Nonno's wisdom. We dedicated ourselves desperately to the sense of smell only to conclude that we were doomed to a miserable existence, since we could detect only three kinds of smells in a woman: the smell of onions from my mother, the smell of vinegar from Miriam, Manuel's mother and a delicate floral perfume that Isabel, Alfredo's mother would put on before going to work.

Alfredo, the eldest of two brothers, was the perfect result of this extraordinary diversity represented by his parents and his grandfather. On one hand, he was a methodical, moderate and responsible individual with a great sense of morality. He could apply himself passionately to any discipline, whether it was sports, studies or strange hobbies, such as dissecting animals, a pastime that occupied him for a long period. On the other hand, Alfredo was lazy, mischievous and drunken, fond of playing jokes and, despite his extensive vocabulary and quite good manners, could be extremely vulgar.

Unlike the Sánchez family, the Piruggis were not flamboyant. For them, money was more like a custom that had grown as solid over the years as the virtues and weaknesses that everyone possessed, but was no big deal.

I loved going to visit them, as they were a pleasant group that got along well together, very similar to my own family, or how my family could have been if it was not for the obsessive hierarchal system that beset us. We were divided by the idea that debating was my father's privilege, overseeing the household was my mother's task, and that my sister and I had different responsibilities which corresponded to our gender.

However, in Alfredo's family, where everyone had complete freedom to follow their own inclinations, no one used rank to instill respect. The adults in the Piruggi family managed to tame their children and the friends of their children effortlessly.

"How are you, sweetheart? I dreamed about you again last night, honey. My princess, as soon as I get back to Caracas I have a cuddly toy to give you…"

Once at the hotel, Alfredo talked at length with Maria Fernanda on the phone again, armed with a handful of sweet nothings while Manuel and I watched a movie. Alfredo's relationship with his girlfriend did not bother us in the slightest; quite the opposite, we took it as a challenge to our linguistic wit:

"Ridiculous, she's got him under her thumb, he's her slave, a lapdog...." The names rained down on our friend even in front of Maria Fernanda who found it amusing, passing them off with childish gestures. For her, Manuel and I were jesters in a court where she was of course the queen, and Alfredo her consort.

Getting on well with Maria Fernanda who was from real Caracas high society had advantages we could not ignore. For as long as her fragile teenage relationship with Alfredo lasted, Manuel and I would get into the best parties at the Caracas Country Club and even occasional brunches with dozens of impatient rich girls desperate to let their hair down.

As Alfredo was still on the phone, Manuel stopped the film to tell me: "Pana, as soon as we get back, we have to meet up with Mafe's friends."

It took me a while to reply as I was distracted by the sudden disappearance of Sharon Stone's legs from the screen.

"Shit, chamo" I said, taking the remote control away from him and switching the TV back on. "Don't you think it sucks how those snobby girls introduce themselves, reeling off their two hundred names as if they're saying the rosary?"

"Hey, Rodrigo," said Manuel, raising his voice. "What sucks is your class resentment. Brother, I'm telling you, you've really got to get over it!" His voice actually sounded angry although it had some of its usual warmth.

"I think they do that shit to make themselves stand out. Those chicks think they're noble, so they don't mix with people and probably end up marrying their own cousins."

"Are you kidding?" Manuel shouted at me jokingly. "What are you talking about?

What about that second cousin of yours? That González-Prieto is so ridiculous! Ha ha, what a jerk! Who the hell are those Gonzalez or Prietos anyway? That poor creep renting a room and pretending to be rich."

I ignored his comments to carry on with my subject.

"And the biggest load of bullshit is that they all have such tacky nicknames: Yayi, Chuchi, Totó... They sound like idiots talking in that sing-song voice that hurts your eardrums."

"Well, I guess you're right, especially Mafe."

"And the worst thing is that they all love cuddly toys. You give them a cuddly toy and the chance of getting laid that night doubles. And if you screw one of these girls in her bedroom, Jesus Christ, she throws herself around like a porn actress, with cuddly toys all over the place, ha ha."

"Ha, ha, ha, Gallego, those beatings you got from your father are screwing you up pal. Why don't you go to the suburbs and marry a poor girl with no cuddly toys or double-barrel name, you faggot! That's it then, no more trips to Miami and swimming pools for you...."

"Honey, wait a second," Alfredo covered the receiver with his hand and leaned back a bit so that Mafe wouldn't be able to hear what he was about to say to us. However, when I saw his face, I knew what was up.

"Shut up Manuel! Don't say that shit in front of the Opus Dei girl," I said in a low voice as he opened another can of beer.

CHAPTER 8

June - September, 1989

It was Sunday. In the dining room at the nursing home, the woman moved her head slightly over a bowl of soup that was going cold. It was as if she was waking up from a long sleep. Her old chauffeur, a black man who was also elderly, although in good condition, took the spoon and began to feed her without showing any surprise at the brutal transformation that she had undergone over the past twoyears.

In a very short time, Miss Daisy had lost her vivacity, a trait that had been far more distinctive in her than the shade of her well-coiffed hair and elegant clothes, both vanished now as if by magic. Wearing a red wool sweater whose only function was to protect her from the cold and staring at an invisible point on her visitor, she was no different from any other woman suffering from dementia.

Before taking the spoon, the chauffeur, Hoke Colburn, looked into her eyes, searching for that stubborn spirit that could never tolerate pity from anyone. Least of all from her own son, the dapper businessman who had offered to take him to the nursing home the previous night and who now watched his mother and the man from a corner of the wide dining room.

Hoke resettled himself in the seat and still inebriated with the pure emotion of being by her side for the first time in months, spoke to her again softly. His sentences were brief and unhurried. In the silences that separated them, he slipped a glance at the other old people who were eating at nearby tables, some with their families and one or two immersed in the solitude that was cruelly and notoriously part of Sundays.

When the scrutiny was over, Hoke looked at Miss Daisy's face with the self- confidence of someone calling at a door with the conviction that someone is at home to answer. He lifted up the spoon for the first time when he was sure that something fizzled in Miss Daisy's blue eyes.

She swallowed the food responding to a reflex. It was only a mechanical reflex as her life no longer wanted to continue. However, the instinct led Miss Daisy to act, perhaps to free herself from the man who was staring at her, delving into the havoc wreaked by her illness. Perhaps she wanted to spare him the sadness of witnessing the dark limbo where she seemed to wander around lost most of the time.

They both stayed like this as the movie ended. He speaking to the flame that burned in the depths of her eyes, she forcing herself out of the dark shadows, trying to meet him half way with her mouth open, ready to swallow another spoonful of soup with her eyes fixed on those of her old friend, who with a smile and a few kind words was slowing trying to lead her to the faraway land of her own memories.

Carmen took my hand. Since we had met, it was the first time that she had initiated contact with me. As I watched her engrossed in what was taking place on the screen as if she was beholding a miracle, I noticed that tears were pouring down her cheeks. She had never seemed vulnerable to me before, but as she gave into the acting skills of Jessica Tandy and Morgan

Freeman, all my defenses vanished, taking with them the shyness that she had always provoked in me. Without hesitation, I drew her face toward me and plucked up the courage to kiss her.

"That wet kiss will be one to remember," she whispered to me with a smile, a little abashed by her own sentimentality. The lights went back on and people started to leave the movie theater.

Of course, I would remember that kiss forever, even though I could never admit to her that she had become real for me in that fit of sobbing that made her seem like the fragile waiflike girls from my romantic fantasies. Her weeping encouraged me to let go of my fear and go straight to her tenderness, leaving behind forever the boring image of perfect student that Carmen had at university. That was it. I only began to see her for who she truly was when I threw everything overboard to go and find her in mydreams.

I remember so little about how Carmen was before that moment, as my memory is obscured by a vision I had nurtured. She wasn't really a woman who stood out for her beauty, which was discreet, although not ordinary. However, I could never tire of her intense gaze, nor of her hands, which came together on her lap when she thought no one was looking, as if she were waiting to separate them when someone needed her or asked her for something. To appreciate Carmen's generous disposition, you only had to study her hands.

Everything that happened at the beginning is still wrapped in a thick haze, although I know that I sat opposite her for the first time in the architecture school's cafeteria, when I was eating there with Publio. It was June 1989. Carmen was with two girlfriends at another table and she waved to my classmate, inviting us to join them.

"You know, María Jóse," Carmen told my mother almost two years after that lunch break, when they were sitting together, sewing. "Rodrigo hasn't the slightest idea how we met. He was wandering around in a daze and hanging onto someone or other. But I do remember when I saw him for the first time. As I say, it was on the first day of class. He was in front of the school, leaning on a wall and looking around as if he had just fallen out of the sky. I asked him if I could borrow a pen to fill in a form. I didn't have one on me. And can you believe that he gave it to me without even looking at me? And the most amazing thing, María Jóse, is that by the time I'd finished the form, he'd vanished. And then I saw him a few times in the faculty corridor, but he never realized I was the one who owed him apen."

When I started at university Carmen was already in her third semester, but we had the same linguistics seminar that I decided to take for some reason and which made very little sense to me. It seemed as though she found everything quite easy, as from her favorite seat in the first row, she would volunteer answers to questions that Professor Froilán asked during the class.

I was not the only one who could not bear to hear her know-it-all answers, but I was the only one who was not noticing her. Once or twice, I entertained myself listening to her in the forums that the students organized. In general, whoever gathered there admired her, because Carmen would quote Marx and Engels as if they were her intimate friends. To me, her voice seemed cold and her face would stiffen when she would regurgitate parrot-fashion what she had probably memorized the night before.

It was obvious that my impressions were fuelled by envy, as I'm incapable of speaking in front of a crowd without my voice trembling and my ideas getting confused. The truth was that when I heard her speak, I felt daunted, because Carmen was not intimidated by anybody and would say things that would never have occurred to me, nor that I would have thought were important.

Maybe that is why I got annoyed with Publio that day we were having lunch in the cafeteria at the Architecture School and she greeted him from the other side of the dining room, waving cheerfully with both arms. She was sitting with two girlfriends, who I later found out were philosophy students. Publio went over to say hello and after a while came back to pick up his tray and ask me if I wanted to join them. I got up reluctantly, feeling betrayed as my friend was obviously prepared to abandon me if I refused to go with him. The truth is that I did not even want to get close to Carmen. It was one thing to show off my cultural knowledge to Alfredo and Manuel, but she would hardly be impressed with my reading habits. If anything, it would show up my childish interest in adventure stories, which of course students looked down upon in the School of Arts andLiterature.

In case the girls might think I was conventional—a word that in the Arts School was synonymous with conformist or loser, I made an effort to avoid the tricky topics of university politics and of course, my literary tastes. For want of a better idea, I ended up telling a stream of gallego jokes that my friends had been telling me since I was a boy. As I got into the rhythm of reeling off one joke after another, forgetting about my food, I was surprised at how well my transatlantic memory, which my old math teacher thought was so bad, could serve me in times of need.

Then as I was telling the joke about the gallego who asked his brother for another shampoo as the one in the bathroom was for dry hair and his was already wet, I heard one of the philosophers, a girl sitting next to me, ask Carmen who this clown was. As she didn't even bother to ask quietly, I lacked the gentlemanliness to ignore her question, although of course, I was far too classy to ask her where she had got her outfit which, fitting in well with the subject of clowns, wrapped her generous amounts of flesh in the most violent tones of the chromatic scale.

At that same instant, I exchanged the gallego jokes for ones about colorblind people. These jokes are not very common but there are some. That was when Carmen burst out laughing, probably much to her regret, as she looked at her friend as if to apologize for her outburst. When she managed to compose herself, she asked me if I had forgotten about the pen that I had lent her on the first day of classes.

After that lunchtime, I said hello to her whenever I happened to run into her somewhere, but whenever possible I avoided her like the plague, as I did not want to have to rely on my collection of jokes every time I saw her. This went on for several months until the French film festival. I found myself at the French Alliance in the line for tickets.

"Hi Rodrigo, how are you? What are you doing here?

"Hey, Carmen! The same as you I imagine, I'm going to see *Betty Blue*."

She paused and looked at the poster with the list of films showing that week: *Betty Blue, Camille Claudel, The Big Blue* and *The Bear*. I noticed that she deliberated on the titles with her lips lightly pressed together. She had her hair tied back with a pink plastic hair band. I remember thinking that it did not really suit her along with the white blouse with little flowers on the buttons, which I had seen her wear on anotheroccasion.

Seeing her absorbed in her thoughts and surrounded by swarms of people who had come to see the movie, I thought that Carmen was similar to all the girls who rode the subway every day. They all had blue jeans, dark skin and long, black hair in common as well as a slightly absent look, as if they had left their souls at home or hidden somewhere and only their bodies battled their way through the city, pushing andshoving.

"Wow, hey! What a list of movies" she said finally. "I haven't seen *The Big Blue* yet but I've heard that it's really good. I think I could watch the other three a hundred times over without getting bored, especially *Betty Blue*.

"This chick is really intense," I thought while she paused again and took another look at the poster and then around her.

"Are you on your own, Rodrigo?"

"Yes. I couldn't find anyone who still hadn't seen *Betty Blue* or who wanted to see it again," I said. "But wait, aren't you here to see the film?

"I came to see if I could get hold of something on Victor Hugo. I'm doing an assignment about investigative literature and I was thinking of discussing *Les Misérables*, so I need some information that I can't find in the university library. Maybe here they have a book I could use."

She said more, but the mere idea that Carmen could grab a French book in the Institute and read it without batting an eyelid overwhelmed me, making me feel like I was next to the spirit of the renowned left-wing author from Cuba, Alejo Carpentier, who by some fatal accident was reincarnated in this young girl whose hair band and Marxist wisdom I hated. When I realized that her big eyes were waiting for some kind of feedback on my behalf and not knowing what to say, I looked around me and finally I jumped into thefray.

"Well, Carmen, I love French novels. I've also read a few…"

"Oh really?" she exclaimed, rather too enthusiastically for my liking. "Which ones?"

"Well, let's see… I've read…. *The Count of Monte Cristo*, and a lot of Jules Verne. *The Mysterious Island, Michael Strogoff, Around the World in Eighty Days,* … Did you know that Vernes tried to run away from home when he was eleven because he wanted to travel around the world by boat?"

"Exactly," she answered, opening her big eyes even wider and looking at me in quite a curious way, but without the same enthusiasm she had shown a few moments before. Then I started telling her about the classes I was taking, about my difficulty with linguistics and about a load of nonsense to do with the essays I had to write that semester. I doubt the brief report I voluntarily gave her went down well as she did not say a thing and instead invited me to join her to dig out information about Victor Hugo. "Anyway," she added, as if to encourage me and straighten out my intellectual wanderings, "it might be useful for you for some class you might take. I'm dying to see *Betty Blue* again, so we could go to see it together at seven o'clock. Have you bought your ticket already?"

"No, Carmen, come on. Leave that till later," I protested, pointing to the bundle of books that she hugged to her chest, "Let's go and watch the movie right now."

She was having none of it. She wasn't going to postpone her work for anything in the world. She said it almost in shame and was in a hurry to justify her dedication to her studies. Her father was a school teacher in La Guaira, a city next to Caracas and right on the Caribbean. Her mother was a teller at the cafe at the port. Since she was a young girl, she had spent all her time studying and looking after her sisters because her mother was of fragile constitution and used up all her energy working.

It was plain to see the immense effort that her family was making to enable Carmen to study in Caracas, although she also helped out by giving classes to two or three unruly children. "I teach them grammar and math. You can already imagine how much I know about math," she told me laughing, "but as they are worse at it than me, I don't feel bad charging for those lessons."

After browsing the Alliance books and watching the film, she told me about the projects she had in the pipeline. Carmen was full of vague plans, drawn out more by her heart than with her head. She wanted to be a university professor, but also to work in the library system. Her dream was to expand the system and open study centers in barrios of cities around the country. Children would have guided readings and adults could learn literacy skills and study with their children. "Illiteracy and ignorance," she told me gravely, "can only be corrected from within. We can't just sit around and expect people in the barrios to battle with rush-hour traffic after work to go to a study center. We have to become their neighbors, go into their homes and convince them to give up some of their time."

"You already know what the poet Rafael Cadenas said, Rodrigo: *without language we can't think. If we can't think, we are dead.*"

She had many more dreams, each one more impossible than the last, but it was pleasant to listen to her while we drank coffee and night fell around us. At around ten thirty, she got up abruptly from her seat and asked me to accompany her to take the bus downtown because, apart from Saturdays, her landlady did not like her to get home after eleven, and she did not want to have problems with her landlady.

I offered her a ride in the old Malibu my father had given me, but she flatly refused, claiming that she was perfectly well able to get home by herself. However, I insisted so strongly, and as I had shown so much interest in her projects, she finally accepted.

While she went on about how she could remedy the country's problems, I thought about how lucky I was to have my Malibu and the books that my parents happily bought for me so that I could concentrate on my studies without having to get a part-time job.

The whole way to Carmen's place, I could not stop feeling guilty about how different I was from all of my classmates.

That day she persuaded me to go with her to the national library to look for material about Victor Hugo. She also convinced me to see the whole cycle of depressing French films. Slowly but surely, our conversations got longer and longer and became a habit. Perhaps it was pride that compelled me to talk to her, to show her that I could also take my studies seriously and that I was not narrow-minded or ignorant. Or maybe it was how different her world seemed from mine, and how I thought of her dreams with a mixture of fascination and pity.

As it was, I began to study hard. I not only read material for my classes but also whatever Carmen recommended, although her books left me numb and bored, a state that I could only overcome after long siestas. I woke up from them feeling ashamed as, although Carmen was barely a year older than I was, I could not understand how she knew so much about everything, and how she had been able to learn so much on top of all the other things she had done for her family.

I was frightened of letting her down, and as time went on, I also became afraid of myself, although at that time, I was making notes and reading them daily. But in spite of my good intentions and fear of failure, even when I gave up the siestas and started reading standing up so as not to fall asleep, the truth was that not one of those new books managed to absorb me in the same way as a single page of *The Count of Monte Cristo.*

Not one single book took me by surprise, or revealed tunnels I could eagerly visualize, imagining with glee and anticipation where their strange winding paths and multiple mysteries might lead. My efforts were useless. All those books, big and small, old or new were written in treacherous languages of other worlds that excluded me.

When she noticed my dejection, since it did not take much shrewdness to see what I was going through, Carmen offered to study with me under the pretext that she needed to revise certain subjects. As time passed, I noticed her bold and almost comical ability to clear the forest of words that I had become lost in.

I felt better having her to show me the way and could open my eyes to the horizon and compare her teachings with those of my professors, who soon started sowing ideas in our heads without expecting miracle results. However, Carmen seemed to take hold of a concept and give it a beating until she got some meaning, without realizing that sometimes the clarity that she found in it was only a mirage.

By the time I had reached this conclusion, I already admired her Marxist version of *The Beauty and the Beast* and the existential dilemmas of *The Ugly Duckling* in the bleak, godless world that being an orphan had dealt out. Although I was a slow burner in the thought department and quite shallow, I recognized that Carmen only kept her crazy stories for me, while in front of others at the student forums, she would stiffen up and launch into tedious sermons.

With vanity residing in my natural charms and already slightly well versed in theoretical jargon, I would sometimes daydream about knowing as much as Carmen and outdoing her, leaving her bowled over with admiration and envy. But my secret and sporadic competitiveness with this girl from La Guaira who had raised her two sisters always stayed in check, not from embarrassment or lucidity, but because the impulse to compete implied a drive that I've always lacked.

As a child, I would often strive to do the same with Alfredo and for days on end, I obsessed about beating him in a match or an exam. But I never managed to defeat him in anything unless he allowed me to. With Carmen it was more sporadic, as my desire to know as much as she did would wear off as soon as it reached my heart, and I always ended up accepting that I was definitely not made to be the first or the best in anything.

A long time after this first impulse appeared with Carmen, just at the same time that I decided that we should have some distance, I thought we had become friends and I would always need to have her close by to escape from the feeling of emptiness and misplacement that I had during my first semester at the School of Arts and Literature. She was my anchor, my residence permit in this environment, the only person who excused me for being so different.

But before vanity and guilt could threaten me from all sides, just as I began to see some light in that arid territory of critical theories, Carmen also revealed to me the city where I was born, and that I thought I knew.

Her restless explanations involving lots of examples called for fresh air and sunshine, which were not to be found in the libraries. It was these explanations that brought us to parts of the city I would have never set foot in: around Los Caobos park up to La Pastora and at weekends, to the El Silencio towers and to the Baralt avenue.

Through her eyes, I saw the same places where I had had thousands of mishaps, including the stabbing that landed me in hospital. As was to be expected, I realized that not even Carmen could pull them out of their sordidness with her stories and ideals.

Street sellers, cripples, starving stray dogs, loud traffic, the smell of urine and excrement strategically placed on the corner, next to some ashen tree or beat-up flowerpot were all still there. But Carmen was adept at moving gracefully around the mess, the sordidness, lowlife and misery because when it came down to it, she seemed to accept whatever she came across without trying to work out how she could erase it from the face of the planet.

One day while we sat at a cafe in the basement between the El Silencio towers, a ragged, dirty old man came up to us, and held out his hand to Carmen.

"Can you spare some coins for my daughter in hospital, bella," said the man to Carmen.

"I bet you put her there," I retorted in a hard voice as I caught a strong whiff of alcohol on his breath. As the drunkard began his sob story in a dazed whisper, I added, raising my voice:

"Ask the boss here for the money that we just paid for these fruit juices. We're broke."

The man did not budge, still reciting his litany.

"And is that why you believe in Communism?" I dared to ask Carmen, looking at the man from the corner of my eye and involuntarily associating the spoutings of the drunkard with the debates at the student forums.

"My father is a diehard communist, Rodrigo," said Carmen somewhat coyly, as it was now she who was trying to pass an exam and I who was her teacher, "Since I was old enough to reason, he's been talking to me about capitalism and class consciousness. I still buy books and sometimes I read paragraphs from "*The Fear of Freedom*" and things like that. You know, so that I don't forget the doctrine."

"Spare some change for my daughter in hospital," repeated the drunkard for the fourth or fifth time, trying to focus on his prisoner.

"What about your mother?"

"She's a devotee of our saint, Jose Gregorio Hernández and controls my father" and as she noticed that I did not get it, she proceeded to explain, this time in a more relaxed and tender voice.

"If my father had been the king of the house, I would have been called Lenina.

Imagine what a fuss that kicked up. My mother insisted on calling me Carmen, and seven years later when Coromoto was born, the poor man tried again. He wanted to call her Marxina," said Carmen with a matter-of-fact expression, pausing.

"And I bet he wanted to call the youngest Stalinina," I added without even thinking.

We both burst into laughter. I looked at her lips and to my surprise and astonishment even, I felt an urge to look down at her small breasts and squeeze her waist. The desire to touch her shot up in me in a matter of seconds, as if it had always been lying there dormant and awoke just at that moment erupting like a huge volcano.

"Spare some change…."

"That's enough, chico," shouted the cafe owner, coming up to us from behind the counter. "Are you going to stop this business or do I have to call the police?"

"And what are they going to do?" he shrieked, getting the attention of everyone sitting around us. "You're the one they should take for being a thief, goddamn Portuguese. No one can touch you rich people. No one!" After a pause in which he almost lost his balance, he carried on muttering curses.

Through compassion or perhaps in the hope that he would leave us alone, Carmen took out a bill of 5 bolivars and pressed it into the man's hands, who without saying "Thank you" stumbled out of the bar, taking his monologue and his stench with him.

I sat there pensively, watching him as he disappeared. Carmen was right, the world was wrong and if we started to be disgusted with it, we would end up not being able to breathe anywhere. Misery seemed to encourage her, while for me the drunken guy was the same loudmouth that I would come across everywhere. With other faces and attitudes, he would ask me for money again, and tell me how hard it was for him, or assault me with his sulky and resentful face on a bus or a street corner, always dreaming of giving me the definitive stab in the back.

Full of sadness or perhaps nostalgia, I realized that there was no way to build a bridge over these waters. One thing I now understood was that by accident and without even real-izing it, Carmen was pulling me away from all of that which really existed for her and which was just a nightmare to me, a bad dream which could only be kept at bay by getting on the subway and getting off at Altamira. Turning my imaginary camera on myself, which was only fair to do, I thought that my own world would never understand her. *"What are you doing with this overexcited ghetto girl who wants to protect the people with her five-dollar bills? Did I break my butt to send you to the Salesians for that?"* my father would ask. What would my friends say if I brought her to a party at the Piruggi's house? *"You've blown it now Rodrigo. Which barrio did you find this little girl in, pana?"*

With shame, sadness and even anger, I felt that the volcano of desire, after an intense but brief eruption, had wrapped itself up like a sick person tucked up in bed, burying its lava deep into the earth once more. I also felt that Carmen, who was now putting her wallet away without noticing me, was still wrapped in that darkness of the unreachable, which we can only contemplate from the other side.

That was when I thought it would be better to get some distance from her, although gradually, so that she wouldn't be offended. After two weeks of making poor excuses and avoiding her, I bumped into her face to face after a class. She had obviously been waiting for me and although she was smiling, her eyes looked sad. I could not refuse to go with her to the botanical gardens, although as far as I could see, the situation was resolved, albeit in a cowardly way without an explanation.

"In that acacia tree Rodrigo, not this one, that one over there, look," she said as we stopped, pointing out the tree to me. "A little thrush lives there. I recognize it because it's the most speckled one. It lives alone. It looks like its partner died or left because they used to have a nest with babies. If you wait, you'll see it come down looking for seeds and worms. I don't know if it's male or female. There it is. Can you see it now? Yes, well," she added with satisfaction as if she were the thrush's mother. "It is what it is."

"Why? Because it's a creature feeding its young?" "Well, yes and no."

"Ah," I replied, thinking that the time for recrimination had come. "So you mean I'm not me?"

"No, no!" she said, waving her hands in the air to shake away the tension she noticed between us. "I'm not talking about you, but about me. What I'm trying to tell you, is that the thrush is what it is because of the acacia. Perhaps at some moment, that magnificent tree wondered who was looking for a home in its branches, and perhaps it even resented the bird for being ugly and scandalous and it would prefer to give a home to a turtledove. But see how the tree can't dwell on these ruminations, because at the end of the day, it's a tree."

"Carmen, I don't get you. Speak to me clearly for once."

"What I was going to tell you, truthfully, Rodrigo, is that for me you're the acacia tree. You wonder who I am, but at the end of the day, and in the hour of truth, for whatever reason, you let me be who I am and you never tell me, look chica, your problem is... I don't know how to put it, but people think that I can be what they want me to be and I don't normally comply, and also because at the end of the day, it's just me.

However, with you, I can afford to be the thrush. And the truth is I like it..."

The night of the kiss, we waited in a long line at the movie theatre. *Driving Miss Daisy* had just won an Oscar and was the in-thing in Caracas.

"Hey listen, Rodrigo, look at that long line. Just think, the movie celebrates the relationship between a high class woman and her servant. God! That would never happen in real life, at least not here. That's a fact."

She looked at me for a long time while a faint smile bloomed on her lips.

CHAPTER 9

November 17, 1989

"Mom. Have you ironed my shirt?"

"Don't pester your mother now, Rodrigo. You know that her soap operas are sacred," said my father slapping his palms on his belly on his way to the armchair where Mom was sitting, serving him coffee.

Friday was the only work day that my father celebrated washing down his dinner with half a bottle of Felipe II brandy and two or three coffees. My mother also celebrated "their night" as she would call them, as every Saturday she would have dinner with some fellow Asturians who preferred to drink Carlos I, being wealthier than us.

Drinking brandy named after such a powerful king, this little Asturian social club finished their Saturday feasts with tears in their eyes, overwhelmed by alcohol and patriotic emotion. Ready to leave the table, at the height of experiencing such noble sentiments, my mother would start singing "*Asturias, my beloved land...*" which is something like "*Alma llanera,*" Venezuela's unofficial national anthem. Before long, Luis's tenor would join her solitary and wavering solo along with the high-pitched voice of his wife, Sinda.

I'm still impressed today by how important this song has always been to my mother and I still don't really understand exactly what makes her sing it. When I was a child, she would sing it to me at crucial points in my life, whether I was behaving myself, getting up to mischief or falling sick. As the occasions were all different, I grew up thinking that there was a confused mix of ideas and facts in Mom's head. I wouldn't have thought twice about this matter if it were not for the fact that, as a teenager, I began to do the same. It's not that the words of the song meant much in particular to me, as I've never been to Asturias, rather that I would hum it in my mind without realizing, whether I had received a good grade or if I was suffering from constipation, for example. This secret habit, over and above my tendency to make mistakes in everything I do, has always made me feel different. And to be honest, and I'm being as serious as I can now, I will always feel I have at least a couple of screws missing until I meet someone else who sings "*Alma llanera*" while straining on the toilet.

Getting back to the main point, as digressing is a big problem of mine, when they were older, my parents rediscovered a closeness they had not enjoyed since Raquel and I were born. Now that I was older, I started to go out with my friends on Fridays and then with Carmen. Then my sister took the opportunity to get out of the house when she started hanging around with Teresa's daughters, two frisky girls who covertly provided her with a solid romantic education.

As Teresa, one of my mother's cousins, lived in Maracay, a small city close to Caracas, Raquel used to take the bus on Friday afternoon, using the argument that her asthma was greatly soothed in El Limón, an area of the city full of trees where our only Venezuelan relations had a small house. It must have been very good for her, as what else would explain the color returning to my sister's cheeks and the knowledge she would gain over the weekends that she spent in the fresh air.

Almost every Friday after three o'clock when Clemencia, our housekeeper, would say goodbye until the following Monday, Mom would put the sewing to one side to shut herself in the kitchen, which she would only leave when the aroma of her Asturian dishes filled the whole building. Afterwards she would set the table and have a bath.

Dad would get home about seven o'clock, exhausted and sweaty but, as showering was not his forte, he would make do with washing his hands and face after putting on his slippers. We would sit down together, drink sidra and chat, or rather, it was Papa who would chat to us as he felt free on these evenings and wanted to be listenedto.

On Fridays when Raquel stayed in Caracas because the cousins, who were both nurses, were working shifts, it was her job to clear the table and wash the dishes. If my sister was in Maracay, which was the case on this particular day, the dirty plates were left sitting in the sink until the next morning. This was because without fail, my mother would fall onto the sofa after dinner, as tired as my father, and watch her soap operas one after another without even pausing to answer the telephone, which she was just as addicted to as the soap operas and *Hola!* magazine. At her side, my father would be busy having coffee and brandy, waiting for the news to come on. At midnight, you could find them with their heads together, snoring in front of the faithful television, which was showing some prehistoric movie in the darkness of the livingroom.

That particular night, my mom noticed I was looking a little drawn, and I explained to her that for the past two days I had been writing about servants in soap operas. My parents understood little or nothing about what I was studying, and to be honest, they had never shown much interest. As my mother was such a great fan of daytime soap operas, her eyes lit up and she asked me again and again to read her my book.

"It's not a book, Mom. Well maybe it is, but not the way you think. It's an essay, and you probably won't like it anyway," I told her, ignoring the maternal curiosity that prompted by her interest in the soap operas, had arisen halfway through the conversation. As she kept on insisting, I got up from the table with the pretext of going to the movies with Alfredo and Manuel.

After a few minutes, when I came out of the room asking about the shirt I had given her that morning to iron, my father ordered me to be quiet without so much as a look before letting out an enormous, volcanic belch. On the other hand, my mother gave me a pained look, as if I had thought for a moment that my parents were unworthy of having my things read to them.

"All right then," I said not too enthusiastically. "If Papa wants me to, I'll read you my work."

"Of course he wants to hear your poems, my dear little Lope de Vega," sang Mom, turning off the television where Papa had already anchored a glazed stare. I was too flustered to even begin to feel flattered by my mother's comparison of me with the celebrated Spanish poet.

"They aren't poems, Mom, I already told you. It's a study about soap operas which...."

"Whatever, son, get on with the damned thing and let your mother rest for a moment," yelled my father, cutting me down flat with his usual authority although displaying the vivacity that took control of him when he was interested in something.

That was how I read an essay, in which I had invested many hours of meditation and discussion with Carmen, to my parents, who had hardly managed to complete their elementary school studies. Slowly and deliberately, to prevent them falling into an irreversible coma, and asking them to stop me whenever there was something they did not understand, I introduced them into the complexities of my intellectual activity.

….In soap operas, which we can class as "pulp fiction" the domestic servant is a worker who logically receives a salary for providing cooking and cleaning services.

However, in real life, this has not always been the case. Until the late 19ᵗʰ century, the servant and her employer would establish an exchange of services; in other words, money was not involved. In exchange for her work, the housekeeper was guaranteed accommodation in the home of her employers. There she would get married, have children and finally die. Her life and interests were completely identified with the life and the interests of her employer.

Many soap operas transform one of their domestics, usually a young, attractive woman, and apparently an orphan, into a "lady" or "lady of the house," following the model of Cinderella. Accompanying her on her journey, there is often an older female servant, who is allied to or an enemy of the main character, and who exercises an indisputable influence over her destiny.

The young princess, who turns out to be the legitimate or bastard daughter of the man of the house, the old woman who tries to kill her or at least reduce her to a disabled state, and the old fairy godmother who guides the naïve young girl along the arduous path of contemporary social life are all literary inventions.

In soap operas, most women employed in the household stay in the background, serving coffee, dusting the house and answering the doorbell.

However, these secondary female characters are used in the soap opera to reflect the true relationship between the modern domestic help and her employers. Like their cups of coffee and aprons, they are symbols of the power and wealth of the bourgeois.

...in our country, the oil boom and urbanization introduced the trend of collecting servants, to the extent that nowadays even the saddest middle class family has one. In this way, the old system disappeared and in its place appeared a morbid symbiosis between wealthy people and their servants.

I stopped as I had started to feel a little nervous and under the pretext of thirst due to the large quantity of salt that Mom had put in the fabada asturiana, I poured myself a glass of water.

For the first time in my life, Papa had let me speak for more than five minutes without interrupting. A completely new sensation gripped my throat. Being soft-hearted, my eyes started to water as all the long hours I had invested in the essay were beginning to fill me with a deep satisfaction. However, I had to confess deep inside that I would have been incapable of coming up with "morbid symbiosis." That was Carmen's work. "...morbid symbiosis ...." Shit! Would my folks think that this was a sexual thing? I turned to look at them, and there they were, sitting side by side in silence, with their hands in their laps and their eyes wide open, looking at me like two simple scholars in the presence of a master. I was so moved by their composure that I went back to the sofa and without asking if they had understood, Icontinued:

In this symbiosis, the domestic servants seem to enjoy a freedom that did not exist in wealthy households or on traditional haciendas at the beginning of the century.

However, their freedom is a false one. Their employers wash their hands of the domestic when she becomes pregnant, or gets into the habit of arriving late or misses work.

It's easy to fire these helpless women, as they have no legal rights. As little time is invested in their training, they are thrown out onto the streets from one day to the next and always without compensation.

For many years, the Venezuelan middle and upper classes have closed their eyes to such injustice, especially considering that domestic servants are usually born and raised in remote villages and are not equipped to deal with their "liberty" in large cities.

To sum up the insult to injury that the employers dole out to their domestic staff, it's necessary to remember that nowadays they are called "cachifas," an extremely derogatory term for "maid."

"Ah, my little Lope, you explain everything so well, my dear boy! Poor servants, what a hard life…!"

That was my Mom, dabbing her teary eyes with the handkerchief that she always carried in her apron pocket, then wringing her hands. But Papa attacked her saying, "Be quiet woman, that's not what it's all about!" and "Let him read!"

In the deathly silence that prevailed at that moment, after checking that Mom still had her handkerchief, I continued reading:

In former times, in the universities of Colombia, a young person who showed alertness and confidence in his or her intellectual abilities from the beginning of classes was called a "cachifo"—a "smarty". A modern day "cachifa" or "maid," belonging to the school of life, is seen as being quite sharp-witted and is a master of the art of survival: do the minimum amount of work, lie to the employers and if given the opportunity, steal from them.[4]

The modern maid, presumably disloyal until the end, lives on a pitiful little shack with several different partners and raises children by different fathers. However, as the employers argue, she's the

---

[4] By 2001, there were at least 4 million registered Colombians in Venezuela. The number of illegal immigrants is unknown. By then, the total population of Venezuela was about 25 million. While the country benefitted from intellectual immigration coming from Argentina, Uruguay and Chile and other countries, its infrastructure was significantly affected by the disproportionate number of illegal immigrants.

master of her own freedom, which amounts to the same thing as saying that the poor woman is responsible for her own misfortune.

Not content with being the facilitators of such freedom, the employers praise themselves when they contract the maids. By performing such a generous gesture, which exposes them to becoming victims of robbery or worse, they change these women's lives, at least during the hours or days they spend with them. "That's how it is," says the employer. "They even get to eat the same food as us." This is the most common phrase in the leisurely conversations of middle and high-class ladies.

The only truth in all of this is that the domestic servant ends up living in two worlds. There is no other job in which one is so exposed to the sharp social contrasts that exist in Venezuela. Eventually, "the change of life" transforms the servant woman into a lens through which she contemplates everything she has longed for and will never be able to have.

It's no exaggeration to say that the social and psychological pressure placed on the maid in our society is terrible, as the huge quantity of unnecessary tasks she carries out on a daily basis is awful, the "freedom" of her working conditions without a union and the contrasts that she experiences within her employer's house and shack. However, no one is doing anything to remedy this drama and neither are there sociological studies on the subject.

Perhaps now it can be understood why soap operas do not try to rescue the domestic servants whose mission it is to open doors and bring cups of coffee from one place to the next: they are part of the social status of those who employ them and they are also part of the social status that the soap operas strive to reinforce.

The insensitivity of the middle and upper classes toward the domestic help is a sad example of everything that is wrong in Venezuelan society and of how democratic ideals are being eroded.

Only when it's too late will our elite wake up from their state of lethargy. And they will have to pay for it.

"You tell me what we'll pay," my father corrected me firmly, "or don't you have a maid, smart aleck?"

My eyes met his which were glassy because of the Felipe II and were looking at me as if I were a schoolboy.

To this day, I don't know if the slap that I felt in my face got to me through his words or his look, or even a distant memory that suddenly blossomed from the void to fill my head with the image of Yuramis. I lowered my eyes in shame, staring at the transparent file that protected my essay, while I relived what had happened two years previously at Manuel's house.

I had spent the night there and the next morning I awoke with a hangover. In a rush to get rid of the dozen beers I had imbibed the night before and as my bladder was full to the brim, I stumbled into the bathroom. Added to the pleasant rushing sound of urine splashing into the toilet were the clatter of plates and the sound of voices coming from the kitchen. I made my way there after quickly splashing some water on my face. The heat was beginning to be unbearable.

Manuel was preparing an arepa, a type of corn bread. When he saw me, he rounded his lips as if he was about to play the trumpet to point out a young girl sitting opposite Miriam. He was watching her with a combination of anxiety and enthusiasm.

Yuramis was probably Colombian; she was small and dark with long straight hair tied back in a ponytail. A few hours later, Manuel would describe her in an admirable way:

"Firm little tits, a round little ass, she looks like an easy lay."

I remember scanning her from the head down to her feet, but the drunkenness of the night before and my libido prevented me from behaving well. I insolently anchored my gaze on her thighs, which were barely covered by her miniskirt.

Then Miriam Sánchez who did not need my visual opinion because Manuel had already shown his on Yuramis' breasts, very suggestive in the tight blouse, soon said,

"Well, see now, chica, I'm thinking…. I don't need really a girl right now. I'm sorry, I think you come all this way for nothing…"

And what a journey! According to Clemencia, who had already worked for us for thirteen years and was like part of the family, getting to our apartment would take just over two hours, and that is because we lived so close to the subway. Getting to more isolated suburbs, like Manuel's, would take at least another hour and a half, with the aggravation of having to walk the last stretch.

"Well, I finish 'bout four. I go down walkin' 'cos the buses don't wanna go into the barrio, hell yeah, it's a pain 'cos everyone knows that's when the thugs go to sleep," explained Clemencia.

I remember Yuramis' sad face as she grabbed her black plastic bag from the table at the back of the kitchen, where the other two servants watched her in silence, eating leftovers from dinner. Yuramis left without a fuss, although she was present in our conversations and fantasies for some time.

"Look Rodrigo," my father said to me, handing me a little glass of Felipe II, his voice a little mellowed now. "Communism has no point. I would love to have been an opera singer, but Christ, even given the opportunity, I could never have sung like Pavarotti, so I don't see how he and I could have the same income. Sure there is injustice, but some are more talented than others and some work harder than others, ok?"

In the midst of the painful humiliation of that evening, I realized that in fact, I had never heard my father sing a single note.

CHAPTER 10

December 14, 1989

What was a woman like Carmen doing with a clumsy oaf like me? For a long time, this question blew around in my head like a whirlwind, which sometimes turned into more of a tornado.

Given my little inclination to live the adventures that I loved to read about in books, I used to dread the currents of this restlessness. More than once, however I dared to give in to it, letting it drag me along the ground or touch the clouds. I wouldn't have exchanged these delirious moments for anything in this world.

Anything could have happened to me at that time, but I knew that my only rock, the only permanent place that I had in the world was Carmen. As her guard lowered, she became happier and more willing to give herself over to her own flight, forever energetic and changing. It was as if my presence had given her the final push to become a daring Amelia Earhart, flying boldly around the sky while the rest of us were left stranded on the ground, struggling with the engines of our crippled little planes.

When I say this, I'm not putting anyone down as it's one thing to love a woman and entirely another to give oneself over to her blindly. If I had any virtues, it would be the ability to look at things in a practical way. Perhaps it's a birth defect rather than a virtue, as Professor Méndez told me before failing me in math, just the day before my birthday, September 14, 1986.

"Rodrigo, you're a blockhead," declared the teacher Pablo Méndez, from the La Candelaria neighborhood like me, "This doesn't mean that you're incapable of a good idea or two, but your mind is inflexible."

It must be true because as everyone already knows, I can calculate a sum using pears or guavas but without them, I understand very little, and much less about linear equations and treacherous parabolic curves that flee to infinity, deliberately leaving me stranded and humble amid a load of fruit.

Finally, and as I think I already said, I began to understand Carmen's explanations and although my knowledge was full of holes, I would have loved to bump into Professor Méndez again and fire off a few of those words that Carmen always had on the tip of her tongue. Recently though, perhaps due to my awkward affection for her, all this stuff about socialism, colonialism, imperialism and so on did not sound so stuffy.

Even if all this waffle was still important to Carmen, the tone of voice she now used was very seldom defiant or rigid, even in those forums and in the presence of the Universidad Central big shots who kept on inviting her to bury her head in the sand. This is saying a lot about my girlfriend who, normally flitting from idea to idea, began to observe and acknowledge her ideas warmly and placidly as if they were old girlfriends. Between her father's teachings and the equally intense orthodoxy of the top students, she finally came to accept that as well as their virtues, her ideas also possessed great defects.

New to playing with words, I used them as if they were lucky charms to protect me against a cult or to score points against those who did not take me seriously. I would day-dream of surprising my old teacher Méndez in a department store for example, buying stuff for his car. After greeting him politely, I would bring up the topic of consumerism and continue in that vein until I had exhausted my repertoire of new vocabulary.

I was not bitter. I've never felt that way toward my teachers, although according to Carmen, I was carrying repressed resentment around in my unconscious. If the truth were told, being a practical type, I'm not convinced of all this stuff about unconsciousness. Far from getting back at Méndez, I just wanted to show all those who had always known me how much I was learning with this little dark girl from La Guaira.

This was impossible with Alfredo and Manuel, as even before I had met Carmen they would call me a pompous idiot if I uttered a word that was remotely refined. Trying again at home wouldn't work either, since Papa had given me such a hard time about the servants. Therefore, distrustful of everyone, I daydreamed for several months of Socratic dialogues, which would leave my old college teachers astounded.

The time I spent lying in bed was excellent for wrapping myself in a misty haze, which worked wonders to cure my old student wounds. I began to surprise myself with my considerable and unusual knowledge until, in my imagination, the phone would ring. Slowly and with false annoyance, as in my musings I received more calls than the president of the republic, I would pick up the receiver of an imaginary telephone on my bedside table to listen to the hectic voices of those who had caused me so much anguish in the Salesian high school. One of my greatest pleasures was to hear the dry voice of Prof. Martín who thought she knew best in matters of grammar, choke to ask me advice on literary questions.

Of course, Méndez' call was the most difficult to imagine as he was only interested in math and his car, in which he would compulsively change the oil every three months. However, I was hoping that he would have a breakdown like those that hit hard after the age of fifty, and that he would come to me asking for a book to resolve his issues.

"*The Confessions of Rousseau* that you recommended was just great Rodrigo!"

He would call me again full of euphoria. "I feel like a new man now, I don't know, how should I put it? That Jean-Jacques, who shirked his responsibilities and gave up his children to an orphanage, was nothing less than the father of the French Revolution. Then there's my wife, listen to this! Asking me to give evening classes so that she can buy fashionable new dining room furniture because she's organizing a canasta club. No brother, honestly! Ah, you can see the connection between Rousseau and my wife. Look, I don't want any new furniture for the house, Rodrigo. I want to write the real confessions of a mathematician who couldn't finish his master's degree because he was so naïve. Hombre, why didn't I think of the orphanage, pana? And my wife and her belly! In the last few years, I've been scared to go near her in case she gets pregnant again. And we so rarely have sex, I got Violetica into my head. Do you remember Violetica, the youngest daughter of the butcher on the corner of Perico street? No, man you're kidding me, you left and you don't even remember the Perico butcher? Well, whatever, pana. Hey, the thing is that every time Elvira sends me to buy ribs or chops, I have to do breathing exercises so I don't keel over at the sight of Violetica. Yes, she's hot, pana. Imagine the confessions I could write if I could give her more than justthe eye! I'm working on it, brother! If I played my cards right maybe I could father a child who doesn't just cry and eat. Intellectual stimulation only leads me to the butchers."

Imagining the conversation and turning it over in my head so often made the image of poor Méndez more and more perverse. I began to feel bad about myself and even about my teacher, who had not changed in all those years. He had only committed adultery with his car, which he had begun to wash scrupulously every Sunday afternoon, probably to avoid the visits to the in-laws'.

Conscience forced me to accept that everyone who knew me judged my newfound knowledge wrong or dull. It was my fate to have grown up with people who could do without it, or even worse, could not believe that I was able to learn something and become a hardworkingprofessional.

The safest option for me was to study literature and everyone agreed with this choice, but after two years of study, I found it humiliating to admit to myself that none of my schoolteachers had objected to my decision because they did not expect much of me. Literature was a bag into which you could put anything, good or bad, but nothing that would put anyone out. Nothing that would produce prosperity or great success, at least not in my case.

I can remember the day I waited until all students had left the class to tell my teacher, Mrs. Martín about my decision. She was absentmindedly clearing away her things and was surprised to see me in front of her desk, staring at her, stagestruck with the same shyness I had felt as a ten-year old boy on the first day of school. Plucking upas much courage as I could, I explained to her that I had chosen literature, and due to my financial situation, would study at Universidad Central.

"You're doing the right thing, Rodrigo," she answered, fixing her shortsighted, wide-open eyes on the textbooks that she gently placed in her briefcase. "You know, Spanish teachers are always in demand," and after a distracted and unenthusiastic pause, she looked at me insipidly before returning to her packing. "Look, when you graduate, get into the public education system. They take even the worst teachers."

Without my furious aviator Carmen, I'm sure that after a year of studying literature, I would have driven in reverse in my old Malibu from the middle of the campus to downtown Caracas and from there who knows, maybe to the building site that my father was in charge of then. I did not see anything wrong with being a builder, except of course the fact that my father was one and he had wagered many years' salary on the dream of having a son at university. Being the man of the house did not seem a privilege just then, but rather an immense burden and from time to time, I sighed with envy at the trap that my sister Raquel was in because of her virginity.

Then everything started to go downhill with Carmen. Not just because of the huge effort she put into teaching me everything she knew, but because of how much she tried to be my tree. Perhaps she thought that I was her acacia, but I was convinced that it was the other way around. She was the new home where I could grow without fear of judgment.

Now I was ashamed of the knives that, with respect to Carmen, I had allowed to stab me in the heart. It was certainly not the wish of having a boyfriend from the east of Caracas or of having a baby to hold in her arms that made her put up with my jokes or the Caracas' baseball team card collection that I kept in a shoebox under my bed. Carmen's hidden child, who had been bursting to get out since she was seven, was good for me.

Being with her gave me a feeling of almost implausible freedom, and at the same time allowed me to indulge in all the things I really loved apart from my playing cards: the music of Rush and the heroes from my books: irredeemable pirates, drunken detectives and fervent medieval knights. I could even make an altar to them without Carmen thinking I was an idiot. On the contrary, she laughed happily and always waited for more, looking at me with wide eyes, childlike and pleasantly surprised.

Because of this, and maybe also due to an explosion of hormones, when the Malibu broke down that Thursday in December, I had the minibus drop me on the corner of Caobos street and Libertador avenue while the driver and its five sleeping passengers continued on to El Silencio. From there, I got to the flower stand just before La Consolación and bought three sunflowers for the price of two, the last ones left. I also got hold of two red roses for nothing as I put on a cute face and the flower seller thought it was my mother's birthday.

With the bunch of flowers and testosterone pumping through my body, I took another cab to Puente Yánez and from there I made my way to Parque Central between the sad crowds, piles of garbage and rough streets.

After I had walked more than half a mile and climbed up twelve flights of stairs, as the elevator had ignored my pleas, Carmen opened the door to me. Speechless with surprise at the flowers or maybe at my disheveled appearance, she gestured to me to come in quietly. She told me in a low voice that Barn Owl—that was the woman who rented her the room—was in the kitchen making dinner. Barn Owl did not like her tenants receiving visitors after seven o'clock. "You know Rodrigo, because visitors always sit and watch TV and she doesn't like to waste electricity that apparently no one paysfor."

Hesitating and concerned about my breathlessness, she quickly pushed me through the dining room toward her room while she shouted to Barn Owl at the top of her voice that whoever had been banging on the door, trying to break it down had the wrong house.

Not knowing what to do, I stood stock still in the shadows holding my flowers while she went to the kitchen to tell her landlady that she was getting a migraine and she was going to bed.

A century later she came back, closed the door and turned on the light. Carmen had let down her beautiful hair that she had been wearing up before. It was wet and she was wrapped in a white bathrobe. She looked like a vestal virgin or a Greek goddess, but instead of holding the scales of justice or the torch of liberty in her right hand, she had a cup of hot coffee whose aroma filled me with courage.

I took two shaky steps toward this woman who was surely a reincarnation of Aphrodite and held out the bunch of flowers to her in such an awkward gesture that her face was practically buried among the petals. Carmen did not move. Her eyes watched me like two stars that had fallen into an overgrown garden.

The bedroom was horribly austere and outside, nightfall and noise invaded the city. From all sides came smells of simple cooking and reheated food: fried eggs, arepas, beans and stew. When Carmen took my hand, I knew that we had been waiting for each other since that first meeting in the School of Arts and Literature. That is how it always is. Lovers know things that we don't and they act without asking questions.

I did not want to complicate matters and least of all with a girl who would be of no advantage to me in this city where we all struggled, if not to get to the top, at least to maintain our position, right there where we were, without falling to the gloomy depths of the underclass.

However, Carmen was neither afraid, nor ashamed of the old deformed mattress and the gaunt blanket that covered it. She pulled me over as if I were a child, making me sit on the squeakiest bed in the whole universe.

I can't tell you what happened after that. I'm lacking in macho pride and would be lying if I said I had the situation under control. I'm not used to writing poetry, nor can I begin to describe the matter with mere words. The only thing to say is that hours later, drenched in Carmen's clean perfume, while she slept in total darkness, I was not thinking of the thousands of people living in the hive downtown nor of what the insipid future would bring us.

As strange as it may seem, taking the last sip of cold coffee, I thought of something that had sown itself in my head years before: On my way home from school one day, a stray, sickly dog crossed my path. My efforts to scare her away were useless and I ended up carrying her to her two puppies, asleep in sheaves of corn piled up in a building site.

Wrapped up in my jacket, I carried them the three blocks to my house. There I settled them in some rags and gave them some milk with a few drops of medicine that my mother got from an old bottle. When my father arrived and saw the animals, he began to shout, yelling at me to get them out of my room, out of the apartment and out of his sight. My mother looked at us not knowing what to say, overcome by tiredness from so much sewing and by the bad mood of my father, who was climbing the walls at the time, trying to make a decent salary. My sister watched us in silence, squeezing a soft toy to her chest, her breathing agitated.

I placed the puppies in our building's parking lot and promised my father that I would take them back to the site the next day. However, that night it rained without mercy, as it has never rained before in Caracas, and the parking lot barely had a proper roof over the door to the building. I never saw them again, despite asking the neighbors and going back to the building site every day for two weeks.

The anger that arose at my father from that episode made me feel like a huge mosaic of Walt Disney films. I could not stop thinking of the child heroes that had rescued animals as I had. After many mishaps and adventures, they ended up more united than ever with their parents, thanks to the dogs, cats, dolphins and whales, who had been mistreated or were in danger of dying at the beginning of the film.

I walked around for a long time with my head down, clinging to those films in a silent reproach to my father, to rid myself of the memory of those little puppies that had broken my heart. It was a very efficient strategy; I never watched another animal film and until that day in downtown Caracas, I had never let the starving look of the puppies come to mind again.

Protected by the closeness of Carmen, I gave in to the possibility that I had rejected back then, when I was eleven: the puppies had died looking for their mother or had been washed into the gutter. Now, while I pictured them squashed beneath the wheels of a lorry, I finally understood that they were part and parcel of life, of the unconscious nature that was ceaselessly deteriorating every day under the indifferent Caracas sky.

CHAPTER 11

January 22, 1992

"Hurry up Rodrigo, our appointment is at nine!" It was a Wednesday.

Several yards away and with my mouth full, I shouted, "I'm coming." I had stopped at a stall that sold the best empanadas in the whole of Caracas. I hurriedly took the last bite and tried to walk quickly, but the coffee I was carrying in a plastic cup was too hot and soon began to burn my fingers. I stopped to change hands and blew on the creamy froth. Carmen shouted to me again with an impatience that I just did not understand.

"But we're only going to see a student!" I objected when I caught up with her, after burning the roof of my mouth. My back tooth had also awakened to the pain and I began to feel like the most miserable man in the world.

At times like that, when Carmen was unapproachable, my ephemeral resentment recalled the sayings of my father, not always wise but at least governed by a simple and comforting pragmatism: "My son," he used to say. "Everything costs something in this life, including a toothache."

The pain was not unbearable, nor did I want to skimp on dental costs. The problem was Carmen, who was involved in one of her many social causes. As usual, I was not able to say no to her and I soon forgot the idea of going to Doctor Panichi, the distinguished dentist who for half a century had been curing all the toothaches in La Candelaria.

One of Carmen's friends, a student of medicine, had told her that we at Universidad Central were part of a community and should help each other mutually.

"So those poor dentistry students," said that old cow whose name I can never remember, "are fighting for a chair for their patients. Imagine chica, that to graduate they have to do thousands of hours of practicals and there aren't even enough dental chairs.

And to top it all off, they only get them if they have the right connections. I don't mind the favoritism, but it's the practical thing, you know me. Because if the rich kids, the ones who graduate first can never actually graduate because of the chairs, which are as old as Columbus by the way, you tell me who is going to go to the rural provinces to do a six- month externship? Who's going to help me to prevent meningitis, abscesses and heart disease in the Orinoco Delta villages? Because you know chica, my thing is public health and my commitment to the people comes before everything..."

Those were the words spoken by a future doctor, who strangely enough, I always imagined sitting in a comfortable practice in a fancy Caracas neighborhood or the most impressive office in the Ministry of Health. Perhaps it was my bad conscience that could not imagine her in a motorboat, making its way through the piranhas and Amazonian mosquitoes to finally arrive at a little hut where a child from the Yanomami tribe was dying from gastroenteritis.

However, Carmen was Carmen and I accepted these facts. That was how I ended up at the Dental School, offering my tooth to a student who according to the receptionist was called

Alberto Arnau. Every night during my long wait, I prayed to God for him. Just before falling asleep, I became very pious before succumbing to agitated dreams where a giant with huge ears took all my teeth out. I was not scared of dentists, but being a guinea pig was another matter.

After walking at a fast pace for more than twenty minutes, we got to the Dental School. The empanada, coffee, and the miles we had walked and finally the flight of stairs all turned my stomach. When we got to the passage on the second floor, we came out into the clinic's hallway. Believe it or not, I immediately recognized the future Doctor Arnau because his ears were huge, if not as pointy as those of my giant. Also because he was working in chair number twenty-one, where I had been told I would find him. He was busy with a patient but when he heard us come in, he interrupted his work and slowly came over to us, turning his back on his poor patient who, with his mouth held wide open by a rubber device began todrool.

"Are you Rodrigo?" he asked with a terse melancholy, as he pushed Carmen and me toward the passage. Without waiting for an answer, he started to speak in a booming voice. I thought that his high forehead and bony gravedigger hands went very well with his ears and with the languid look that he shot us at that moment.

"Look," he said with an eerie slowness. "It's how the saying goes here, first come first served. You snooze, you lose." At this point, he made such a long pause that I instinctively looked around for somewhere to sit. There was no need to go to such extremes as Arnau went on speaking as if he had read my mind:

"I waited for you for fifteen minutes and then I had to give your slot to another patient."

"But we had to pay and the counter only opened ten minutes ago. And where did he come from?" I said abruptly pointing to the dribbling boy. "Did he spend the night here or what?" I added to make the injustice clear.

"Brother," the curt man said, "Just behind you, don't turn around now because he's watching us… he's another guy like me with his three patients. If mine don't come, his herd gets the seat. We only have forty-five dental units here," he paused again with his gaze lost somewhere beyond my head. "Forty-five for ninety students. So you'll have to wait until I've finished with this one, ok?"

Doctor Arnau treated my tooth two hours later. After studying it with an intensity that did not bode well, he worked in silence and with tenacity, captivated by the cavity as if it were a bomb that he was painstakingly disarming. His movements were as slow as the brief sentences that he offered at the end of the treatment.

Carmen had gone to the library on the ground floor. My dentist's frugalness and the trance that he had entered in his contemplation of drills, hooks and tongs were making me feel very uncomfortable. After all, we were two men united by a cavity and I would expect some degree of intimacy to surface under such circumstances.

My dear Doctor Panichi, the dentist from La Candelaria, would have told me about a few Euro cup matches, with his heroes the Italian team. Or for the umpteenth time how his father stole stones from the Coliseum in the mid fifties, hid them under the baby's blanket then sold them to tourists who came to Rome. "Those were the days," he would exclaim, giving me some gentle slaps that I could not feel thanks to the anesthesia. "Yes, dear Rodri, you only get men like my father on the soccer pitch." We would both finish the session feeling happy, him with his memories and me with my numbed wooziness.

"Hah muk wonger?" I asked Arnau, with hunger pangs attacking my stomach, trying to ignore the device, which now trapped the left side of my jaw, making me salivate like a fountain.

"Don't worry, we're almost done."

As he spoke, he looked around him searching for the clinical teacher, a large man who was doing rounds of the room and inspecting the students' treatments with the mistrust of a police officer.

"Dr. Morales, my patient has classes and has to leave. Please could you check the filling that I did on him?

"Listen," barked the Professor, sounding normal for that yellow room that reeked of disinfectants. "I have nine students on my list and you're number five, so please wait your turn."

Just at that moment, Carmen came in agitated. Without stopping to take a breath, she told me we had to leave. People in hoods were throwing stones and burning tires at the main door of the university campus. They were students who had covered their faces with hoods and were protesting violently against the government. The police were getting ready to shoot at them, and as the students were also armed, it could easily escalate into a shoot-out. Just then, there was an explosion, which seemed to act as a trigger for Arnau, who with his eyes coming out of orbit began to shout out a litany of expletives.[5]

"...fuck those hooded jerks," concluded Dr. Arnau. "Where the hell do they get the weapons from? How can people complain about the rise of one bolivar in public transport? One bolivar!"

---

[5] According to Venezuelan law, security forces cannot enter the university campus. This along with a culture of public protest created an eternal battleground at the entrances of public universities. The entrance of the School of Dentistry was particularly violent during the times describes here. The hooded protestors were sometimes but not always students. Some of them are currently involved in the leadership of the Chávez administration.

"Well, that one bolivar," said Carmen staring firmly at Arnau, "added to the three bolivars in the student cafeteria and multiplied by five days in the week is a lot of bolivars, don't you think? And while we're on the topic, we came to you at the school to help you, because you tell me who wants to come for treatment with a novice."

Arnau ignored the insult but came back to his attack against the hoods, who in my opinion should not have been judged too harshly since they were working wonders on this man's spirit. Barely moments before, he seemed to be on the planet of the zombies. Now, trapped in a current of high voltage, he reminded me of Panichi.

According to Arnau, the hoods were useless layabouts who were being paid to study for decades and were just ripping everyone off. He had lost two terms due to the university strikes and was about to lose the third one.

"Why don't they kick up a fuss on the weekend or on national holidays, or better yet, at five o'clock in the afternoon, when my practicals are over? Why, for God's sake?" continued the future Doctor Arnau at full speed.

"I gagree wig him...ang wig you," I added hastily, but the damage was already done. Carmen looked at me hurt, and I smiled at her as best I could while a dribble of saliva escaped from the left corner of my mouth.

"A teargas bomb!" shouted Doctor Morales, flinging his hands in the air. The smell had entered through one of the windows at the back of the room and many began to throw themselves toward the passage.

Still talking, Arnau took the rubber dam off and covered the hole in my tooth with paste that he said would have to be replaced by a permanent amalgam. Looking at Carmen, he added that as Doctor Morales was about to flee, he wouldn't be signing the supervision of the treatment. He had lost the credit. However, he certainly had not lost the miraculous vitality that the hoods aroused in him. He began to smile at us, and to dampen strips of cotton in vinegar.

"Here you are. Put these over your nose and hold them there with these surgical masks. Follow me."

We started to go down the stairs. My eyes were burning and it was difficult to keep them open. Clutching the handrail, with Carmen close by my side, we formed a clumsy mass until Arnau, still in front, began to shout:

"Come on, come down, there's a landing here. Take two steps forward, now the first step down, last landing...."

Many people were overtaking us. Some fell and went tumbling down the stairs. Others were pushing us. Everyone was in a panic to leave the building. The vinegar was making me feel sick but without the mask, the burning was much more intense.

"Damn the stupid law that says that the police can't enter the university to kill those assholes," condemned Arnau when we got to the ground floor.

"Yeah, sure! Let's not complain about the economy, the bigwigs, the corruption and the lack of basic goods and services. You don't understand because you have everything. You don't know what it's like not to have those two stupid bolivars so you can eat in the cafeteria or take the bus," Carmen was saying, or rather shouting to herself, or perhaps to me because Arnau was not there anymore.

On our right outside the building, just behind the door of the university campus, the police were still throwing teargas bombs and pellets. The 1980 "Caracazo," that wave of protests and looting due to the rise in transport costs and fuel, had returned with a renewed impetus, on a smaller scale but regularly, once a week, right at the doors of our university's Dental School.

Hiding behind trees and cars in the university compound, people wearing hoods were throwing stones at the police. A distance of about twenty-five yards and a small, abandoned surveillance post separated the two groups.

The leader of the hoods was chanting slogans to address his group while shooting at the police with a short-range gun.

"Sing, comrades sing! Shoot with your voices! The people won't sing without weapons!"

He had taken refuge behind a garbage truck, filled with burning tires. It was Florencio Alvarez, a third year student in political science and well known because he had been studying for nine years at the university. Every now and then, he changed programs. He had studied literature for a while and then switched to sociology. He had also indoctrinated numerous young students and then abandoned them without scruples. One of them was Elena, a friend of Carmen's. She hated him now.

Right in the middle of the street, in front of the small hut at the entrance of the school, watching the police with defiance, another hooded man ignored the danger of the pellets, breathing in the smell of the bombs as if it were the morning coffee. I recognized him by the back of his t-shirt, illustrated with the Jamaican flag and Bob Marley's face. At the top in black letters was the legendary phrase: *Get up, Stand up for your rights.*

This reckless man was no layabout, nor was he being paid. We knew that he was trying hard to finish his studies and he adored Carmen, who often passed him her notes and helped him to write essays.

"Maikel! Chico, what are you doing? Come over here!"

Carmen's voice resonated several times in the passage outside the Dental School where some students and patients had congregated, full of fear and frustration. Maikel, who was holding a stone in his hand, did not bat an eyelid.

CHAPTER 12

February 3 and 4, 1992

They found a tumor in Oscar Sánchez's stomach. More tests were needed to make the full diagnosis but fearing the worst, Manuel wanted to spend more time with his father, with whom he felt he had shared very little.

He was right. I remember seeing Mr. Sánchez on those Sunday mornings when I had slept over at Manuel's house, and Manuel, Alfredo and I would sit around the kitchen table while Miriam made breakfast for us. This was always a complicated affair, which consisted of ham, beans, eggs, fried plantains and other light dishes that Miriam believed young people needed. We thought it was only a matter of heating some food up or throwing stuff into a pan, but Miriam always made life difficult for herself when Alfredo and I were visiting. After serving breakfast, the poor woman looked exhausted and ready to cancel the rest of Sunday.

Mr. Sánchez used to come into the kitchen just as the coffee was brewing. He was extremely pleasant to us, taking the trouble to crack a little joke with each of us and comment on something we might have told him a few Sundays before and that by that stage we had already forgotten. But he had not. His prodigious memory was capable of recalling those bland anecdotes we confided in him charitably, as if to give him the impression that our souls were open books. In turn, he would reciprocate, injecting a few touches of heroic fiction into his memories in order to make us feel special, while surely he suspected that our confidences were not sincere.

His triumphant entrance fascinated me because some time before, Alfredo, Manuel and I were more like a pack of dogs who had lost their dog warden than teenagers and would bark wildly, competing to see who could be the loudest and fiercest. At Manuel's house, we would create plenty of havoc even when we were too old for such exploits, perhaps because Miriam's temperament was a continuous source of inspiration. Perhaps it was her cooking, as we only did it with her food and at her house. On more than one occasion, I received a wet, raw egg in the eye, or I launched my portion of plantain onto someone's t-shirt with no respect for the culinary sensibilities of Miriam, who, yelled at us, telling us in no uncertain terms to clean up themess.

However, Mr. Sánchez would come into the kitchen long before the attacks would start and manage to keep us under control while his conversation lasted. At those moments, I thought of him as an amazing dog tamer, although a little later I realized that his performance was not just out of huge affection for us, but it also displayed his impressive sales skills.

He had a high voice, which he liked to modulate, perhaps to have the opportunity to show off his perfectly aligned white teeth, slightly yellowed from nicotine.

When he would smile or pronounce the "a," "e," or "i" before or after a consonant, the long narrow little moustache that was his pride and joy would move up or to the side, acting like a hood for his teeth. Mr. Sánchez always offered us a great hooded chat while demonstrating his great sales skills.

However, his dazzling personality would be gone in a flash, as once he had drunk his coffee, he would go to the other end of the counter to sit on the only stool that the Sánchez family had and bury himself in the horseracing paper, deaf to the commotion and to the food fights that ensued in his silence. He could spend most of the morning reading and taking notes on a small scrap of paper that he then put in his shirt pocket.

Later, dressed in a suit and tie, Manuel's father would saunter around the house without bothering anyone. At these times, already completely forgotten by his profession, he became a caged ghost, so ethereal that if we had not witnessed his comings and goings from the master bedroom to the balcony and vice versa, with an occasional stop in the bathroom, we would never have noticed his existence. Only around half past eleven, we would hear a very faint but unmistakable slam of the door, followed by the metallic, sonorous closure of the gate. This was the Sunday "see you later" of Mr. Sánchez, who was on his way to spend his evening at the racing track until nine or ten o'clock at night.

When he was fired from Jeep Venezuela, his mood brought an end to the jokes and his taste for heroic episodes, but he would still greet us affably. The change made Mr. Sánchez's day quite grim and much more ghostlike than the quiet strolls around the house. He got up very late every day and without really tidying himself up or stopping in the kitchen for a coffee, he would go to the "spa" as he and his new friends would call the steak houses or rather, their bars. They would spend many long hours there, united in drunken pleasure and a common interest inhorseracing.

"I don't know, Rodrigo. The doctor says that it's stomach cancer but he thinks that it's spread. They have to do a biopsy of a spot that they've found in his left lung,"

Manuel told me on the phone before asking if Alfredo and I would join him to go to the racecourse to spend a bit of time with his father.

A couple of hours later, we arrived at the restaurant at the second stand. There was Mr. Sánchez as if nothing had happened, sharing a second bottle of scotch with his drinking pals, four men who had their ties knotted up wrong and binoculars hanging from their necks. Apart from Mr. Sánchez and one guy who looked like a dry, baked cheese stick, the others were hiding their belt buckles under volumes of springy belly flesh. They were all clutching the horseracingnews.

After spending a little while in the company of his drinking partners, I discovered that they shared a strong sense of humor and a remarkable interest in gambling. As none of them showed much interest in talking to us, not even Mr. Sánchez, whose joy at seeing us was short-lived, we had to make deductions from their comments: Ismael Urdaneta was "Billy Goat," Pedrito Gutierrez was "Big Ant," Julio Colmenares was "The Whisperer" from the sound of it and the dried out cheese straw was Omar Quintero, who they called "Cheese Whiz."

"Hey, Cheese Whiz?" said Big Ant. "Don't bother putting a three nil-nil down on that old horse." He was pointing to Catfish, who was none other than Mr. Sánchez, perhaps because the hairs of his moustache stuck out as far as the corners of his mouth. The small man with a stoop answered with a piece of blood sausage in his mouth.

"Three nil-nil? No way, nor an "eight bet." He'll come in crippled after the ambulance."

Their comments referred to a type of illegal bet in horseracing. In the "three nil- nil," the gambler wins if the horse comes in first or second. If it finishes third, neither gambler nor the house wins. In the case of an "eight bet," the horse has to finish in the first eight places for the gambler to win something. Obviously, Oscar Sánchez was the sick horse, unable to finish among the first eight. In the remote case that he crossed the finishing line, he would be behind the ambulance, which always drives about three hundred feet behind the horses to rescue any poor unfortunate jockey who had fallen from the saddle.

"No kidding, Big Ant, that horse ain't even running. He didn't pass the vet's exam. They pulled him out," Billy Goat said.

By the fifth race, the continuous jokes about the dying Mr. Sánchez outraged us, although he managed to put on a little smile from time to time. Manuel, saddened by his father's illness and in a vain attempt to get close to him through the horseracing, wanted to leave, and Alfredo suggested a game of dominos at his house.

As we could not take Manuel's father with us, since he was set upon staying with his friends until the sixth race, we entrusted him to The Whisperer. He was an older man and a neighbor of the Sánchez family who earned his nickname thanks to a stroke he suffered ten years before. Since that day, half of his face was paralyzed, making him look as if he was telling someone a secret.

At around eight o'clock, we sat around a table on the back patio of the Piruggi house. It was one of four tables gathered around a grill area on one side of the house. They were made of cement with a large circular leg. The top was decorated with small, sparkling mosaic tiles, the same color as the ones on the ground, although these were opaque and more rustic. Surrounding the tiled area, which continued in a wide strip around the back of the house, was the garden with an immaculate Chinese lawn. At the end of the lawn, right next to the wall, which separated the neighboring patio from the Piruggi's, grew a lemon tree and several papaya plants. The quadrant of the patio was closed with a huge palm tree and a row of rose bushes. Behind that was a slope with small terraces to prevent mudslides. It was a beautiful patio and above all, it was well equipped for those who wanted to while away the time since the paved walkway had a roof. As well as the tables, it had two hammocks, several bamboo chairs and a television. From any angle, you could see the eastern part of Caracas and El Ávila mountain.

Nonno joined us. We used to play together against Manuel and Alfredo, who made an invincible pair, but that evening Manuel could not stop thinking about his father's problems, ruining his teammate's pieces in the process. Seeing that it was a good time for a comeback, Nonno urged Manuel sweetly to continue indulging his sorrows while Nonno busied himself with his pieces, making signs for me to follow his example, Italian style. We carried on in this way for several hours until Alfredo told his grandfather off, warning him that winning was not everything in this life. After that, he looked at Manuel very seriously and asked him if he was ready to throw in the towel, without a last fight.

Just when Manuel was starting to regain his position and had Nonno and I cornered, we heard a blast that sounded like thunder, followed by a series of whistles, bursts of machine-gun fire and many other different types of explosions. Isabel and Roberto came running down to the garden and speechless, we all watched the conflict unfold in the La Carlota airport, a small military airport in Caracas. A little later on, the television channels showed a video of President Carlos Andrés Pérez appealing to the people to stay calm. His nervousness was noticeable, although he asserted that the situation was under control. The shooting continued waking up Caracas.

The next day Mr. Sánchez's health was already old news, although we were far from knowing that the following month he would have a successful operation. His routine would continue in the same way for many years, unlike Caracas, whose cordoned streets full of soldiers were a prelude to the end of an era.

For several days, in case there was someone in the country who had not heard about the failed coup, the television channels showed the same video insistently in- between commercials that were no less insistent.

"*Comrades,*" said lieutenant colonel Hugo Chávez, accepting his defeat with a solemn yet optimistic voice, "*Unfortunately, for now, the objectives that we intended have not been accomplished in the capital.*"

In effect, while the leaders of the coup had taken Maracaibo and Maracay successfully, the attempt to take Caracas led by Chávez had failed.

"If it wasn't for that useless Chávez," said Manuel around six in the morning, when the face of our future leader appeared for the first time on our television screen, "we would be living under military rule now—who knows. Just like what happened in Chile, Argentina or Uruguay! Well, I guess we don't have to worry, at least not *for now.*"[6]

Just like Manuel, many people interpreted the words "*for now*" as a threat. To me, it was just any old phrase, used by someone with very limited vocabulary in an attempt to impress. However, in Universidad Central, they turned it into a prophetic phrase and its author into a mysterious martyr, a brave man who had not yet had the last say.

"Manuel, don't joke about these things, muchacho," said Isabel Piruggi, horrified. "It would be terrible."

---

[6] On February 4th, 1992 there was a failed coup against Carlos Andrés Pérez, led by the then Lieutenant Colonel Hugo Chávez, Francisco Arias Cárdenas, Yoel Acosta and Jesus Urdaneta.

Isabel's face made me think of a Venezuela with thousands of people being tortured and disappearing. In a flash, all the romanticism of a radical change like the one university students were hoping for seemed like a nightmare to me.

However, Carmen was much more optimistic when I called her from the Piruggi's garden, where for the first time in my life I felt under siege.

"Don't get me wrong, Rodrigo. I'm not saying the military coup is a good thing. But I'm telling you, this is the end of the *Acción Democrática* party. Now they know they can fall. No, no, let me speak. You're right. We'll be the ones to suffer in a coup. Us poor bastards as you say. But someone had to tell the politicians that enough is enough, right? Enough abuse and corruption!"

"Let her be, pana," said Manuel, who had come up to me quietly and had guessed what we were discussing. "She has her ideas and you have yours. Or is politics also going to separate us from our family and friends? Don't let it get you down, chico, it's not worthit."

The others stayed glued to the television and the telephone did not stop ringing.

Everyone was offering their own political predictions and were trying to make themselves heard, perhaps to convince themselves that the clashes in La Carlota were not that important. Everyone apart from Alfredo, who sat in silence, watching Chávez's speech over and over, in close detail.

"This motherfucker looks like a baboon," he said almost accidentally.

CHAPTER 13

"You idiot, did they never teach you to use condoms?"

"No! The priests thought it was your job!" I almost said but I contained myself. Red with fury, my father paced around the room cursing and asking God for patience to hold back from throttling me.

The house was infused with a strong smell of onion as my mother had made a Spanish omelet just before I had decided to drop the bombshell. A little upset, although much calmer than me, Carmen watched my father with her mouth half open.

I decided to have her over that night through pure cowardliness, predicting that my father would refrain from throwing a lamp at my head in her presence. I was also counting on my mother's help, as I knew she wouldn't mind the idea of becoming a grandmother. The truth is that becoming a father did not bother me, although I would have preferred not having the responsibility and to just carry on being Carmen's boyfriend for infinity. However, when she told me the news, my world collapsed. It was on August 3, at the huge party that Mr. and Mrs. Piruggi threw to celebrate their twenty-fifth wedding anniversary.

We arrived late, as usual, because Manuel came over to pick us up almost three hours later than we had arranged. "You have to get to parties when everything is nicely warmed up, panas, so you don't have to do all that small talk," Manuel told us by way of excuse, adjusting the knot on his tie as we entered the living room of the extravagant Quinta Esmerelda party venue.

I was holding Carmen's arm and noticed her astonishment at what she saw in front of her. It was no less than La Billo's Caracas Boys playing *Piano Merengue*. The guests were extremely elegant, making a train in the middle of the dance floor to the rhythm of the music and flitting around, greeting people. On one side of the room were the instruments from a string quartet who were also going to play later that evening; on the other side were tables laden with assorted cheeses, bottles of wine and platters filled with caviar and smoked salmon. The windows were dressed with blue velvet curtains, which fell in a cascade over the floor, and the ceiling was lit up with hundreds of little crystal stars distributed symmetrically.

I took Carmen's hand so that she would continue walking as she had stopped and was rooted to the spot. For the first time that evening, I noticed how beautiful she looked. Her hair was tied back in a ponytail, which was decorated with an intricate red hair accessory. Her dress was also red and very simple, although it cleverly emphasized her curves, revealing her splendid dark back.

Carmen smiled and naughtily said to me, "If you don't know how to dance salsa, today I'm teaching you." Then she turned toward Manuel who looked like a different man in his sober grey trench coat suit to exclaim, "How beautiful! I've never seen anything like it in my life!"

Her comment reawakened all the fears that had tormented me at the beginning of our relationship. What would these people think of my girlfriend from La Guaira? What would

Carmen say when she noticed the tremendous distance between them? As we went further into the room, I imagined María Fernanda's look of contempt and the secret gestures that she would make to her friends. I also imagined the fierce comments Carmen would make about the squandering of rich people.

However, as had happened on so many other occasions during our years of courtship, my fears were almost immediately dissipated when I saw Roberto Piruggi's happy face. He was dressed impeccably in a dinner suit and was waving at us, pointing out to Alfredo that we had arrived.

"How are you, Carmen? Welcome. Come here, give me a kiss. Hey, you got here at last."

"Yeah, pana, so…," Alfredo was saying to Vicente. "The chick didn't know that Pedrito was with us in the car. He was hiding in the back, waiting for the right moment to give her a scare. I parked across from the bakery with the excuse of going to get some beers and they both stayed there. You know, a simple joke, but it was heavy. Then when Pedrito was just about to get up and say 'boo', the girl goes and lets off a great stinking fart. She opens the window and shakes her miniskirt to get rid of the smell. Can you imagine?! Pedrito couldn't help laughing and when she heard him, the chick screamed and shot out of the car. Well, pana, what to say. I haven't seen her since that day."

"Carmen, just so you know that what these animals are talking about has nothing to do with me," María Fernanda informed her, not without sarcasm, passing Alfredo's arm around her neck, perhaps with the intention of showing off her bracelet that was ten times more expensive than the whole of Carmen's outfit.

When Vicente had dried up the tears from laughing at Alfredo's absurd anecdote, I introduced him to Carmen and after hugging her, he began to tell her stories from our student days. When Alfredo saw that Vicente was monopolizing Carmen without giving her a second's break, he decided to go to her rescue.

"Did you guys hear about the earthquake in Iran? About fifty thousand are dead and it looks like a real disaster."

"Hey, can we talk about something less depressing? We are here. They are there.

There's nothing we can do," said María Fernanda, looking annoyed.

"Yes, Alfredo, it's a disaster for sure," replied Carmen gracefully, giving him an appreciative look for rescuing her from Vicente's verbal onslaught. "The last time I listened to the news, about four hundred thousand people were homeless. You know, the problem is the same as the one we have here, people living in miserable conditions. And as you know, the government is just not prepared. Please God; spare us a natural disaster like that!"

"I'm going to invite you to my place so you can give that lefty speech to my mother. Let's see if she can understand that not everything can be resolved with crates of rum," Manuel said to Carmen, approving of her comment but not wanting to go deeper into the topic of the earthquake, because at that time Manuel did not even know where Tehran was. Just at that moment, I noticed that Carmen went pale and placed her hand on her stomach.

"Rodri, come with me to get some food. All this excitement is making me hungry."

It was only an excuse, as when we got to the tables, she refused to eat anything and asked me if we could find somewhere private. There were many people in the villa's garden, so I suggested going up to the second floor. There we found a seating area.

Carmen asked me to sit down, and then told me she was almost three months pregnant. She was completely sure because she had been to the doctor.

I don't know what I said or what she said. Nor how we even came to the decision that we would go through with the pregnancy. In fact, it was Carmen's decision, as my mind was completely blank. If she had wanted to have an abortion, I would have accepted it without a protest, not because I was frightened or for the sake of convenience, but because at that moment I was in a state of shock. A baby was an abstract thing to me, a problem that had taken me by surprise and that I did not really know how to deal with. Only the heat of the little body when I held it in my arms for the first time made it my child. I remember telling Carmen something that I probably heard in a soapopera:

"I'll support you in whatever you decide, my love. It's your decision. It's your baby."

The egoism of such a cop-out irritated her, and she corrected me straight away. It was our baby. However, from that day on, she was the boss in planning everything, from doctor's visits to the most trivial details.

"If it's a boy, we'll call him Emilio. Your father will be so happy," she said one evening to break the silence that had come over us while we were sitting in the garden in the main square of the university campus. Now I wonder if she had sensed my anxiety and the hours I had spent thinking of how I would break the news to my parents. Carmen was hurrying me to tell them, because she wanted my parents to know first. I practiced my little speech day and night. But after so much preparation, there I stood, ashamed in my living room, which stank of fried onions, on the receiving end of insults and well-deserved admonishments.

"How could you do this to us? Your father will have a heart attack, dear boy.

What about poor Carmen now?"

My mother had decided that sex was just about one person and said these things with tears in her eyes, taking Carmen's hand while Papa carried on pacing around the room like a bull about to charge.

Somewhat upset by so much drama, I thought that my father looked down on Carmen because I had heard him speaking savagely about dark-skinned people. His son marrying a little negrita from the provinces is not what this young man from Gijón had imagined twenty-three years ago, when he ventured across the Atlantic. Although Emiliano was abrupt like the Asturian coastline, he had also grown up in a country of kings and ceremonious courts.

"Explain to me how you're going to support a family now, you idiot."

Despite the insult, I noticed a change in my father's tone. Full of sorrow, he let himself fall into the armchair, looking directly into my eyes. Not with fury but with shame. At that moment, I understood my stupidity, my absolute blindness next to this man whose greatest hardship was not being able to give me anything just when his grandson was coming into the world.

Six months before, my father had spent whole days in a never-ending line in the main branch of the Latino bank. Finally one evening, with tears in his eyes, he told us that he had lost everything. My mother took his hand to tell him energetically that they would start again; her sewing business was going very well. He smiled but said nothing more. Now I realized that there was no new start for my father.

The banking crisis at the beginning of the nineties was the first big blow to fall on my family and on many others like us.

When the oil prices fell, rumors about banking insolvency and the constant devaluation of the Bolivar caused panic among those who had savings. Many transferred their money abroad and this sped up the crisis. The Latino bank where my father had put his savings went bankrupt, due to irresponsible business dealings abroad, among other things. Those who reacted quickly were able to recuperate part of their money just before the government took over the running of the bank, along with sixty percent of the banking institutions in Venezuela. The loss that people like us had suffered had been caused by white-collar criminals: the private Venezuelan bankers.

I felt like hugging my father, as I had never seen him look so small as in that moment. Of course, the hurried marriage and the public shame bothered him, but more than anything his helplessness infuriated him. My father's dream was that my sister and I could have a better life than his. With a baby on the way, my hopes of getting ahead were quite diminished. He knew this and understood much better than I did the difficulties that lay waiting for Carmen and me. In his way, Emiliano Fernández adored his family and would do anything for us; he just did not know how to express it.

"Papa, don't worry, ok? We're going to live in Carmen's apartment until we graduate."

"In one room? Why? You can live here with us. Carmen is going to need our help."

"Mom, Mom, let me finish please. We're going to live in Parque Central. I've only got a year of studies left and look, Isabel Piruggi already knows and she's going to give Carmen a job with the Salesian people, first as a charity work coordinator and then as a teacher in the school."

My mother looked horrified, either because she realized that the news was already in the public domain or because she had not been the first to know. "I'm going to get any old job for now and then when I've graduated, I'll teach somewhere. Look, these things happen, we were careful, believe it or not… And look at Isabel Piruggi, well, you know how Manuel takes note of everything. Carmen told me the news at that big bash the Piruggis had and well, he spoke to Isabel… you know what Manuel is like, he knew about Isabel's educational projects in the ghettos with the Salesian ladies…. Basically, Carmen is perfect for that kind of thing."

"Emiliano," Carmen was one of the few people who dared to call my father by his first name, "Why don't you see this as a blessing? Wow, you're going to have a grandchild crawling around on the carpet and gurgling on your tummy." She said this enthusiastically while she opened the balcony door. "Forget about what other people think or about our financial future. We're going to be ok. I'm so happy, because finally I feel as though I'm officially part of the family." Now she addressed the both of them. "I adore you and this baby…this is what I want. This is the happiest moment of my life.

And yes, I'm just as worried as you are, but I'm trying not to torture myself with what hasn't happened yet, and might never happen."

Once more, Emiliano succumbed to Carmen's simplicity and once more was unable to express it.

"Yes, well, you'll have to think everything through, but I think your mother is right, Rodrigo," my official name came back to the surface. "It would definitely make sense for you to move in with us. The unnecessary rent, Parque Central, with all this violence everywhere, there's no question."

Mixed with the racket coming from Altamira square and the air coming in from the balcony, the onion smell was almost unnoticeable.

CHAPTER 14

February 1, 1997

At the beginning of 1997, her belly looked like a huge soccer ball, bursting out of the braces and buttons of my shirts, two sizes bigger than hers, which Carmen began to wear in the last months of her pregnancy.

Sometimes, when she wore one of my t-shirts, which she borrowed without asking, you could see her little belly button camouflaged by the tense and slightly stretched skin of her belly. I would watch her with delight, telling her that her navel was nothing less than a periscope through which Emilio could look out at the world. Who knows what he liked to watch floating in his little sack. Maybe he was attracted to trees and birds, or maybe the numerous movies that Carmen watched, just so that she could sit with her legs raised up. Maybe Emilio enjoyed watching them, seeing how the good guys found a solution for everything, as if life could be better for all, except for the baddies.

Wearing one of my shirts, Carmen would walk like a penguin every day to the Don Bosco School, until the time came when the effort of walking a single block left her exhausted. She did not want to miss classes and as we only had the Malibu, I had to get used to the Caracas subway and its miraculous stations, where in those days, people still let old people pass and did not jump lines.

I became well trained in giving and receiving pushes and shoves to get on buses and mini buses. After a few weeks, I was already an expert at getting on and off moving buses and above all, travelling with half of my body hanging out of the bus, grabbing on to the folding door to get some fresh air. During the rush hour, the heat and fumes in those sardine cans were unbearable.

The journey home was much more civilized as it was usually night. When I left the high school where I was working full-time, I went to give private classes to bump up my meager teaching salary, just as Carmen had done as a student. I would get home at about nine or ten o'clock, to find my wife fast asleep on the sofa next to the TV, despite her stubborn wish to stay awake and wait for me.

My mother would take me to the kitchen to serve dinner and then she would go to the bedroom where Papa was reading the newspaper, waiting for her to switch off the light. Raquel would already have her room closed and when she was not asleep, she would tuck herself up in bed up to her ears and watch a horror movie. Only baby Emilio, from inside his mother's belly, would make signs to me and whisper, "She's fallen asleep again, she's been snoring for the last hour."

"Carmen, wake up now, come on. Let's go to bed," I would say softly. Wrapped in the cotton wool of tiredness, she would let herself be led to the bedroom of my adolescence, which was still the same as ever as I had no time to paint it. Only now, it had a double bed, which made it seem smaller.

Carmen loved ham cachitos, a kind of croissant. Every Saturday, before she awoke, I would go to the bakery and get some freshly baked ones. On my return, I would find her ready to go to Parque del Este, a large park in Caracas, or to the university botanical gardens. We would sit under a tree, eat the cachitos and have coffee from a flask, while some fanatical joggers would stop near us, working their butts off. Then we would lie on a blanket and read a passage or two from the books we loved rereading together: *The Madman* by Khalil Gibran, a Jorge Luis Borges short story or Carmen's favorite, *Platero and I*.

"Hey Rodrigo, I really feel like going for pizza at El León," Carmen would say almost every Saturday, interrupting our reading sessions to sigh under the beautiful Chaguaramos trees of the Parque del Este or a rubber bush in the botanical Gardens. I knew it was not pizza she craved but the company of our friends and the jovial atmosphere of Saturday evenings on the pizzeria's little terrace. She always got the craving when she'd barely finished breakfast.

"Call the guys as soon as we get home, honey, just in case they make other plans," she would say at least three times on the way home.

The group had grown bigger thanks to Carmen. Maikel, her best friend had met my two old friends, Manuel and Alfredo some time back, when I had decided to invite all three to a restaurant to celebrate Carmen's birthday. After that, they carried on meeting more regularly, and together we'd go to watch baseball games, with Caracas playing La Guaira. Carmen liked to invite Maikel along to give her moral support; otherwise, "the three Caracateers," as she called us, would drive her crazy.

From the stadium, we would go to get some arepas, until one day Manuel discovered a cafe where we could get pizza and beer for a good price, and after years of going unnoticed, it came to be quite fashionable. We adopted El León as a regular haunt where we could while away the time talking bullshit.

At one of these get-togethers, at about eleven thirty at night, the volume of our voices and our coarse chatter inundated the terrace. As we loved baseball slang, we used the word "inning" for the rounds of beers we ordered, which usually added up to about nine, unless we were engrossed in a conversation, in which case we would go for an extra inning. That evening, we were already on the eighth, and no one seemed to be getting tired.

Maikel was telling us about when he was a kid making a sandwich, and instead of bringing the jar of mayonnaise over to where he was, he leant over several times to get some on his knife. His mother Anselma was sitting in the middle between Maikel and the mayo jar, eating in silence. Since Maikel was strictly forbidden from dirtying the floor of the shack, he passed the knife on his mother's shoulders.

Maikel bent over several times to load his knife with mayo and let it drip on his mother several more times. The floor was immaculate unlike Anselma's shoulders, especially on her right hand side, nearest to Maikel's plate. The process was repeated two or three times, until Anselma moved her head, covering her hair and chin in copious amounts of mayonnaise. But she still said nothing and patiently waited until Maikel had finished spreading a thick layer of mayo and had crowned it with a fine slice of liver sausage. "Has the chef finished?" she asked her son pleasantly, showing him her shoulder, her hair and her jaw which were all covered in mayonnaise just to save the kitchen floor. Just as he was about to take the first bite of his sandwich, Maikel had to shoot out of the shack as fast as he could, fleeing from his mother who was in hot pursuit, ready to give him a hiding.

"Shit, Maikel! That reminds me of something," laughed Alfredo. "Five years ago, Rodrigo's folks went to the beach with some friends. I think that must have been the only time in his life that Emiliano didn't work on a Saturday. Anyway, we went to Rodrigo's place to drink and play dominoes. But in the middle of the table where we wanted to play was a huge jigsaw puzzle. It was almost finished and had at least five hundred tiny pieces. So you know, pana, in a collective idiot attack—because don't forget we were in a Gallego house—we got the idea to slide the puzzle toward the edge of the table, and lift it into the air with our hands and arms to place it on the sideboard. As you can imagine, there was no domino match thatnight."

We all laughed, and Carmen, seeing Alfredo so jovial, thought it was the right time to ask him about his breakup with María Fernanda.

"Well, come on, tell us everything, Alfredo," Carmen insisted with feline curiosity.

"Well, as I said, the relationship wasn't working anymore. Honestly, I just got sick of Mafe's dumb stuff. And shit, everything was a problem in the end, you know…"

"Well, what do you expect, Alfredo?" Carmen interrupted him. "You did cheat on her."

"Are you kidding me, Carmen? Don't play the judge. It was just a few stupid little kisses with that chick from the School of Medicine. She had nothing to do with it. Our relationship wasn't working before that happened…"

Alfredo defended himself astutely, bringing up his cousin.

"At least I'm not like that guy. He cheated on his girlfriend who was a virgin to avoid disrespecting her. I mean, to sow his oats, he thought it would be better to cheat on her than to have sex with her. José Antonio is such a caveman! I wonder if he's found another virgin to cheat on."

Our guffaws did not deter Carmen, who kept on insisting:

"Don't play dumb, Alfredo, I can see things exactly how they are. You did the same thing our ex-president Lusinchi and his lover Blanca Ibáñez did when they fled from Venezuela. They left with no bad feelings about the mess they left behind them, with all their money tucked away in Switzerland and Costa Rica. If you ask me, Mafe was open like the Venezuelan people. She put her trust in you and you swindled her. Then, just the way Jaime and Blanquita did, you ran away having had your fill, leaving her furious and just as ignorant as at the start."

Alfredo laughed, denying the accusations with a shake of his head, but he had understood the analogy. Then Maikel took off on politics, without giving Alfredo a chance to contest Carmen's remarks.

"My mother used to follow the *Acción Democrática* party, but not anymore. She felt deceived, exactly as Carmen said. She was the sort who would go to all the *Acción Democrática* meetings, and helped in the cooperatives for free and everything. I come from a very poor family as you all know, and during the election campaign, the AD knew all the tricks. They've always been good at getting to the poorest households. I remember before the elections, the regional leaders let the campaigners speak about the things the village needed. Then they would come and wave their magic wand, making things appear: water, electricity, medicine, a few drains, a tiny playground and maybe even a bit of asphalt. But like in Cinderella, the fairy tale disappeared or turned into a complex issue after a while. But the people were happy because to celebrate our new and short-lived progress, the AD would organize a huge bash with plenty of rum, music and free t- shirts."

When he said that, Manuel and I glanced at each other, remembering the unforgettable party that his mother Miriam had organized in Baruta with three hundred crates of liquor.

"I'm telling you, guys," continued Maikel, "I would shoot Lusinchi in the head. What's more, last Thursday I had a dream: I dreamed I had the whole bunch of those ex- presidents together, Jaime and his lover Blanquita, that Carlos Andrés and

Luis Herrera.[7] In my dream, I torture them and try to get information about their bank accounts, something like what that guy from the TV show "On Our Streets" does. The one that kills the corrupt guys and leaves a card that says "irretrievable." Only I don't kill them straight away, I mess them up just the way a lot of people were messed up because of them."

Manuel and Alfredo laughed, but I knew that Maikel was not joking. I could still remember that afternoon at the Dental School, when he was throwing stones at the police who replied with teargas bombs.

"Well, that is why Chávez is going up in the polls. He already has the support of 30% of the people and there is still another year to go until the elections," Carmen pointed out.

"No, forget it, Carmen," said Alfredo firmly. "That man has no chance. He's a military man, the leader of a coup. With that speech he made, he is just scary. No way!"

"Alfredo," said Carmen, the only one at the table not drinking beer. "What do you mean leader of a coup? What, so you mean his accomplice, Arias Cárdenas didn't win the elections in the state of Zulia? That coup was legitimate. It was nothing. Anyway, that idiot Caldera[8] forgave Chávez and let him out of jail."

---

[7] Luis Herrera was President of Venezuela from 1979 to 1984 and was a member of the Social Christian Party of Venezuela (COPEI party). Jaime Lusinchi was president from 1984 to 1989. Carlos Andrés Pérez was president twice, from 1974 to 1979 and then again from 1989 to 1993. They were both members of *Acción Democrática*. These two parties have shared power since 1958. Their administrations were corrupt and ignored the lower class. Chávez represented change and hope for the neglected part of the population.

[8] Rafael Caldera was president of Venezuela for the second time from 1994 to 1999. The fact that he pardoned Hugo Chávez for leading a coup contributed to Chávez succeeding him in 1999.

"If the people have any sense, they'll realize Chávez is just another populist. This country churns out corrupt people and demagogues. They're all a bunch of opportunists," advised Alfredo, emptying the last of his beer into his glass while he prepared himself for the counter. When it came to politics, Alfredo was like those sports commentators who think they know everything but have never held a ball in their hands.

"I don't know, chamo, we'll see. I think their plan is going to backfire on them," I said, hurrying to contradict him. "People admire Chávez because they think he's the only one who can change the situation in this country. Forget the *Acción Democrática* and the Christian party. If not, look how Caldera won the last elections. Just changing the name of the party and saying that he was the change, people lapped it up. But Chávez really does present a change."

"Yeah, sure Gallego, I get your point. You've been saying that for a while. Of course we need a change, but for Christ's sake, just because that gorilla is reciting Whitman's poetry doesn't mean people are going to vote for him. Those bastards led a coup, and don't forget that Venezuelans prefer democracy. What change, anyway? That guy's rhetoric doesn't say a thing. It's totally abstract and Manichean: We're the victims and they're the sons of bitches. Revolution, change... it's all bullshit."

"Well, what exactly did Lusinchi say in his campaign?" asked Maikel, realizing that the moment had come for him to justify his support for Chávez. "To tell you the truth Alfredo, I prefer to vote for a dude who's had a hard life, like me, who can represent me properly; an honest type even if he doesn't have the gift of the gab. I prefer that to not voting, because those are the only two alternatives for me."

"Which is pretty sad," added Manuel, raising his voice just before downing the last of his bottle of beer. "Look, Alfredo, if

I put my dog forward as a candidate in this country's election, and I made him bark with a different bark, I'm sure he would win. And I'm telling you, even I would vote for him."

"What dog, dumbass? You don't have a dog," retorted Alfredo.

"I'm bushed," I said, waving to the barkeeper to get the check. "Shall we go, Carmen?" Everyone protested in unison.

"No, honey, we're not going," she replied calmly. While Manuel began to laugh at her reply, Carmen fixed her hair gently, making a kind of knot to keep it out of her face and turned to Alfredo:

"The change has already happened. That's what they're trying to tell you. What is yet to be seen is who will take advantage of the people's disappointment. Maybe Chávez, who is an extremist for sure, but at least he had the guts to sacrifice himself for something he believed was right. I think I would vote for him if he didn't make a pact with the usual suspects."

The check arrived. Without looking at it, I put some bills in the black folder, knowing that my share consisted of nine beers, two pizzas, and Carmen's pineapple juice. While I did that, I complained under my breath:

"Jesus. So much for criticizing my father and here I am, pana. Tomorrow is Sunday, back to those damned private classes."

"First, stop whining." Manuel intervened euphorically, taking the folder from me and giving me back the money. "Second, we already told you. You're not paying a cent right now. Also, Carmen is in charge here, and she doesn't want to leave." As he said the last thing, he glanced at the bill and exclaimed even more triumphantly:

"Shit! These dudes must have got it wrong. It's so cheap."

Alfredo quickly came to back up Manuel's comment, and with identical glee, shouted to the bartender:

"Boss! Another round over here. We're going for another inning!"

"No, stop. One thing is for you to pay, but we're going now. I'm tired and anyway, why the waste?"

"Honey, I already said we're not leaving, and definitely not now. Alfredo and Manuel are getting another round," Carmen said to me with a long but sweet face. When she saw Alfredo's quizzical look, Carmen sighed and tried to explain. "It's just that I'm fed up with this money business. Thank God, I got paid the other day so I'm ok. Let me tell you about something that happened." Carmen was speaking as if I was not there. "Two weeks ago we went down to La Guaira to visit my family and my father took us out to eat fried fish. You know, Manuel, the place I took you guys to that day at the beach.

Well, you already know my father is pretty broke. He's always been broke, but whenever we visit, he gets money from somewhere because he likes Rodrigo. Papa always tells me that soon we'll convert Rodrigo to communism because that boy has it in him. Anyway, as soon as Papa tells me he's taking us out to eat, Rodrigo starts with his whining. "Hey, chiquita. Why's your dad spending money on this meal?"

Carmen imitated me, lowering her voice to sound depressed. "Hey, I should pay half, shouldn't I?"

"For Christ's sake, Carmen, don't make stuff up!" I protested, more tired than bothered by the joke.

"Shut up, Gallego! We all know what you're like. That stuff is true. Let her finish the story—it's a good one. I already know the rest...."

I looked at Carmen in surprise at Manuel's comment. For some time now, he seemed to speak to her more than to me. They seemed like two best friends when they spoke on the phone. Rather than being jealous, I felt quite pleased that they were getting on well. Carmen was like the sister that Manuel never had.

"Well, I thought, I'm going to tease him back, I'm fed up with this. So I told him," she paused for a moment to swallow and continued. "Honey, when they serve you your fish, you have to eat the eyes, the tail and suck the head. You know what a big sacrifice my father's making to take us out to eat and how much he hates wasting food."

"Ha ha ha!" Alfredo was crying with laughter. "Don't tell me any more. I can already imagine the Gallego eating fish eyes with a disgusted look on his face, and feeling like he's doing something for the cause." Everyone laughed, and Carmen, the queen of the situation, put her arm around my shoulders and planted a huge kiss on my cheek.

"What to do, Rodrigo? Have another beer, for God's sake. Did I tell you about the nine year old girl in that coastal town who put her you-know-what in my face when we were dancing to drums?" Alfredo did not wait for anyone to beg him and began to tell the story.

"The little girl wanted to teach me to dance to Afro-Venezuelan drums. Well, don't forget I was doing my externship in Capaya and I was just the coolest guy there, you know, like a god. They start playing the drums, she starts to dance, and there I was, standing still in the middle of a circle, feeling awkward in the spotlight. Then her mom shouts out to the girl, "Get him to smell, Gertrudis! Get him to smell!" Well, what then? The people got me on the ground and the girl opened her legs, with a foot on each side of my ribs. She made small steps with her hips toward my head and then she started bending her knees to go down bit by bit. She was waving her hips around like crazy with her arms in the air until finally she squats on my face, pana. The idea was that I could smell her sweat. But shit, nine years old! Thank God she was wearing panties. How embarrassing. If Father Bernardo had seen that shit he would have excommunicated me."

"What are you saying, you stupid Caracas shithead? Us people from the coast are perverts or what? Or are you the pervert because of what you thought would happen?

That little thing only wanted to dance with you. Imagine what her family would do to you if they heard you talking now." As he said that, Maikel made as if he was throttling Alfredo amid the laughter brought on by the beer.

With a tight game and no races, the night was long and did not end until the fifteenth inning. Two months later, our son Emilio was born, and he also became a regular at El León. Later came the elections and we all voted for the winning candidate, Hugo Chávez. Everyone except for Alfredo, of course, who suddenly took off to the States to do a postgraduate degree. At least that was what we told him jokingly, as he never spoke about going to study in Chicago. Something must have been right in our reasoning because after Chávez won, Alfredo never stopped talking about the misfortunes that our country would suffer with that man. But that is another story. That night in El León, we were dealing with our problems like the rest of the people of Caracas: celebrating with friends.

PART TWO.
THE AWAKENING
(1999 – 2007)

CHAPTER 15

October 14, 1999

"Ah, Manuel dear, we're finally going to find out if you're a cock with vision. Can you imagine? A cock that can see, as well as all its other skills!" Those were the words of Vilma Montilla, the daughter of the most important minister in Chávez's cabinet.

Manuel had met her a few months before graduation, when Miriam Sánchez, worried about the possibility that her son would end up working in an ordinary law firm, called on her most valuable contacts to get him into a decent notary's office. Vilma's office did not particularly stand out on its own merits, but Pedro Montilla was then the leader of the *Movement for Socialism* (MAS), a political party that took over the candidacy of Rafael Caldera in 1993 after fusing with *Convergencia,* the first big block of political parties in Venezuela.

Manuel was practically dragged to the luxurious office by Miriam, who first explained to Vilma that she had bumped into her son in the street and had decided to join him. Then she claimed a chair opposite the desk and began to talk about the heat, the traffic, and the distinguished Rigo Figueroa and Ernesto Piñero, who were so fond of dear Manuel and who had recommended him so highly. When she heard the name

Rigoberto, Vilma's ears pricked up as only Piñero had called her to talk about Manuel Sánchez.

The last time Rigoberto had spoken to Vilma was the day they had both graduated from Law school together with thirty other students. The whole class, unaware of the sacrifices that some of its members would make, threw a huge, stylish party. It was there, twenty years ago, under the glow of oil-lamps decorating the table, when Rigoberto said to her, "I'll be back in a minute, just getting a drink." She waited for him in her fuchsia pink dress, clutching the glass of whisky that another new graduate had given her, until she heard that Rigoberto was no longer there. He had left with the woman who would become his first wife, a Caracas club member, who would enable him to climb into the higher ranks at the Ministry of Justice. Ten years later, he left with another woman, and finally with yet another, always at parties and always advancing in his political career, without any of the women he left in the lurch ever so much as lifting a finger to deal the blow that would settle him down once and for all.

Having been born under a lucky star, Rigo never came face to face with Vilma again. She did not believe in playing the victim, even though no one could say for sure that she was a violent person. Far from pursuing the enemy, she believed it was a great virtue to stay put and to feel the sting of the slapped cheek. With a wry smile, she thought that if fate brought them face to face again, then it would be destiny, and not she who would claim revenge, and the only thing left to do would be to follow its course until the opposition's blood spilled.

The image of the young, good-natured Rigoberto, recently arrived from Táchira, made her feel slightly uncomfortable, and she suddenly felt like cancelling this interview that in essence, had been forced upon her. Then, seeing Manuel's embarrassed reaction to his mother's wild enthusiasm, she felt something resembling compassion, and for a few brief seconds she wavered, lost in the flow of this charitable sentiment.

An ugly nervous tick that suddenly appeared in Miriam's right eye brought her back down to earth. Then, noticing Miriam's nervous state and not knowing how far this woman would be prepared to go if things did not go her way, Vilma thought that good will among party members was de rigueur, and that she could do without enemies in *Acción Democrática* lines. She employed Manuel on the spot, ushering Miriam and her great volume toward the door in an effort to get away from her incessant chattering and the crazy eye, which had just begun to water.

When they reached the exit to the street, Vilma confirmed the details of the contract. With premature generosity or perhaps due to habitual and unconscious cruelty, she explained to Miriam that in a matter of no more than two years, Manuel would be promoted to Head of Department if he worked hard and above all, if he kept his eyes open.

During the next years, Vilma and Manuel worked together in harmony; at least according to Vilma, who never bothered to hide her preference for "Manuel dear," who she would call to her office every day for coffee. In these moments that were ill-fated for Manuel, Vilma lounged in a splendid swivel chair which she got from Capuy, and listened to the agenda that her star employee would read to her, while she adjusted her bra and raised the steaming cup to her lips, leaving on it a bruised red lipstick smear.

After making a couple of observations out of force of habit or to show her status as boss, Vilma would instruct Manuel on political topics of the moment, savoring the most scandalous details with the last cold sip of coffee.

Sometimes she spoke in a somber, sardonic tone of voice in an effort to intimidate Manuel. As he only laughed and replied evasively, Vilma would jump to other subjects, such as the renovation of the office, with which she was obsessed for a while, and the incompetence of her staff, who she could talk about for hours and weeks, repeating like a scratched record tales of their numerous mistakes and endless ignorance.

After exactly two years, Manuel became Head of Department. That was when he had to sit down to discuss the renewal of contracts and when he learned to control his words and his facial muscles, stiffened in a type of disdainful smile, keeping his eyes half closed to look distracted. He had learned from experience that Vilma could be even more ruthless if she had a hint of him looking condescending, or if she let slip a vaguely kindhearted word.

For Manuel, it was incredibly difficult to calculate when and how to intervene in the purging of staff members that Vilma would carry out behind closed doors, hissing like a snake. But such was the nature of the job he would tell himself, especially when it came to young female members of staff, who he considered very helpless, as very few of them managed to grow old prematurely or find a husband who would beat them, the only situations in which employment with Vilma would be relatively safe-guarded.

In this way, letting very little show, staying focused and fine-tuning his ear, like a good orchestral conductor, Manuel managed to transform his boss's screeching into a harmonic and human melody. He did it so successfully that Vilma began to consider herself one of the most generous people in her position, since she gave incredible second chances to even the most useless individuals. And the kinder she appeared, the more sterility and cruelty she blamed on Manuel, silently congratulating herself for having employed him, as after all, thought Vilma, those are the sort of men she wanted around her.

Very seldom did Vilma manage to ruffle Manuel's feathers. Manuel, however, became adept at finding patience in an array of images, some of them childish but no less effective. While he listened to Vilma violently declare who she would fire, he imagined silent bombs and guided missiles, full of lethal chemical agents, which would leave his boss completely bald or dissolve her curved eagle claws into the air. Most of the time, Vilma was like the Cruella de Vil who had fascinated Manuel when he was a kid. Except that in his version of the film, he was the hero who, after defeating the despicable and petulant butler Alonso, would save the Dalmatian puppies and stop Cruella Montilla from getting her hands on them, and also from making those unbearable noises she made when she sipped her coffee and obsessively chewed the ice in every Cuba Libre.

Such childishness was far from enjoyable as, in his worst moments, Manuel realized that he was trapped in the same hole that he thought he had crawled out of when he gained independence from his mother. However, on days when he felt more optimistic, his crazy imaginings lent him a certain composure, paradoxically bringing him back down to earth, where he was earning a fantastic salary, doing what he would be expected to do in any other notary's office. Furthermore, it was obvious that Cruella appreciated him very much, and needed him to run the office smoothly. Manuel had never experienced this seductive power over anyone else, nor the moral superiority that separated him from his boss, a mature woman, alone and unhappy with a yellowed face, creased like the delta of a river. He also felt compassion for her.

"Manuel, dear." She said to him one afternoon that they bumped into each other in the city center and decided to go to a nearby restaurant. "You really are the cock with vision. I don't know what I would do without you. Can you imagine how my life would be if that idiot Yolanda was in your job?"

Smiling back, Manuel clinked his bottle of Polar with Vilma's while in his throat he felt a stab of guilt. The mere mention of the clerk took him back to a few days before, when Yolanda and he had stayed late to work. They had to write up various documents for the following day, and after a few hours, when the task was almost done, Manuel took a bottle of aged rum out of his office. He needed a little break before revising the documents for the last time. Without a second thought, he poured Yolanda a glass. From there they started laughing and making jokes about clients, colleagues and Vilma.

Yolanda was a young woman with delicious hips and a great sense of humor. She had a boyfriend or husband, but that night Manuel chose to ignore the details of his subordinate's personal life, and caressed her from head to her toe, after carrying her, staggering to the biggest and most spacious office in the company. With his foot, he pushed to one side the magnificent swivel chair from Capuy, which swung around, hitting a filing cabinet. He placed her on the very old and well-polished oak surface.

There they united, spontaneously and full of fervor, seeking the human contact they barely experienced in their daily routine. In the early hours of the morning, after getting dressed, they looked at each other, shyly and gratefully.

In 1999, when Chávez became President, Pedro Montilla became his right hand man and the Minister of Food and Nutrition. That was when Vilma's life would change forever, when her father took her on as a trusted employee, and with her, she dragged Manuel, whose services she could not do without.

Within a short time, Vilma and Manuel filled their pockets, charging commissions to food importers, a group that had begun to multiply due to the damage that Chávez' government had wreaked on the country's food industry. However, while Manuel maintained a discreet and contained attitude toward his unexpected prosperity, partly because he had begun to understand Carmen and Maikel's naïve social passion, Vilma was seized by a euphoria that barely let her sleep. She spent all her time traveling back and forth to Miami, returning laden with random items such as imported aspirin.

According to her, the Venezuelan version could not help cure the headaches that were brought on by the Caracas traffic, door-to-door salesmen and her two housekeepers, and that would afflict her as soon as her official car would leave the airport for the highway.

During the few appearances that she made in the Ministry, Vilma would go directly to her office without bothering to look around her, or to find out the name of her own secretary. She no longer had to deal with all the staff nonsense, which she happily passed on to Manuel, who was great at getting on with the mobs. Her world was one of big decisions, which if the truth be told, only took up a few hours of the week, as her job was simply to revise and approve import requests, and to fix the commissions which she would then distribute, without much regard for justice, between the civil servants involved in the process.

Manuel stayed in charge of running the division and processing the sordid paperwork which, in less than a year, produced enough profit so that he was able to buy a luxurious penthouse in the exclusive neighborhood of Valle Arriba.

Sometimes the Ministry's political decisions and Vilma's ambitions made him feel extremely uneasy, but his new position freed him from the mid-morning coffee break and his previous responsibility with the notary office staff. Once he found his own rhythm and felt confident of his own skills as head of administration, he let himself dream of having his own law practice far away from Caracas and Vilma, and far away from politics, near a small ranch with trees, some horses and a river. But no matter how often he ran through the map of Venezuela in his head, Manuel could not find his "Garden ofEden."

When Vilma grew tired of gallivanting around Miami Beach, socializing with high-ranking civil servants and trying to ruin Rigo's life—for a while she thought that destiny had finally brought her face to face with him, and that it was time to tear him to shreds, which she effectively did—she resorted to using Manuel for entertainment. She would invite him to the best restaurants in Caracas, and update him on the current political gossip, but now accompanied by a bottle of 18-year old Buchanan.

On one of these decadent afternoons, stepping out of a well-known steakhouse, Manuel was dazzled by the intense sunlight and had to lean on Vilma's right shoulder. She was much shorter than him, and made a perfect guide dog.

"Manuel dear, I'm taking you home. We're leaving your car here and we'll get it tomorrow. Christ, you're so drunk," laughed Vilma jovially, showing off her dental work, faded by the years and stained with nicotine.

In the car, Manuel rested his head on the top of the seat and closed his eyes, trying to doze. But halfway through the journey, he began to feel Vilma Montilla's cold hand stroking his left leg, up and down and in a circular motion so that on the way up, her little finger brushed against his genitals. Neither one said a word until they had parked, and the same hand, now warm and sweaty, took him by the neck and pulled him toward her.

Manuel stretched out his right arm with the intention of stopping the snake, but instead, a cowardly reflex made him surrender and place his fingers just below Vilma Montilla's armpit. Aroused by the contact, and with her hand grasping Manuel's member, she suddenly began to kiss him, invading his mouth with her viper's tongue, still impregnated with anisette and cigarettes. When she finally let him take a breath, she whispered,

"Ah, Manuel dear, we're finally going to find out if you're a cock with vision.

Can you imagine? A cock that can see, as well as all its other skills!"

At this moment, Manuel had no other option but to accept the double meaning of Vilma's epithet. Humiliated and drained by this recognition, he let her shake him around like a ragdoll to extract bodily fluids that he would have preferred to exchange with other women. Between his drunken state and Vilma Montilla's acidic perfume, his conscience managed to remind him of how harshly he had judged his own unbearable mother, whom he had always held responsible for buying the house in Prados del Este, when he himself, only a few months before, had received the first big commission which enabled him to buy the apartment he now lived in.

Since that afternoon, the frequency of meetings with Vilma Montilla had increased or decreased, depending on which was stronger: her desire or his repulsion. But when they were together, Manuel carried out his part conscientiously, sometimes even enjoying the carefree feeling of days gone by. Trapped in the haze of excess, he thought he was still able to control Vilma's lack of moderation and prevent their parallel lives from crossing, interwoven in a web that his disregard, conformity and eagerness for financial security had given them by fate.

CHAPTER 16

December 6, 2002

Two years after the tragic death of her parents and sisters in the mudslides of La Guaira, Carmen was still hammering herself in the head, deeply regretting not having paid more attention to the ones she loved so dearly. To compensate, she tried to be attentive to everyone, and to be aware of those next to her and who would not always be with her. But her rage continued unabated. She dwelt on the numerous mudslides and storms that, according to her, the La Guaira tragedy would bring.

Her endless monologues—as Rodrigo, Manuel and Maikel ended up letting her speak alone—always went in a full circle, starting somewhere and always stopping on December 15, 1998, when Hugo Chávez betrayed her for the first time by ignoring the landslides that had already started on the coast. "Instead," she would say, shaking her head angrily, "Mr. President continued with his daily agenda, asking people to go out and vote for the new constitution that he desperately needed to stay in power."[9] Chávez justified his indifference to the tragic

---

[9] As said before, the referendum approved a change in the constituion that gave Chávez incredible powers and control over the country's institutions. It also allowed the dissolution of congress. Only 45% of the population voted due to the heavy rains all over the country.

events by quoting the famous phrase uttered by Bolívar after the earthquake that struck the city of Caracas in 1812, and which today even primary school children, for some peculiar reason, know by heart: "If nature goes against us, we will fight it and make it obey us." That is what Bolívar said to a city in rubble. That is what the children recite in school and that is what is written in big golden letters in the old headquarters of the now defunct Comercio Bank, a beautiful white marble building from the 70s, built next to Bolívar's birthplace. For these reasons and perhaps for others too, the phrase lived on. While children repeated it at school, adults passing through the center of Caracas in front of the white building remembered it as they read the words, always asking themselves what nature had to do with banks, and never receiving an answer.

No doubt, Chávez, who had also learned this phrase by rote as a child, or at some point had seen it in the center of Caracas, said it opportunely to quiet the people who had to go out to vote. But ironically, far from bowing in submission before the leaders of the Venezuelan government, nature rebelled with fatal fury on December 15, 1989. Neither Chávez nor anyone in his cabinet foresaw the colossal disobedience of the strong winds which mercilessly unraveled a gigantic mass of clouds hanging over La Guaira.

In this way, nature asserted its independence from politics and to leave no doubt, the mudslides that nature unleashed with all its might that December 15 left behind it a death toll of fifty thousand in less than forty-eight hours. No-one watching on television could believe their ears or eyes.[10]

---

[10] This was according to the Red Cross and most organizations involved in the rescue operation. In fact, the Red Cross called it the worst disaster in Latin American of the 20th Century. The number of victims

But Chávez certainly did believe it, because he saw it with his own eyes. And in spite of that, he betrayed Carmen again as he flew over the cursed area in the presidential helicopter. Cruising in his comfortable cabin, with his bright red beret and his impassive expression, he spoke to the television cameras and to the people about the cruel, oligarchic past and of the grandiose future that lay ahead for the country. He spoke for a long time, showing his satisfaction with the electoral vote, without paying much attention to the freakish hell that he was flying over and that was bringing grief to thousands of families on the coast.

Sobbing, Carmen could not believe the images on the television and those she would see a few hours later, when Hugo refused to let the two US ships disembark with engineers, marines and equipment to move debris. She could not understand why, after calling the gringos for help, Chávez denied them entry and instead asked them for money.[11]

No, she definitely did not understand what was going on in Hugo's head, although on December 18 she suddenly understood, when they were digging out her family who had been trapped under a thick layer of debris, that she would never again hear her mother complaining of her arthritis, nor

---

is unknown, but it was likely to be over 130,000. According to the 2012 Guinness Book of Records, this is the largest number of fatalities produced by a mudslide in history. While some of the leaders of the Venezuelan government admitted that the number of fatalaties was at least 30,000, the official declaration made on December 20th was 7,000. Little has been done to rebuild thearea.

[11] When rejecting the offer, Chávez argued that he needed money and equipment instead. However, the US Department of State received a letter from the Venezuelan Ministry of Defense specifically asking for military Engineers.

the adolescent giggles of her sisters, nor her father shouting to celebrate Antonio Armas' homeruns.

"What goddamn revolution?" She started saying to the four walls, fusing what she imagined of the president's psyche together with an immense resentment of his voracious appetite for power. After a few months, tired of shouting because no-one was paying attention any longer, she became silent, and every night, after putting Emilio to bed, she went to her room and sat down at the little desk that she and Rodrigo shared.

There, Carmen read as much as she could get hold of from Universidad Central on political philosophy. She read through this material as if it were foreign and new, a different knowledge, words that were mysteriously registered on pages that she had memorized as a young girl, and others that she came across for the first time. Dispensing with the old Carmen, she read absolutely everything, with so much eagerness and so much unease that her husband, whose surprise grew as the weeks went by, began to fear that she would abandon her graduate degree in linguistics, just as she was approaching the final stretch. But she was determined to write about the hatred, this ghost that woke her up in the night and covered her in sweat. There was no way to dissuade her, or to get her to explain what this wretched project was about and why it could not wait until she had graduated.

She began writing exactly two years after the tragedy, the same Friday that she offered a mass for her family, first asking her late father to forgive her for going to church, *the opium of the people.* That same night, after putting Emilio to bed, and under the pretext of working on her thesis, she left her parents-in-law alone in front of the TV and went to the small desk in her room with a spiral bound notebook she had bought the day before in Paco's bookshop. Paco was a neighbor from the building where many years before, Rodrigo's parents had bought an apartment with the intention of moving to the east of Caracas for good.

Against his frugal nature and as if he had read her mind, old Paco, an avid anti- chavista, gave her a box of pencils and two more notebooks with no explanation. He had never shown any compassion toward Carmen's misfortune, and even at this point, when she shared his political vision, he seemed reluctant and perhaps even wondered what Rodrigo had seen in this communist girl from the provinces.

Armed with her nicely sharpened pencils, Carmen would write every night for an hour or two, after bathing little Emilio and putting him to bed. Her parents-in-law told her not to work so hard, asking her to sit with them for a while, at least until Rodrigo arrived home from his evening classes, but Carmen was in a hurry. It was as if she could foresee her own death, which was to take place on December 6 of 2002 in Plaza Altamira, just opposite her in-laws' apartment, only a few yards away from the balcony where her husband stood, watching her tenderly.

By the time of her death, Carmen had filled three thick notebooks and had outlined two chapters. Rodrigo only had the courage to read them a long time after, sitting on the bed where, late at night, he had often begged her in a whisper to finish her thesis so she could find a decent job, because he was exhausted with teaching so many classes. Also in the same bed, a gift from her in-laws, Carmen would sometimes answer that he was right, and in a trembling voice, ask him to forgive her for her incredible egoism, although she could not promise him anything.

Sitting on the worn mattress that had witnessed the only difference of opinion in their married life, Rodrigo had the courage to open Carmen's notebooks. It was a Saturday morning. His parents had decided to visit Raquel, who had been living with her cousins in Maracay for some time. Her parents wanted to persuade Raquel to move back to Caracas, and she, now a graduate nurse, was indecisive. To bribe her, they promised her the absolute freedom she had desired as an adolescent. The thought of living with the family again only made her smile condescendingly, as in Maracay, Raquel was as free as a bird. But she adored her nephew, and the idea of living with him was more and more tempting as she saw her own chances of having a family diminish. Because she still looked younger than her thirty-something years, those who knew her called her "Mrs. Raquel" and those who did not called her "Miss," which upset her. In a country where the largest part of the population is extremely young, on turning thirty, Raquel abandoned her dream of seeing a prince climb up into the tower where her parents had shut her away.

With little hope of having her own family, Emilio was her great joy. Fully aware of her little weakness and prepared to resort to bribery, her parents had gone with their grandchild to Maracay that Saturday. It was the first time since Carmen's death that Rodrigo was completely alone in Altamira.

He thought he would spend the day correcting exams, but mid-morning a corrosive loneliness took hold of him, depriving him of the defenses that had protected him from Carmen's absence until then. Vulnerable, he shambled around for hours with an emptiness that had kept itself hidden until then and which that Saturday began to gush out of his soul. Then he went to find Carmen's notebooks which, in his bitterness, he had hidden in the highest part of the closet, amid soft toys and books. With trembling hands, he took them out of their hiding place and began to read them, understanding very little, as the presence of his wife emerged strongly and clearly from the big, scrawling handwriting whose spontaneous expression he knew so well.

It took a long time to pull himself together, but when he had managed to, he took the notebooks firmly in his hands and read them again without stopping. His mouth hung open, since he was expecting an academic essay, and not this ghostly fantasy that had been secretly brewing in his wife's heart. Between her scribblings and smudges, Rodrigo discovered a confusing, surreal story that reminded him of Dante's *Divine Comedy* and which he later interpreted in the following way:

Carmen's Notebooks

In the first chapter, the Helicoide appears, standing erect, and veiled in mist. This marvelous building was commissioned in the mid-fifties by dictator Marcos Pérez Jiménez and was built according to his orders in the small, steep Tarpeian rock, one of the many hills at the south entrance of the Caracas valley, where the avenue Medina Angarita joins the Fuerzas Armadas, the only main street of the city that runs from north to south.

Though the building remains unfinished, and has been surrounded by a row of sad little shacks since the dawn of democracy, its serene beauty lives on. It was called Helicoide because its triangular floors were built up like a pyramid, and are bordered by six protruding vehicle ramps linked together. The whole thing becomes a wide, floating lane for cars in the shape of a spiral which rises up to the last terrace on the outside of the building.

In his summary, Rodrigo always starts explaining to a sparse, but loyal imaginary audience that when Carmen saw the Helicoide, she always thought of the Helicon, the holy mountain where the Muses lived and where the great artists of ancient Greece would make a pilgrimage to pay them homage. "I bet you anything," she said some time before, when she had stopped talking about Chávez, "This building was designed with the purpose of reinforcing the rock, so that it's like a new holy hill."

"Wow Carmen, that's great!" he would say, unable to hide his relief that his wife had finally found a topic to talk about that was not politics, although she, feeling threatened by how the rift caused by her thesis was affecting Rodrigo's mood, recognized a slightly mocking tone in his voice. This irritated her immensely. It was as if her cultural observations, so well-received in times gone by, now seemed to her husband to be nothing but banal remarks.

"What is really great," she said to him one day, fed up with the stupid line Rodrigo had adopted to celebrate her comments, "is the idea of building the Helicon on the Tarpeian Rock. See, honey," she added, taking a deep breath and counting to ten in silence, "there are several Tarpeian Rocks. The original is southeast of Rome, on one of the seven hills. Before the city existed, the Sabines, from a nearby village, fought brutal battles against those barbarians from the south who were descended from the orphan of a fratricide: the Romans. After years and years of war, peace was finally made between them and that was how Rome was created. But the rock was immortalized way before that, when the Sabines, who used to throw traitors off it, decided to push a Roman woman from it. Apparently, she was jealous because the men of her village had very few women and had stolen a group of Sabine women. And without thinking twice, the woman revealed strategic information to the enemy, who nevertheless sentenced her forbetrayal.

"Christ, Carmen, so what we have with our Tarpeian Rock is historimyth."

Carmen nodded, wondering what "historimyth" meant, but leaning toward prudence, a virtue that she had learned to cultivate with her husband, she made do with enthralling him with the story.

"What we have here in Venezuela is mental chaos. And the hill jinxed the building for sure."

"Carmen was right." Rodrigo began to tell everyone after reading the notebooks.

Because no matter which brilliant idea had inspired its design, and despite the wonder that it aroused in the Museum of Modern Art in New York, the Helicoide had certainly been conceived under an unlucky star. Three years after Pérez Jiménez had fled to Spain and just before the New York exhibition where its model was on show, construction was halted because the new democracy refused to be associated with a project launched by the ex-dictator, or maybe it was dictatorial corruption later within the democracy that halted construction work.

Even when the idea of finishing something that was almost finished finally crossed the minds of politicians as well as city planners, after several decades of dwelling on it, no one calling themselves democratic could bring themselves to rehouse the shack owners who had settled in the immediate vicinity of the magnificent building. The neighborhood was already too dangerous for the old project of clubs, luxurious boutiques and a theater, which Pérez Jiménez had dreamed would bring modernity to Caracas with the Helicoide.

Nevertheless, perhaps foreseeing the uprising of the new Sabines, Chávez moved some army offices into the huge space and even managed to repair the glamorous dome which in 1988, the twice ex-president Carlos Andrés Pérez erected on the last terrace.

Just as the shining helmet of a fierce warrior reflected back to Jupiter the rays that wounded him, the defiant dome maintained its gleam in the sun until fate, weary of so much audacity, had a large bomb fall on it and smashed it to smithereens in March 2002, during the coup attempt against Chávez.

Back to the content of the notebooks, at the beginning of the first chapter of the notebooks, floating like a ghost, Carmen perceives a dense fog filling the silent space where she is suspended. As soon as she manages to overcome her surprise at her own lightness, the mist thins. The peace is suddenly broken by the sound of a nearby cement mixer.

Her vision free of the misty frame, she guesses that she's in front of the Helicoide, recognizing the area and the intersection of the avenues. However, the big building is in a pitiful condition: its columns, now curved like the shoulders of a sad, old man, have transformed the upper terraces into concrete precipices and the triangular stories, almost united in the angle that looks down on Las Fuerzas Armadas avenue, form a gigantic accordion with its bellows pressed in on one side. Bent all over, the concrete mass opens up with hundreds of cracks where tall grayish weeds, whose willowy heads sway in rhythm with a breeze that Carmen can't feel, are growing.

She levitates slightly, searching for the air brushing against her, but as she's unable to burst the bubble that protects her from its friction, she soon abandons her interest in this strangeness and concentrates instead on the monotonous rhythm of the mixer, which she can't see. Lifting her head, she makes out Hugo Chávez on the last terrace, next to the dome whose damage is neatly described in the notebook, even though it had already been rebuilt in 2002.

Wearing combats and a black beret, Chávez comes out between the woeful greenery of the weeds and the ashen building and waves his arms and hands desperately, shouting to someone who, like the invisible mixer, Carmen is unable to see.

"Hugo, what are you doing up there?" she now calls out, from the bottom of the Helicoide.

Although he's heard the question, he decides to ignore Carmen and continues giving orders while she, looking up to the sky, sees a big cluster of dark clouds racing over until they gather just above the president. The wind suddenly whips up, and seized by its chaotic impulse, a flock of blackbirds flap their wings in confusion and squawk in distress. Livid with anger at the storm and because the irreverent gusts of wind have blown his beret off, Chávez finally decides to answer Carmen, who in the midst of the grimness and not knowing what to do, continues asking the same question.

"I have to finish building it! It's my project," he answers her, on the edge of desperation. He goes on giving orders.

The loud storm and the noise from the mixer prevent her from hearing whether he had said "finish it" or "demolish it," and Carmen rises up to the building's terrace just as Chávez is demanding that they finish correcting the damned columns.

"But why? Don't you know that in Caracas, people hate each other? They'll kill you for your cell phone or just to vent their anger at how things are."

Hanging on to a twisted metal railing to stop the fierce wind from throwing him into the void, Chávez looks at her again with disdain, as if the presence of such an insolent woman is part of nature's curse. Finally he regains his balance, and turning his back on Carmen, he shouts for workers to bring a crane and to finish correcting the goddamned columns.

Upset by his aggressiveness and still unable to watch the poor laborers being subjected to Chávez's bad temper, she sets off down to the avenue, but after barely a few yards, she hears a great commotion. Curious, she stops on the cracked ramp that drains off on the fifth floor and watches in the semi-darkness of the large space as a group of men dance clownishly, joking and hurling insults at each other. All over their bodies they have hundred-dollar bills stapled onto their flesh. In their euphoria, they don't even feel the pain of the staples or their own infected wounds, although Carmen has to cover her nose to avoid the stench reaching her in the wind. Astonished by the scene, and also because she's finally able to feel the current of air over the Helicoide, she stands still, unable to react.

"It's the floor of greed," erupts a deep voice at her shoulders.

Spinning around, she sees a small, pale man, shivering from the cold although he's draped with an old poncho. She instantly recognizes him as Simón Bolívar[12], whose severe face and fine looks from the paintings have disappeared. But nevertheless, his presence comes to Carmen wrapped in an invisible light that caresses her with a hand firmer than the wind. Seized by childish shyness, she blushes and lowers her head, trying to hide her embarrassment, but the joy of seeing the national hero is stronger than her shame. Soon she looks back at him, exuding purity, as if she's already been cleansed by the downpour threatened by the furious clouds.

"Come," he says to her, taking her hand and leading her to one of the last few floors, where the concrete can't be seen,

---

[12] Simón Bolívar (Venezuela, 1783-1830) is one of the most important and influential politicians and military leaders in the history of the Americas. He led the independence of Venezuela, Colombia, Ecuador and Bolivia from Spain. In Venezuela, Bolívar is a national hero, almost to cult level. Due to his universality, many use, abuse and distort his views, particularly modern Venezuelan politicians, especially Hugo Chávez.

the scene resembling an endless midnight desert with small sand dunes.

Strewn on the cold sand are hundreds of skeletal people, in a severely weakened state. Circling fearlessly but cautiously, hundreds of vultures come toward them, preparing for the final feast. But no one notices the vile creatures or is intimidated by their presence. The only thing these people can see and feel is the promised future that never comes. As though a film is playing in front of their eyes, they think they are robust, living in big houses and driving impressive cars.

"This is the floor of the starving people, paralyzed by promises," Carmen tells Bolívar, giving him the impression that she already knows where they are.

"There is more," he adds, his glassy look becoming sad, before descending a good distance to rest on the first floor.

When Carmen catches up with him, with some effort since Bolívar is a great levitator, he leads her around the floor, which like the ones above is sloping on the outside, although perfectly horizontal on the inside. Large partitions divide the space into compartments, and the light is blinding. In one of the rooms, Carmen recognizes Paco, the owner of the bookstore, accompanied by Maikel. Alfredo and his family are in another room, and in the next one, she sees herself with Rodrigo, Manuel and many others. Overcome by rage, they're ripping each other to shreds and looking at each other in mirrors, which multiply their reflections to infinity.

Filled with anguish because she can sense what she's about to see, she continues walking around the first floor, looking for her father, and soon she finds him almost dismembered, with his mouth twisted and full of huge teeth, sharpened like knives. In front of his bedroom mirror, he laughs at the sight of a hole in his chest that someone has ripped open with their teeth.

Carmen is paralyzed by disgust and fear. At her side, Bolívar asks her to breathe deeply, and closing her eyes, she manages to inhale some of the air blowing on the Helicoide and whose chill helps her to react. But as soon as she regains the sensation of her own blood pumping throughout her body, a strange compassion seizes her. She wants to caress her father, to cradle his smashed head, to take his battered limbs and put them back together, as if the arms and legs that lay around the floor were fragile treasures.

Bolívar guesses her intention and stops her.

"If you go in, you will never come out again. Everything you see is, and is not true, although it will happen, has happened or is happening. But if you go in, that will be the end of you."

Carmen frees herself from Bolívar, feeling the new pain that causes her impotence. She turns again to face Chávez and shouts to him:

"Hugo! Look down here. Everyone is killing each other like cats and dogs. They're the children of your people. Make them stop, Hugo, tell them to stop it!"

"This is my project," answers the president, infuriated more than ever by Carmen's constant interruptions. "I will finish it even if it's here, in *hell*. The oligarchs of the world will not get the better of me."

After saying this, he turns toward the city, the one he had turned his back on until now and shouting to the wind, he cries out belligerently:

"Beware, oligarchs of the world!"

Bolívar takes Carmen's hand again and leads her down to the second-to-last floor. Once there, after wiping away her tears with one hand, she comes across Carlos Andrés Pérez. In a monotone whimper, he repeats that the people did not forgive him as he looks at knotted nests of worms where his hands once were.[13]

"Please do something" Carmen implores Bolívar.

"I was just one man," he replies breathlessly, exhausted by going up and down. "Just one man, Carmen." he continued, without a trace of light in his eyes. "I was convinced that Reason was the only grace, the higher good and absolute common goal that we should all aspire to. I'm not the one to stop this madness, which I feared much more in life than death itself. What you're seeing today, muchacha, is also my last delirium."[14]

---

[13] It is believed that Pérez made a fortune during his first administration in the early 70's through corruption. He was ousted during the middle of his second term for the embezzlement of 250 million bolivars belonging to a presidential discretionary fund. It was during this time that he delivered his farewell speech, stating that the people "did not forgive him" for the many accomplishments he had made during his politicalcareer.

[14] While he believed in freedom and social opportunity, Bolívar who was ultimately a white creole and an aristocrat, feared the rising of the lower class to power. He was in line with the social divisions of his era. This is contrary to the image Chávez portrays of the national hero.

CHAPTER 17

The same day

The second chapter is long, complex and with very little action. Reading it, Rodrigo curses his brain again for its limited capacity for abstract thought, but more than anything, he curses the lack of interest he displayed toward his wife's nightmares and lucubration over the last few years. The pages of the second and third notebooks remain an unfathomable mystery to him. During the very few moments in which he thinks he might shed some light upon them, a strange, dense and tangled mess of concepts emerges, bringing his anguish to the surface. Sometimes, Rodrigo has the feeling that it is not the notebooks, but his own wife who, brandishing a sword of fire, is pushing him out of this universe scattered withwords.

However, no one notices error or insecurity in her stories, perhaps because Rodrigo succumbs to the temptation of imbuing her words with his own imaginings. Rodrigo's imaginary, attentive reader would have expected a few exaggerations, particularly regarding his wife's questionable wisdom and the phantoms that pursued her. But not completely insensitive to his reader, and thanks to the notebooks, Rodrigo is aware of his tendency to misinterpret what he reads, although he doesn't try to fix it. So filling in the gaps with his own imagination, Rodrigo conjures up an image of them galloping together over the words, and as before, Carmen laughing at the nonsense that he comes upwith.

Although he tones it down, the only thing that Rodrigo doesn't change, out of respect for the notebooks' intentions, is Carmen's new and indifferent attitude. At the beginning of the second chapter, she's next to Bolívar, facing Carlos Andrés Pérez, who is still whimpering, covered with now fully grown worms, multiplied by hundreds in his bloody wounds. She and her guide stand open-mouthed, watching while a wide lane of worms crawl up the arms and neck of the ex-president and bore into the orifices of his remorseful face.

Suddenly Carmen breaks the silence to challenge Bolívar, asking him abrasively what he's doing there, why he's with her and if he somehow hopes to save her. "From what?" she continues defiantly. What can he save her from? Her only liberation runs parallel with the fate of Chávez. Why does Bolívar do nothing? Why doesn't anyone do something to thwart the fury growing in Hugo's heart?

According to Rodrigo, Bolívar is quiet, coughing and nodding while Carmen begins a long monologue. Perhaps Rodrigo exaggerates the concern his wife feels for the sickly looking hero, whose deterioration she describes in the notebooks. But she could not have been that worried about his condition, as she needs all her energy to escape from him, as if Bolívar was the devil himself. Carmen flees, devoting all her passion to the other extreme, toward what she herself preached when she was alive. At this moment, perhaps affected by having witnessed her father's punishment, she finds Bolivar's European, Rousseauian way of thinking ineffective. To her, this philosophy is adept at predicting things, but incapable of solvinganything.

154

"What we read are recipes: everything in the *Social Contract* is cooking recipes. If you use the wrong ingredient, you get poisoned. Look at me, Bolívar, take a good look at me," she continues, raising her voice. "Don't you understand who I am? You're so blind that you can't see in me, or in Chávez the humble creatures of this earth. And tell me something: How can we contain the pain and fury of the voices mingled in our heads? There are thousands, millions of voices of those who are suffering, all the time, all the time, here in my head. If you were to hear them, thinking you can fight chaos, you would go mad in less than an hour."

"Arise to birth with me, my brother," continues Carmen, quoting Pablo Neruda. "To birth?" she repeats with fire in her eyes, while Bolívar is quiet and Rodrigo interrupts this tense scene to explain that Carmen's anger isn't real, just fictional. "It's a rhetorical fit of anger," the enamored widower adds, "as we all know that writers and their heroines are temperamental creatures."

"Be born? Be resuscitated? Find a voice?" continues Carmen. "But we who are the working classes have never been dead or voiceless. Correct me if I'm wrong, but can humiliation and insult die or be suppressed? Can the people be subdued by the passing of laws, and their troubles and anxieties be suspended while sociologists and psychologists reason? But I repeat that they do not die. They are life, but also the poison. And in the good ways of western reasoning, no stomach is strong enough to digest such a recipe."

Bolívar bears the reprimand and appears absorbed, although Rodrigo affirms that far from being distracted, he is focused on everything Carmen says, and she in turn enters suddenly on the thorny territory of despair. She quotes Hobbes and Nietzsche, highlighting how their philosophies delight in the bad conscience of mankind.

"Who are they talking about? Who allowed them to speak on your behalf or mine, or my father's, trapped and destroyed in this hell?" It all seems pointless and arrogant to Carmen, although more than once, she falters and uses the wrong quotes to try to prove her point.

She seems much more comfortable with twentieth century thought. There she stops to comment on a curious and almost forgotten book written by the psychiatrist, Gregorio Marañon.

"Resentment is incurable. Its only medicine is generosity," Carmen quotes from the book, and she asks Bolívar irritably:

"But what parts of the body or soul does generosity come from? How can you demand generosity of Chávez? Who can give something they haven't acquired?" she concludes in a ghostly but triumphant tone, as the hills of Caracas suddenly tremble with a large quake, wiping out route 905, a highway that joins the Helicoide with the old residential development, El Paraíso.

Bolívar takes advantage of the chaos to take Carmen to see something he wanted to show her from the beginning. Quickly, without giving her the chance to react, he leads her by the hand to the black depths of the Tarpeian Rock, through a narrow tunnel ending in a wrought iron gate. Above, hanging over the beam, a small, dilapidated sign reads "shroud" and through the bars, in a small, cold cave is Chávez, his face barely lit from above by an oil lamp. Still and silent, he's watching something that must be incredibly frightening, as he's crossing his arms in a shield to protect himself from what he sees. Although his hands show no sign of injury, blood is running down them, and every so often, he opens them to rub them on his trousers. This is a useless gesture, as the blood flows straight out again.

"Help him! Help us!" Carmen begs Bolívar, now with the voice of a lost child. And as there is no reaction to her plea, she begins to open the gate, but is stopped by a new earth tremor and by the dizziness of her guide who, leaning on her for support, feels a fire burning in his body. He slowly starts to evaporate.

Bolívar wants to speak to Carmen, but he can't articulate a single word, and after several attempts, he says in an almost inaudible whisper that we humans have to grow:

"Like almost all passions, resentment is a childish one, and like most of them, it serves no purpose."

Carmen is profoundly disgusted. She feels that he's thrown this trite observation at her feet and is waiting for her to pick it up gratefully, like a hungry dog that has been thrown a scrap. But she is no dog and looks at him coldly, while he is seized by a sudden and indescribable pain, and fades away, leaving no trace but for two words that follow him through the tunnel to the surface.

"My bones! My bones!" cries the faint echo.

Carmen turns back to Chávez with the intention of opening the bars but she stops, as at that instant, the sky darkens and thousands of gigantic Kapok trees emerge from the earth, engulfing the city.

It was night when Rodrigo returned the notebooks to their hiding place. He began to talk about them a few days later, shyly at first, but that Saturday he snapped them shut, wondering if his wife had lost her sanity, or if on the contrary, the Dantesque dialogues were a terrible and brave form of exorcism. After reading them, he began to understand how attached she had been to the philosophical language of social classes and the indelible rubric it left behind, scarring her heart forever. She was carrying such a weight, and had been so deeply and violently indoctrinated. How could she have loved him? And had he not immaturely branded Carmen before bringing her to meet his friends?

As if shaken by guilt, the need to understand the love she had felt for him made him examine every single word in the notebooks. He sought a hidden sign written only for him, but he couldn't find any, despite studying the books that Carmen had written of, as well as the texts by Bolívar. Then he cursed himself for not being able to find that trace of salvation. Later, he cursed himself even more when he realized that Carmen was closing the doors of her hell on him, as he had done so little to ease her burden.

However, on that December 2, when Rodrigo slammed the notebooks shut, his only preoccupation was Carmen's suffering. He gladly went to soothe her spirit, which was maybe still wandering in the world of man, and still obsessed by the chapter that her own death had prevented her from writing.

"No one is just a social class, Carmen," Rodrigo whispered gently, remembering with disgust his own unfortunate attempt to write about domestic servants. Suddenly, as if a light had just been switched on, he grabbed a small and weathered little book. It was by Ernesto Sábato. He found the phrase he was looking for, which he had underlined in red ink, despite his wife's protests.

"... *the best socialist revolutionaries do not arise from the dispossessed masses but from the bourgeois and aristocracy... the "children of the people": they are almost always resentful and become involved in the revolutionary movement as a result of their feelings of inferiority.*"

After reading it several times, he lay down on the bed with the book open on his chest and repeated the lines mechanically, watching the spider's web that had been growing in the corner for the last few days. Only when he made out its small creator coming down on a thin thread did he recover the serenity that he had lost that morning, and feel able to go back to the afternoon that Carmen died.

It happened on December 6. She was sitting on a bench in Plaza Altamira with one of the spiral notebooks resting on her lap. She was revising the second chapter and decided to cross out a line.

Months before, fourteen officials from the Armed Forces had sworn to stay in the square until Chávez gave himself up. There they created a center of opposition that many civilians joined, making banners which fluttered under the Obelisk: "Chávez, imposter! Student murderer!" "This is how we govern, say the Chavistas rolling in their shit!"

Rodrigo used to watch Carmen from the balcony of the apartment. Due to the tense atmosphere in Venezuela—months before there had been a failed coup against Chávez, as well as the Puente Llaguno massacre—he was not keen on the idea of his wife giving out coffee to the demonstrators every afternoon, but she had given herself to the civil movement.

About seven o'clock, when the sun had already set, shots could be heard, followed by shouts and people stampeding in all directions. As if she was awaking from a long sleep, Carmen lifted her head and immediately raised the notebook to her chest. Still deep in thought, she did not know that Joao De Gouveia had opened fire on the people who were gathered around a little table near the bench where she was sitting. Standing up, and without even setting eyes on her executioner, Carmen received two bullets.[15]

Incredulous, witnessing the scene from the balcony of the apartment, Rodrigo saw Carmen collapse. He ran down the stairs to help her, but it was Maikel who got to her first, from the subway entrance on the square.

---

[15] In reality, nineteen people were injured and three lost their lives in the Altamira tragedy. But out of respect for the victims and to avoid any possible association, our character became the fourth victim as it will be seen in future chapters.

Maikel had arranged to meet the couple around seven o'clock and was walking up the subway steps when the shots went off. He wanted to go back down to take cover, but his curiosity was stronger than his fear, and he crouched down on the last step, against the wall of the subway exit which led to the square.

It was not long before he realized that Carmen was lying on the ground a few meters away from him, and without thinking of the danger, he came out of his hiding place to help her. When he reached her side, he kneeled down to her, after yelling at the top of his lungs for a doctor.

Carmen's head fell sharply backwards as if she were trying to avoid the unexpected embrace. Maikel realized that blood was gushing from his friend's neck, and changed his position slightly to support her neck and shoulders with his left forearm.

Rodrigo managed to push through the people coming toward him, fleeing from the shots on Altamira square, only to see Maikel's arm bent, his right shoulder raised up to his ears, his hand holding Carmen's neck and his knees on the ground, wide apart.

The two men's eyes met for the split second that it took Rodrigo to fall to the left of his wife and see the thick line of blood running down Maikel's right thigh, forming a glistening, round puddle around his knee.

Someone rescued the notebook from the ground where it lay, and gave it to Rodrigo as he got into the ambulance, pale and waxen, and still not understanding that Carmen was not breathing. The book miraculously survived in his hands, despite the anguish with which he cried and embraced his wife, the hours he spent waiting in the hospital, the certificate pronouncing her dead, and the journey home which he could not remember. But sitting at the dining room table, when his father passed him a brandy, he was surprised to see it there at his side, in perfect condition except for a reddish colored spot in one of the corners, which several days later, before Rodrigo put it in the closet along with Carmen's things, had been cleaned off.

Motionless, watching the spider's web again, Rodrigo thought that it must have been his mother who had skillfully removed the stubborn stain, which he now thought came not from Carmen's veins, but from the story contained in its pages. Remembering Sábato's phrase again, he sighed and repeated aloud again that no one was just a social class.

"No one is just that," Rodrigo continued saying "But envy and revenge shift everything."

The sound of the door and noisy activity made him get out of bed in a hurry. His parents and Emilio had just arrived.

CHAPTER 18

March 13, 2005

At 7 o'clock in the morning, when a gust of wind filtered through the dense clouds from the west, the only palm tree planted in the Piruggi garden shook its large leaves to disperse the intense heat that had been so oppressive during the night.

Its light movements did not distract Alfredo, who lying down wearing shorts, was reading a newspaper article about El Charcote. That was the name of a 12,000-hectare cattle ranch located in the heart of the Venezuelan plains. Until recently, it had belonged to a British group represented in Venezuela by Andrew Stone, or simply "Andrés" to his friends at the Country Club. Alfredo felt sad about how president Chávez was expropriating the ranch from its British owners. He had visited it as a child with his uncle from his mother's side, Arturo Bocay, who had been a tough dairy cow breeder until a bad investment and Parkinson's disease brought his business dealings to an end.

He folded the large newspaper sheet and held it closer to his eyes to look at the photos with the article. There were four pictures in total, showing some farm workers to whom Chávez had given the El Charcote land so that it could be cultivated. Alfredo resettled his head on the cushions to study the fourth picture, whose ironic and lazy humor had escaped censure.

It was a photo of a man in front of some plots of land where a few bean plants were sprouting. The inscription at the foot of the image said: "Colombian peasant protecting his crop from cattle." And effectively, the man was standing between the plants and a small calf that was sniffing the ground, perhaps wondering what had happened to its pastureland. "Shit!" said Alfredo out loud, unable to resist laughing as he looked at the calf. "That thing's the only Venezuelan here," he thought.

He left the newspaper on the bed to take refuge in the tranquility of the palm tree but once again, his glance met the *Zeta* magazines, compulsively organized in sequence and spread in three columns. He had gone through them by chance, taking a few issues from each year out of the pile, only to realize that since 2002, when he had started his job at the Chicago Hospital, most of the characters were unknown to him, all involved in turbulent business and political scandals. More disheartened by the new faces than by the country's never-ending corruption, he left the *Zeta* magazines and began to read the newspaper that had been placed on his bedside table. El Charcote and its pastures were refreshing to him, because although they were gone, they represented a fluorescent buoy in a sea of news he had been swimming in for five days.

The *Zeta* magazines were a gift from his father, Roberto Piruggi, who had decided to collect them on June 23, 1997, just when Alfredo flew over to Illinois to become a notable neurosurgeon.

"I should have asked him to mail them over to me, or taken time to check on the internet," he said to himself, remembering his father's lectures every time they crossed paths in the house or ate together. "Can you see what I was telling you about on the phone, Alfredo? That son of a bitch is taking this country down. And what's around the corner for me? The same as what happened to that Juan Mendizábal? You see, he went to hell with his investment company."

Alfredo was about to remind his father that the "hell" the poor man had ended up in was a mansion on Long Island, and to escape from the tedious holiday season, a luxury apartment in Majorca. However, at thirty-five years of age, Alfredo had resigned himself to the stubbornness and never-ending hidden messages that, after so much time and with considerable theatricality, Roberto still kept sending him through the magazines, and above all, with his Sunday telephone calls.

Alfredo could not imagine his father being seriously worried, unlike Nonno, who had lived with his head buried in a big notebook with black covers and full of numbers, while Alfredo, then still a child, hung on to his sleeves or ran around him to get his attention. But Nonno's son, Roberto Piruggi, was something else. Risk exhilarated him. Alfredo was sure that his father would have died of boredom if he had not lived that way until now, balancing on a tightrope, his acrobatic poise sometimes leaning him toward fraudulent fields of activity, other times dipping him into the sterile waters where respectable citizens swam.

For Roberto Piruggi, Chávez was just an inconvenience, a challenge to his considerable skills and his business dealings, which included a horse ranch in the state of Apure. Aware of his competence in difficult times, and of his good reputation, he thought that the Chavistas would soon fall. Even if they stayed in power, he was sure that he could still survive in the new republic while he continued to drink scotch with his bosses, sucking up to them and telling them they were geniuses while designing their white- marbled mansions.

The *Zeta* magazines were not a cry for help, but a mixture of nostalgia and the same fastidious hope that as a child,

Alfredo had read in his father's eyes, encouraging him to go to lengths that Alfredo could never attain, as they called for him to give himself over to "serious" matters. According to Roberto, serious matters were construction, horses, the stock exchange and some transactions shrouded in mystery that made Alfredo nervous.

On the contrary, to Paolo, his younger son, who had chosen to be a musician and lived in London, Roberto directed a boring repertoire of trivialities. "How did your concert go last night, Paolito? Is it cold over there? Alfredo could never understand why his father, who never asked anything of Paolo, kept on hoping with futility that Alfredo would be interested in his matters.

Much more similar to Nonno, the eldest Piruggi son dedicated his passion and effort to only one very limited and absolutely legitimate activity. Although Alfredo by no means hated his father, he felt tremendously uneasy when he heard him brag about his business dealings, which, as he kept on saying, were all legal until they could be shown to beotherwise.

The gulf between Alfredo and his father made him seek out the immense distance between Caracas and Chicago. He preferred to go far away for a few years to come to accept this man whose audacious Creole attitude he could neither identify with nor judge. Once here, giving into his father, Alfredo made an effort to read some of the *Zeta* articles, taking notes here and there in small handwriting, uncharacteristic of a doctor. His colleagues in Chicago joked about Alfredo's compulsion to write everything down with childish scruple, using his fine-tipped Mont Blanc: ideas and questions about medical treatments, recommendations from his supervisor, and thousands of other notes, even personal things, wrapped up in a book he called his "diary," bound in black covers, just like Nonno's.

He got into this habit as an adolescent, when he put all his effort into being the best student in the class, discovering that it was only a question of willpower. For Alfredo, studying was not preceded by an intense vocation, like it was for Paolo; it was enough if it were a constant activity, firmly attached to the ground, just like railroads that, protecting him from chance, brought him to the next port.

Tired of reading and writing all morning, he lay on his side, facing the palm tree whose huge plumes caressed the bedroom balcony every time they swayed in the breeze. Alfredo was amazed by how much it had grown in the last seven years and for a long time, he lost himself in the movement of its leaves and the moving shadows that appeared on the carpet each time the sun peeked out from between the clouds. He was overcome by a feeling that he could not define when he reflected that maybe on his next visit, this magnificent palm tree that was now trying to reach him would be balancing against the roof of the house. Then he would only see the trimmed and fibrous trunk whose shadow of fallen timber would penetrate the room in themornings.

He rubbed his eyes hard as he remembered that it was Sunday. Everyone would probably be sleeping at this time of day, except Salomé, the old servant woman, who used to take a bath early in the morning before her morning prayers. According to her, God only listened to those who are clean in body and in spirit. Maybe she would be in the kitchen, thought Alfredo, imagining the robust woman, from the Afro-Venezuelan town of Choroní, straining coffee and kneading arepas for the first round of breakfast.

Very soon, Pedro, the chauffeur and gardener, and Juliana, the young girl just arrived from the province, who hid from Alfredo out of pure shyness, would sit down to eat with Salomé at the other end of the house, in the garden area where the papaya shrubs were. Or perhaps it would be more accurate to say that the chauffeur and the new servant girl would eat under the pensive gaze of Salomé, who on days of religious observance only had two cups of sugar cane juice, accompanied by a cigar.

Every Sunday, except Easter Sunday, Salomé examined the future in the burning top of the cigar. As a child, this ritual had made an impression on Alfredo. It was not particularly ceremonious. On the contrary, Salomé let her gaze wander as she inhaled the smoke, and every now and again she would whisper something as she watched the mass of ash formed by the fire.

He tried to get up, but his body felt rusty. "It's the lack of exercise," he told himself, to justify the lack of enthusiasm he had felt since he had arrived at Maiquetía airport. In Chicago, he continued to himself, still aware of his physiological changes, he never stopped, and in Caracas, he was surprised to find that nothing or no one needed him, nothing except the scandalous amount of *Zeta* magazines, with which his father had practically blocked the entrance to his bedroom balcony. During the five days that he had already been there, he spent his time eating and reading, having a beer or two with friends and observing the unfortunate transformation of Caracas.

He glanced at the small calendar leaning on his bedside table. It was one of those mass-produced Christmas gifts, with a transparent plastic stand with the words "Piruggi Construction" printed on it. He sighed as he realized that a week remained before he could return to the United States and he made an effort to control the total state of despondency he felt himself falling into. That was when he remembered the daytrip to El Ávila that he had planned with Rodrigo and Emilio for that day.

El Ávila had always been much more to Alfredo than an enormous mountain that separated Caracas from the north-central coastline of the country. Not just because as a child he had wandered on its side, or because he had cried there out of fear and frustration when things were going wrong. El Ávila was much more than child's hiding place for Alfredo, because each time he closed his eyes and breathed in its air, he felt the whole planet teeming and he was unable to say where his feet ended and where the enormous force coming from the earth began. With this feeling alone, Alfredo could stop thinking so much and feel deepstillness.

He yawned several times and changed position. Lifted by the view of the passage, he gave in to a pleasure less intense than the one provoked by the mountain, but one newly discovered during this trip: looking at his bedroom. The middle shelf of the large bookcase stretching all the way over to the balcony was still full of books from his adolescence. On the wall that led to the bathroom and the left wall, leading to the passage that crossed from one side of the house to the other, his favorite posters were still hanging, although quite yellowed now: U2, Talking Heads and the great striker Zico. Alfredo noticed that one of the bottom corners of the U2 poster had come unstuck and in a brief moment of euphoria, he decided to fix it right away, or perhaps, he thought after a moment, after his bath, when he might feel more energetic.

After yawning again, his eyes jumped from the U2 picture to the large pine desk that his mother had bought him when he was in his second year of high school. Although the only extraordinary feature of the desk was its great length, Alfredo wanted it for his birthday after seeing it in a shop. At first, his mother refused, as it did not match the colonial style of the room, but Alfredo's insistence made her call the shop to have it delivered to the house one August 8, just as her son was blowing out the candles on a large chocolate cake.

On this desk, helped by the lazy Vicente, Rodrigo had written cheat sheets that he would later copy in exams, while Manuel, with the help of the Alfredo's huge dictionary, amused himself translating U2 songs, later locking them away in the same drawer that was the hiding place for the group's most precious treasure: *Playboy* magazines whose little bunnies they all admired open-mouthed, except for Vicente, who wouldn't stop eating even to look at those amazing bodies.

Alfredo had kept few things from his university days: some pathology books, a dictionary and a medical encyclopedia, several pairs of shoes and the clothes he left behind when he left home. Most of his instruments were probably in the hands of some medical students or buried in the dump. Without giving it much thought, Alfredo had donated them to the university along with most of his university books the same day he was accepted at the University of Chicago.

The palm tree shook again more energetically, and this time the wind took its crown from the handrail which not long before, it had tried to cling to. The fog in Alfredo's head began to dissipate and he gathered up the strength to go to the bathroom. Also to accept with clarity what he was seeing: the number of objects from his university life had been drastically reduced. This was not the case for the records, posters, books and magazines from his adolescence, which next to his old hi-fi system and the stereo his mother gave him later to listen to CDs, all formed a type of museum where the presence of the young boy, to whom Alfredo reverted in his most difficult moments, still lived on voluntarily.

Far from being upset at the discovery, he thought he should keep the room that way until an earthquake destroyed the house or, more likely, until his parents decided to move and boxed everything up to leave it in storage. He did not have anything to worry about for now, as his mother and Salomé looked after the room as if it were a temple.

The thought of his mother filled him with tenderness. Alfredo was sure that, dissatisfied with the adolescent relics, she had searched out ones from his childhood. Only this nostalgia could explain the presence of Mickey there, sitting in the only armchair in the room, in front of a large cupboard, facing the bed. From the armchair, the gigantic toy that had lived for more than two decades in the attic stared at Alfredo.

Mickey had come to live in the room long before the pine desk, although also on December 8, just in time for the candles of his seventh birthday. Against his custom, Amador, at one time the Piruggi family's chauffeur, raced like mad down the highway to bring Nonno and the huge toy that he had brought from Miami. "Do you like him, Alfredo?" his grandfather asked him excitedly, partly because of his purchase and also because he had managed to arrive on time for his favorite grandson's birthday party.

Alfredo smiled but said nothing because at that time, he had all the toys in his room that he'd been given since a very tender age. He would pile them up in a corner, in the shape of a mountain where he would hide a little piece of cheese. Then he would get his pet hamster out of its cage, place him on the summit and then sit down and wait.

Mickey seemed too big, even for his splendid spacious room, although it was going to be amazing to watch Pipo, after a couple of days of fasting, dig around the gigantic landscape of Mickey. To increase the entertainment factor, Alfredo took some scissors and discreetly cut the fur on several sides of the toy to bury some pieces of ham and cheese in the stuffing.

Mickey's torture lasted less than 6 months, until Pipo, with a swollen belly, ceased to be, due to the continuous ingestion of synthetic fibers. For several days, Alfredo felt sad and guilty about his experiments on Pipo but one night just when he had forgotten the episode, he awoke at midnight and wanted to see what was on the television while the whole house slept. To his misfortune, they were showing a film in which a terrifying ventriloquist doll came to life and sought its revenge for the way its owner had mistreated it. From that night on, Alfredo projected the guilty feelings he had about Pipo onto Mickey. He could see him from his bed, expecting the toy's huge arms to slowly lower and his gloved hands to lean on the seat of the chair. At one moment, he thoughthe noticed Mickey's body moving slightly forwards to stretch its legs and stand up straight with murderous intent.

Mickey never got up, or at least that is what Alfredo believed after spending hours awake, incessantly imagining complicated escape routes from his bedroom. But he could not run the risk of leaving him there. More and more terrified of the image of the enormous animal creeping up on him while he slept, he began thinking about how to get rid of him.

Confessing his fear to Roberto was out of the question. His mother did not seem like the right person either, and the only one who might have understood his problem, his grandfather, was distant and sad, due to the recent death of Nonna. In his anguish, he thought of asking Paolo for help who, only six years of age, was wrapped up in the world of garden vermin. Alfredo felt dislike, disgust or even fear for the collection of big ants, spiders and a disemboweled lizard or two that Paolo kept in a cardboard box. Looking at the box one day, a few months after the film incident, Alfredo knew that his fears only belonged to him and that the rest of the family did not share them.

That was when he told his mother that he was too old for toys and please could she take Mickey and the other ones away. From then on, he would only collect toy cars, trains and Lego monsters that could be taken apart. He did not have the courage to look at her directly in the eyes to defend his reasoning, but even so, his mother congratulated him for being a young man already. Without thinking twice about the matter, he took Mickey in his arms to bring him to a place full of small children who would be amazed by him, so big, with his shorts and beautiful yellowbird.

Alfredo's shame of his own fears lasted much longer than his guilty feelings about Pipo and Mickey. But by the time he was eleven, he hardly remembered it as he had turned into the child he had wished to be when he was eight: the best hunter of frogs, lizards and insects in the Country Club and the bold boy who would take bets on staying for hours in dark rooms or watching terrifying films without screaming. At that time, he was brave enough to ask his mother what had become of Mickey, this time without avoiding her gaze.

Surprised, she admitted that he was still in the roof terrace closet. On many occasions, she had told Salomé to put it in Amador's van and donate it to an orphanage, but it was too big and awkward to transport. With so much going on, they both ended up forgetting about it. At the end of the day, he did not bother anyone in that cupboard but if Alfredo wanted, Mickey would be back in his bedroom the next morning.

Sincerely convinced of how ridiculous it would be to have Mickey again, he rejected the offer with the same argument he had used when he was seven. But from that moment on, he was not satisfied with testing his courage against ghosts and lizards.

The following year, he was already one of the best strikers in the school football team. He trained with determination, obsessed with competing and winning. He also started fighting anyone who insulted him or made the slightest attempt to attack his brother or friends. Disciplined, and with great physical strength, even if he did not win as many admirers as he had hoped, at least he had the respect of his classmates. Nobody wanted to provoke Alfredo, because behind his well-mannered facade, a wild animal was hidden.

His best friends, those who had known him before he had developed an obsession for sports, did not think the same. Although cautious and sometimes rough, Alfredo was noble. They were never surprised at his interest in dissecting frogs and looking for scorpions underneath stones, nor his games with pebbles, mind-blowing because they were full of screaming ghosts and malignant spirits.

However, the new Alfredo was incredible. Rodrigo was amazed by his speed on the football pitch and the integrity with which he received kicks and blows if he managed to gain control of the ball. The most memorable time was when he collapsed as he scored a goal. A tackle twisted his left ankle, but putting up with the pain, Alfredo got up and carried on running until he found the ball and the shooting angle. The doctor who examined him could not explain how he had managed it.

In reality, no one noticed the immense rigor that Alfredo imposed on himself during those years, not even his mother, who always seemed to be following what her children were doing. Perhaps she had an inkling that Alfredo was too obsessive, to the point of becoming quite unbearable the night before a match, but as long as he did not neglect his studies, she could see no reason to complain.

He certainly was not neglecting his studies, although Father Marcial, his second- year high school supervisor, would insist that the boy was capable of a lot more. With the patience that his small frame and mature years lent him, he would ask Alfredo to make time to come and see him and talk about the future; it was important to be well prepared, as life can be extremely unpredictable.

Alfredo accepted the invitation after receiving a kick in the groin from center fielder Mauro Ortega, a boy from the Andean province of Trujillo who had won a scholarship to study with the Salesians. In one of many football practices, Ortega tackled him for the ball, but Alfredo slipped slightly and lost his balance. It was an accident, he told Alfredo not very convincingly, helping him to his feet.

The boy from Trujillo apologized again. Full of rage, Alfredo told him to go to hell. "Sure, typical rich kid. Always complaining, but not much up here," said the scholarship student, pointing to his forehead with his finger.

The comment was enough to make Alfredo launch a silent battle against Ortega, who was the best student in the class at that time. That very night, he prepared notebooks where he would make meticulous notes, and began to study as if he were possessed.

Little by little, his grades improved without harming his football game, for which he was notorious in the school. Every afternoon he ran a mile, in sunshine or rain, reciting mathematic formulas and mentally revising his art, history and geography lessons. The end of the school year was no surprise to Ortega, who after the 1987 Christmas vacation, began to receive the first of many blows and kicks which Alfredo gave him in every subject. He never quite imagined to what extent Alfredo would beat him, because unknown to him, Manuel, Rodrigo, Ricardo and Vicente, complete clowns according to Ortega, had teamed up with Alfredo in a group project for Physics class and had got the highest grade. While the worst students in the class starting getting the best marks, Ortega would be relegated to the mediocre student pile. Then the mild, studious boy's scholarship would be indanger.

Ortega always had Alfredo on his mind, who after his victory in physics could visualize the total destruction of the scholarship student. It was hard to convince his friends and to do it using the word "honor" instead of "revenge," an error of judgment, since 'honor' was a word that only Rodrigo understood at that time, as he was reading a short version of *The Three Musketeers*.

It was a question of showing everyone—Alfredo emphasized the word "everyone" because they probably all had their own Ortega punching them in the stomach—in other words, showing that they were not weak through necessity but because of their own will. Being a good student was not just about smiling at the priests and helping the poor teachers to load the trunk of the car with piles of homework to take home. In summary, Alfredo asked them to go to war, for at least one year.

With resignation, Ricardo confessed that getting good grades was risky. His mother was a child psychologist and always spoke about kids who were under a lot of pressure at home. They ended up like pressure cookers; first they exploded, then came the straight jacket and everything, pana. Rodrigo added that the only Ortega in his life was his own father, who thought only a miracle or an insane teacher would give his son top marks in math or physics. Manuel and Vicente, after whispering together for a while, started laughing. REO Speedwagon, a rock band that was fashionable at that time, were playing in the bullring in the city of Valencia the following Saturday. If Alfredo could get them tickets, the deal wasdone.

Amador took the five boys to the concert with tickets that Alfredo, or rather his mother, had paid an exorbitant amount of money for, and which would be subtracted from her son's monthly allowance. Once again, on the way to Valencia, Alfredo showed how cautious and calculating he could be when he wanted. Knowing that his friends would never win prizes for their excellence, Alfredo told them not to worry, as he was creating an elaborate system of cheating.

From transparent 10-inch rulers to erasers, including mini rolls of paper and pencils, all their tools were skillfully adapted to each subject, to the type of exam and the habits of the teachers that were giving them. Vicente's huge size would give cover to Alfredo, sitting directly behind him, at the back and against the wall. In that corner, they would prepare the materials during the first few minutes of the exam, then pass them to Ricardo, who in turn would pass them to Manuel and so on. When Alfredo and the copier were at risk, the rest would get up from their desks, one by one if necessary, to distract the teacher, firing questions at him or her.

During the last three months of the school year, the five students managed to synchronize the operation perfectly without detection, apart from the incident in which Rodrigo whispered furiously to Alfredo to write clearly, for God's sake. Alfredo's success was so great that, at the beginning of the fourth year of high school, wanting to follow in his footsteps, Rodrigo insisted on making the cheat sheets for language and literature.

Informed by Ortega or perhaps by an anonymous and intolerant classmate, the Spanish teacher grabbed Rodrigo's first cheat sheet from Vicente. Loyal to the end, Vicente swore that no one had passed it to him: it was his and his alone, but written by his neighbor, a large girl who had a crush on him. Nevertheless, everyone knew that Rodrigo was the only possible author of the cheat, as who else would write that irregular verbs behaved so irregularly because of the abuse they had suffered throughout history.

The cheating system broke down immediately after a sermon full of serious warnings. That was when Alfredo's friends went back to being themselves, except for Rodrigo, who began to study grammar under his own steam to win back his honor.

Alfredo, free from the fear that he had felt up until then, stopped sweating profusely during exams and continued alone in his private battle to defeat Ortega, year after year, until graduation.

The group broke up at the end of the fifth year of high school, when they chose their university programs. But Alfredo could never do without Manuel, and even less Rodrigo. Apart from them, there was no one in the whole world that he admired as much. At university, even with the immense workload and emotional pressure from his studies, he always found time to see them and tell them about his exploits.

"That Alfredo has balls! Now he's into manhandling dead bodies," said Manuel as Rodrigo looked at Alfredo, dazzled, thinking that at least one of them was going to succeed. The deadpan jokes and the shows of admiration made him happy, along with their chants in times gone by of "Go, Alfredo, go" during his best sporting moments, and "come on, Alfredo, pull the ace out of your ass" from their cheating days.

This had been the best time of Alfredo's life, even though sometimes Ortega's sting of defeat played on his conscience, because secretly Alfredo knew that he was not and could not be the best, rather that he wouldn't allow himself to be defeated or overcome by fear. Although Alfredo was now aware of this aspect of his character which, if he could, he would have pulled out at the roots, he had certainly become used to dealing with it by force of determination, thanks to his adolescence. He still needed to be considered the best, as deep down he was just a child grown old, attracting shadows instead of pure light.

He got up lazily from the lounger to go to the bathroom, and passing the armchair he tugged Mickey's ear, but the huge, heavy toy did not move. The stream of the day's first urine was dark and liberating. Alfredo turned the faucet to wash his hands and face with the anti-bacterial soap he had brought from the hospital.

Looking at himself in the mirror, after drying himself and inspecting his face, the skin a little irritated by the Venezuelan shaving cream, he thought that it was ironic to find Mickey in his room. In the end, he thought he had already made peace with him. It would have been better to put him in Paolo's room. After all, his brother forgot the cruel realities of the world before becoming aware of them. Paolo was seven when he started to play the trumpet and since then had talked about nothing other than music. He still lived in London and would stay there until his lips no longer parted or his lungs no longer inflated.

The year before, Alfredo had gone to Boston to see him perform. Paolo introduced him to his girlfriend, a smiley Belgian cellist who stooped, as if she was always cold. They spoke to each other in English, but she used *"mon chéri"* to order him around every five minutes. Once when Alfredo invited them to dinner in a restaurant, the woman chose what Paolo would eat and what he should wear the following day. She emphasized the *"mon chéri"* in particular to remind Paolo that she had a lot of rehearsals the following season and so, they wouldn't have time to visit his charming parents in their lovely house in beautiful Caracas. Why couldn't Alfredo be more like his brother, so simple that he did not even realize he wassuffering?

In the United States, Alfredo experienced fear that his imagination was incapable of foreseeing. He never had classmates like Manuel or Rodrigo, but a bunch of Ortegas who competed with him for the post of program director which he now held. He won it with his own bare hands, with insomnia and continuous stomach ache, brought on by his daily fear of practicals. The hospital was a real jungle which swallowed up the careless and the nicest.

He had fallen for Lucy for her generosity, for loving him too much and distracting him with the pregnancy of a child that was never born. Alfredo did not know what to say to her. Lucy was like a precipice: seeing her in the hospital bed, he understood what he should have done for her. Perhaps if the baby had been born, he would have found the strength from somewhere to repair such negligence. But now it did not matter what he did. Her presence, her smell and even the light that began to shine again in her face, would go on reminding him of the coward he was inside. He thought of Manuel's spontaneity and how much he envied it, as well as how he envied the absurd way that Rodrigo dealt with problems, talking his way around them as if they would solve themselves, but always as if he were concealed in a hollow, expecting the storms to pass overhead. He must have been mad to envy that, but he could not help it, above all that morning, standing in front of the mirror. Deep down, and contrary to his own jealous feelings, Alfredo believed that the lethargy of his friends had to do with the deep disdain they felt for life.

Or maybe not. It was enough to look at Rodrigo now. It was as if a hurricane had torn him to pieces. He recognized it immediately when they left customs. The same fringe, the same long nose as seven years ago, but his body was much thinner and his eyes were wrapped in a dark mist. When they hugged, he noticed that the Gallego was trembling as if he was about to sob, but the feeling only lasted an instant as Rodrigo took his suitcase and began to make his way through the hysterical crowds who, as usual, had amassed in the passageway at the customs hall exit. "Come and see Emilio," he said, turning his back to him.

Emilio was with Manuel in front of the exchange booth. He was eight years old and had the candid look of the Gallego he remembered saying goodbye to right there, seven years before. Neither the phone calls nor the email correspondence had prepared Alfredo for the impact he would feel seeing him again. On the other hand, Manuel seemed exactly the same, although his jokes were a little more scathing and a new, almost unnoticeable shyness made him move a little awkwardly, as if his body was heavy. After hugging him, Manuel said goodbye as he had something to do in La Guaira. "Ok, so now I'm off to pretend to do some work, but I'll call by and see you later whenever I can."

Once on the motorway, Rodrigo asked him how he was, but without waiting for an answer, he began to sound off about everything. Opportunists had become Chavistas and were reaping the rewards. Everything was bullshit; it was enough to see what they were teaching Emilio at school to see that progress was never going to be made. "It's the same country, Alfredo, but infinitely more pitiful."

Alfredo let him talk while he watched the little lights of the ranches, spreading like gangrene on both sides of the highway. He was about to tell him to go to Spain with Emilio; he would help him to get settled down there, at least until he managed to find a job teaching in a school, who knows. Had his own father not immigrated to Venezuela with a lot less? What was he expecting? But Rodrigo only wanted to complain and let off such a dense hatred like the smell of a dead dog they were leaving behind, lying on the curb.

"So Emilio, Who do you prefer, Barcelona or Real Madrid? Or does your Pops have you supporting Deportivo La Coruña? Ha ha!"

At only eight years old, Emilio understood the joke. For a while, he thought that his Papa's name was "Gallego" from hearing Manuel say it so often.

"Papi, can we go to McDonalds? I'm hungry."

Alfredo took the opportunity to change the subject of the conversation and started lecturing the little boy. Junk food has no nutritional value, just pure processed corn, sugar and salt. Organic food is much better for you, free of pesticides.

"Shit," exclaimed Rodrigo, remembering the soft spot that Alfredo always had for a hamburger. "You've really gone crazy, brother!"

After making that comment, Rodrigo stepped on the gas to enter the second tunnel on the highway and covered the last stretch that separated them from Caracas.

CHAPTER 19

The t-shirt was black and said "The Cure" in big letters. On the back was the cover of the album, "*Boys Don't Cry*" with the picture of the lead guitarist Robert Smith painted in yellow.

Alfredo always had trouble expressing his emotions, so he could not tell Manuel that while he was standing in line to buy the shirt at one of the stands that packed the stadium's passages, while he was being buffeted by the crowds, and in turn, pushing some guy who was trying to jump the line, he had felt like a teenager again. He also did not tell him that, at that exact moment, just when the southern wind was interrupting winter in Chicago, he thought he was in Miami again, or perhaps Valencia or Maracay. He could not pinpoint his location but he could anticipate with great precision the shoves he received in the back and the elbow that someone poked in his ribs. He could feel Manuel and Rodrigo's presence with him. So great was his joy, so crystal clear was the feeling that time had gone back, that when it was his turn, he blurted out his order in Spanish, "Dame una eme."

The man at the stall, an aging punk whose ears, lips and nose were adorned with a dozen piercings, looked at him, taken aback. Alfredo had to retrace his deja vu to repeat his request in English and took out twenty five dollars from his wallet. Then he put the change in his pants pocket and with the packet under his arm, he went to the parking lot, where hundreds of cars already had their engines running.

He had to wait a long time in another line—this time sitting comfortably in his Mercedes—until he turned onto the highway from an intensely and pleasantly lit street. He checked his cell phone and seeing that he had no emergencies, he sighed with relief. It was the first time that he had requested so much time off since they had made him head of residents in Neurosurgery, and he thanked heaven that he could go home without stopping at the hospital. With the pleasant prospect of a nice, warm shower and a piece of lasagna waiting for him in the fridge, he started imagining Rodrigo's face when he saw the t-shirt.

"Look what I brought you," he said to the Gallego, the next day when he got to Caracas, while he held it between them, like a curtain.

He waited an instant which seemed never-ending before popping out his head with a childlike gesture. To his surprise, he saw a forced smile on Rodrigo's face and he had to quickly swallow his disappointment. It would have been humiliating to tell him how difficult it was to get the ticket for The Cure concert, and the many shifts he had to negotiate with Peter Boyd, the departmental boss, in exchange for that afternoon of nostalgia. Once or twice, he told himself that it was no big deal. He would have believed it himself if it had not been for the Ávila trip.

That Sunday morning, the Gallego came with Emilio to pick him up in the second-hand Toyota Corolla that replaced the old Malibu. Alfredo took a bag with beers, soda and some delicious sandwiches that Salomé had insisted on preparing. When he saw the car arrive, he made signs to Rodrigo to open the trunk. While he packed the refreshments, he noticed the t-shirt. It was next to some tools, rolled up and looking like an old, oily rag.

Alfredo told the story to a sleepy-eyed Manuel, who was taking him to Maiquetía airport, his eyes fixed on the highway. He mentioned it in passing, just for something to say in the budding dawn of the day he was returning to the States. He did not mention the happiness that had come over him in the stadium, or his huge disappointment at seeing Robert Smith's oily face.

Despite his exhaustion, it was easy for Manuel to visualize Alfredo's frustration about the anecdote. But he did not catch the shadow, also present, of real concern for the Gallego. Snowed under by the work load his boss, Vilma was piling on his desk and also, reluctant to reject it, distracted by the possibility of buying himself a luxurious penthouse in Valle Arriba, Manuel let himself be taken by the feeling that Alfredo was missing the boat.

"See it like this, Alfredo," he said to him in a serious but gentle voice, like a father who doesn't want to scold his son but to his regret, feels that he has to put the cards on the table. "You haven't been back to Caracas for seven years, brother. A lot has changed here, but you can see that Rodrigo is adjusting. You know what he's like. There are days you don't even realize that Carmen died. He's... I don't know...," Manuel went on without reaching a conclusion, until in a fit of boldness he found the words to tell Alfredo that he should have jumped on a plane back, the very day that Rodrigo losthis wife. "But like I say, if there is one person that will never hold it against you, it's the Gallego".

Serious conversations were always difficult for Manuel, and he would have given anything to avoid the scolding that he never thought he would be giving to Alfredo, the only one of his friends who, as Manuel himself would say, was extremely sensible. At that moment, too late to take it all back, he saw out of the corner of his eye that Alfredo was defenseless: anguished and boxed in against the window of his seat, as if Manuel's light and breezy sermon had been a hailstorm.

He felt like stopping the car that very moment, just as he was heading toward the entrance of the airport, along a short straight road where he would drop Alfredo and his baggage off, opposite the American Airlines sign. Through tiredness and due to this inexplicable inertia that took hold of him at dramatic moments in his life, he did not stop the car on the curb, nor did Alfredo get to hear what he was thinking.

"What the hell am I doing, telling you when and why you should come to Caracas?" That's what Manuel would have said to the scolded Alfredo, so that he would go back happy to his hospital, his classes and his research on a strange device to operate on brains. He would have said just that. And to resolve his inner torment, he would have exclaimed out loud, waving his hands: "Christ, which of us could do what you've done over there! We should've seen you off with banners and TV cameras and not like this, for God's sake!"

But at five thirty in the morning, Manuel crashed against one of these dramatic moments in his life and let it pass, because that was how he was. Or perhaps because on that occasion, although drained by tiredness and regretting the telling off, he was lucid enough to be sure, not so deep down in his soul, that everything he had said to Alfredo was true. A small, modest truth that stung like a mosquito bite.

Manuel remembered that time Alfredo called from Chicago. It was just a month before Carmen died, already three years ago, when things seemed normal in Caracas.

Alfredo wanted his friends to travel to Mérida to meet him there. Despite being a mere resident—that's what he said to Manuel, laughing as if he were embarrassed at his success in the medical field—he was taking part in a neurology conference with some research on infectious brain diseases. But he would have time to meet them and have a couple of beers. "And why don't you come to Caracas for a few days?" "Impossible!" Alfredo had told him categorically.

It was also impossible for them to go to the beautiful Andean city of Mérida, even though Alfredo was prepared to pay for their flights. They had to shoot off to Maiquetía to see him while he changed planes, even though the connection time with Mérida was very tight. In less than two hours, they had to make do with telling each other everything they had not said in four years. While Rodrigo talked non-stop about little Emilio and Vicente about the great job they were going to give him in Polar but that never came to be, Manuel wondered, with no trace of anger that time, but only a little annoyance, why Alfredo had not given them a little more warning about the conference in Mérida, and why he was so slow returning calls and answering emails.

But at the end of the joyous meeting, when everyone hugged Alfredo so tightly that they almost broke his bones, Manuel told himself that he had no right to interfere with his friend's life. Things were probably quite hard over there in the hospital, or maybe he had got together with a very jealous girlfriend who checked his emails. Smiling at this absurd possibility, Manuel decided to accept that everything Alfredo did, he did well.

"Go back to Caracas, Manuel. This is an ant's nest," Alfredo told him firmly after looking through the glass front of the international terminal and seeing the vast number of passengers lining up in front of the American Airline counter.

Manuel got out of the car with the intention of saying goodbye. As an airport employee brought over a baggage trolley, he stood lost in thought, staring at the fine leather briefcase and the thick coat that Alfredo was taking out of the trunk. Manuel finally looked at Alfredo, noticing again, for the second or third time during this last visit, how his friend's face had thinned over the last few years, and the deep furrows which went from his nostrils to the sides of his mouth.

"Call me whenever you get a chance, ok?" he told him, giving him a hug. And feeling the warmth from the hug that Alfredo gave back to him, he forgot about Mérida and the unanswered telephone calls.

An hour later, right in the center of Caracas, Manuel was still giving himself a hard time about the scolding. In the midst of his mea culpa, the image of Vilma came to him, more foolish now that they had both started working at the Ministry of Food and Nutrition. To escape from his boss's viperous face and his sadness about Alfredo, he clung onto the only ray of light that had reached him in the last few weeks: the penthouse in Valle Arriba. Crowning a fifteen-story high building, the luxurious apartment rose above the other buildings and immense trees that had survived the area's urbanization. From there he could see the hills of Prados del Este, full of nice houses, and a little further away, the uneven horizon where the great round solar disc rose over the city.

He had been to see the apartment just before Alfredo came back to Caracas. The real estate agent left him alone inside the four walls to let him feel the "vibes" that his new house had. It was an unnecessary gesture on the part of his kind agent, because as soon as he had set foot in the deserted room, he knew he had found what he needed so much. Sealed with double windows which completely isolated it from the noise of the motorway, the penthouse was like the point of a needle cutting into the sky: an introverted sky that Manuel was ashamed for many to see if he could manage to make a decent offer. "And to pay its high price," he told himself coldly, "I'd go down to hell every day for many a year to come."

With his forehead leaning on the window, Alfredo could see the scars that streaked across the long body of La Guaira. Eight years after the mudslides there, they had not shrunk and were just as rough as they had been in 2002, when another American Airlines Boeing had flown him home after the conference in Mérida.

At night, they were invisible, but at seven o'clock in the morning, with the sun bathing them in an oblique white light, their short, ocher stains were diluted in huge extensions of clayey soil, outlined by a thin, blackish border. It looked like a lunar landscape, but being so close to the barrios that had been saved and with a great quantity of debris still lying there after so many years, whoever saw them from high up could not escape the reality. They were what they were, petrified wounds, stopped in time, like everything or almost everything in Venezuela, thought Alfredo, feeling downcast. His bedroom at home in Caracas had also been stuck in a time warp but nevertheless, he was pleased that his mother and Salomé had transformed it into an altar.

A brief feeling of regret ran from his head down to his feet as he thought of his mother and the little time they had spent together. The plane banked suddenly toward the north, leaving the coast to fly over the Caribbean Sea. For a few minutes, he had the blue water before him, so close that he was able to make out the crest of the waves. One after another, they followed each other in the futile attempt to go nowhere, before the wind that had made them blew them away. Alfredo felt kindred to the warm sea whose waters he knew so well. In a sudden burst of emotion, he felt like a brother to the foam, to the waves that existed thanks to the complicated joining of the wind and the water, and how he would hoist up the sails to escape, always fleeing to nowhere.

When he finished his studies in Chicago and had time to think, he suspected in his heart that he would always be running away from something his whole life. It came to him the same morning that he opened his eyes and missed Lucy's body next to his. It made no sense to think of her at that moment, as it was a long time since he had stopped seeing her. But that morning he missed her more than ever, even though things were going full steam ahead. He had just been made head of the Neurosurgery residency program and although it was a position that he did not like, he ended up accepting it, after the hospital promised to let him continue with his research. If he could endure two years supervising the students, they would give him the funds he needed to develop a new surgical method that he had conceived during his career.

For years, Alfredo had dreamed of the day when he would be able to dedicate most of his time to research. Absorbed in this goal, and without realizing, little by little he forgot the image of a future that most men aspire to.

During the several, always brief visits from his parents, Alfredo could anticipate the questions that his discreet mother dared to ask him: "Why don't you take a break, hijito? Why don't you get married, have kids and buy a nice, big house where your father and I can come and visit our grandchildren?" But for Alfredo, it seemed more than reasonable to continue living in that apartment complex where he ended up in his second year in Chicago; more than reasonable to live in a dark, inhospitable place with just a woman who came to clean it once every fortnight.

Isabel had only been to that apartment twice, and just in passing. She and her husband always stayed at the Hilton on Michigan Avenue for the week, every two years that they had come to visit him in Chicago, since 1997. Unable to comment on it to Roberto or even Nonno, Isabel could not understand that this son of hers, so methodical and meticulous to the point of obsession, slept in an unmade bed with his books lying around gathering dust. But removed from such thoughts and far from accepting even the minimum responsibility for his slovenliness, Alfredo showed his parents the apartment with the indescribable pride of living alongside these young doctors from the hospital, still paying off their student debts. He would have hated to compete with any of them in inequality of conditions and he would never have allowed himself to have an advantage over them, other than his excellent car which he drove everywhere, covering the long distances between Chicago and its suburbs.

When the fasten-seat-belt sign had disappeared, Alfredo realized that the plane had reached official cruising altitude and that a huge blanket of clouds was hiding the view of the sea from him. Then Caracas was no more than a hazy memory and suddenly, before lethargy could take hold of him, he got up to get the notebook with black covers that he kept in his briefcase.

Standing up, he looked all around him and realized that he was the only passenger in first class. Curious, he peered around the blue curtain that separated him from economy class. It was full of a silent crowd with languid faces. He had never noticed that on previous trips from Caracas to Miami. On the contrary, the passengers always exuded a contagious holiday happiness that made them get up and visit people they knew in other seats or go constantly to the bathroom. The only unhappiness during those three hours came from the air stewardesses, who spent all their time asking people not to block the plane's gangway, otherwise it would be impossible for them to serve thefood.

The flight to Caracas had been just like the ones he had in his memory and the opposite of this flight: gigantic bags, soft toys, boxes of scotch and sometimes packets of Huggies diapers crammed the overhead compartments, when not even a third of the passengers had boarded. As usual on these flights, the passengers waiting outside had to give their hand luggage to the stewardesses to put in the hold. To top it all off, many passengers already on the plane had gone up and down looking for a locker to put their masses of stuff, without realizing that it would be impossible to return to their seats as the narrow gangway was bursting with people.

When the stewardesses finished seating the passengers and the plane was finally able to make its way to the runway, there was a fifty-minute delay. Then they had to wait another fifteen minutes for the control tower to give them the green light. In this period, among murmurs, laughter and a joke or two, which resonated with the noise of the turbines, Alfredo's eyes met those of an exhausted air stewardess who, used to the Venezuelan oil money chaos, smiled at him and sighed.

The memory of the plane transported Alfredo to his adventures on the streets of Caracas, whose colorful disarray he had totally forgotten about. Endless street sellers trading pirated films, coffee and potato chips could be seen at the highway exit and on all the main avenues, doing their best to slow down traffic, unbearable in itself, to tout their wares.

Recently, added to this simple and effective commercial strategy were the hordes of motorcycles that mobbed the city. Many Caracas residents suspected that there was a Machiavellian pact between them and the sellers, as the motorcycles appeared like hungry flies, irritating the cars with the scandalous buzzing of their exhaust pipes. On such occasions, especially when a traffic light brought the slow flow of traffic completely to a halt, the improvised salespeople were added to the windscreen cleaners, desperate to serve, and the clowns, desperate to distract the car drivers with their pirouettes in exchange for a fewbolivars.

One or two brave drivers would wind their windows down, adding shouts of "epa" and "give my windscreen a bit of a clean, pana" to the chaos. But the bigger the mob, the increasingly tense were the drivers, shut away in their metallic boxes, waiting for the Machiavellian plan to unfold completely, not in selling them some rubbish or other, but in robbing them with impunity. Robbery by motorcyclists was on the increase in Caracas, and the drivers knew that sooner or later one of these bikers, ready to kill for a watch or a cell phone, would brandish a pistol to rob them.

The day that he decided to ask his mother for the car to amuse himself for awhile, Alfredo saw with his own eyes exactly what she meant when she said nervously, "Don't even think about going to downtown, or you're a dead man. And be careful in the east end too, that can also be tricky. In this country, everyone is hoppingmad."

Alfredo found this out for himself when he was leaving the highway, near Libertador avenue. Stopped at a traffic light, he got distracted looking at those buildings he had thought were marvelous as a young boy and that were now dilapidated with time and neglect. When the light went green, the driver of a station wagon behind him began to sound his horn steadily. Annoyed, Alfredo turned to look him in the face while at the same time, the driver poked his head out of the window to shout at him: "Get moving or I'll move you myself, guevón!"

One second was enough to know that the man was not joking. His face was contorted and instinctively, Alfredo put his foot on the accelerator to get away from him, but not satisfied with his threat, the man followed him for a good stretch on the sidestreets of Altamira, pressing on his horn and suddenly accelerating to hit the back trunk of his victim's car. After receiving several bumps, the terrified Alfredo was able to drive into a restaurant car park. Trembling, although ready for anything, he got out of the car, but the station wagon had already disappeared.

That same evening, with the word "guevón" still pounding in his temples, he went to a dinner that a group from the Country Club had prepared for him. Not one of them, whom Alfredo had known since his childhood and sometimes mixed with, asked him how he was or what he was doing in Chicago. From the moment he entered into Daniella's magnificent mansion, he only heard complaints about Chávez'sgovernment.

When the guests made a ceasefire to wolf down the steaks brought from Carora, Alfredo saw his opportunity to stir things up a bit and, making a few detours, he voiced his approval of the Chavista literacy program, which he saw as positive progress amid all the disasters. "Also the health system," he began to say, excited when he noticed that everyone was listening attentively to him.

But he could not finish his sentence. For the second time in one day, the word "guevón" hit him again, this time from Daniella, who sitting at his side and who had not finished chewing a huge piece of asparagus which was stuck between her teeth, said to him furiously:

"Ok, then. Well, move back here, if you think things are so damn great. Come and have a walk around your new Caracas and see if a literate Chavista punches you in the face a couple of times. Shut your mouth if you don't know what you're talking about, guevón. It's easy for you to talk all that bullshit when you're over there, living your American dream…"

"What dream?" Alfredo wondered, staring at the untimely thread of asparagus which had wedged itself between the teeth of a girl who had been his sweet, fashionable girlfriend when he was younger.

Not sure whether to go to the bathroom in search of dental floss or to indignantly take it out herself with her fingers, Daniella swung away in her chair, even angrier with him and no doubt with the asparagus, which was so bad, thought Alfredo, about to grin like an idiot, it must be Chavista as well. But he held back when Daniella looked at him with fiery eyes, as if he were a traitor.

For a brief instant, he was captivated by this look, understanding that for the Country Club lot, beyond the frivolity and excess they had grown up with, Venezuela was their country. And almost immediately, he imagined Daniella, with all the money in the world, in turbulent New York or in Paris or Vienna. Surely she would have no trouble getting hold of two or three servant ladies, and organizing dinner for her compatriots. But in New York, Paris or Vienna, Daniella could not live on her family name, Goicoechea, but would be just another rich woman, fleeing from the poor republics of the third world. Because even if her children managed to fit in with the international jetset, she would always be an expat, daughter of an ex-boss in the oil industry, and judging by how things were going, soon he would be an ex-landowner. Her life would always be elsewhere and always in the past. And now and again, his old girlfriend would call him, the 'guevón', to complain about the cold weather and the isolation in her newlife.

A stewardess came up to Alfredo and asked him if he felt all right. He was standing up, absorbed in something, holding the black bound notebook in one hand while the other grabbed the headrest of the seat. Although the plane was hardly moving, the stewardess explained that passengers had to stay seated, looking at him intensely to make sure that her only passenger was not having a nervous breakdown. Alfredo asked her for a tomato juice so that she would leave him alone.

Sitting down again next to the second row window, he folded down the table on the seat in front of him and placed on it the notebook and the Mont Blanc he had taken out of his shirt pocket. But he made no attempt to write anything. He was still thinking of Daniella's anger.

"What is this craziness all about?" he wondered, suddenly noticing the huge nightmare that the American Airlines Boeing was leaving behind at full speed. What was happening in his country? How could one man have caused so much hatred? What kind of nonsense was going on with the opposition, for them to allow Chávez to return to the presidency after the coup? Because it was after that, Alfredo said, looking to place the blame, and forgetting his own ignorance about the *Zeta* magazines, that everyone either became Chavistas or furious anti-Chavistas and began coming out with their own motives to fight a deadly war. And behind everyone was the great instigator, on his ridiculous clown's throne, wheezing complacently faced with crime and the absence of warnings.

He slowly opened the notebook, almost filled with the magnificent handwritten notes about medical problems at the beginning and at the end, information from the *Zeta* magazines and some Venezuelan newspapers. There were only three pages left and Alfredo started to write on them, taking the lid off the fine nib which he liked so much.

"What dream?" he asked himself again, unsure of what to tell his notebook and remembering, next to Daniella's furious face, the insistent political sermons that everyone seemed hell bent on giving him during his short vacation. Alfredo's only real dream was buried in Caracas, in the spring evenings and the youthful trips he had made with his best friends down the coast and to the plains. This had been his true dream, the one that went with him everywhere like a faithful dog and that never really turned sour. And now, he was not only upset by Daniella's rudeness, but also by his father, so determined to lecture him, and by his friends who sometimes went off the deep end at any comment he made. It hurt that no one was interested in his opinion, and that everyone was too caught up in their own business and anger to listen to him, and to realize that he was still one of them. He felt he had also lost hisworld.

The ink pen glided smoothly across the blank page, leaving behind a twisted trail of grey-colored blood.

March 20, 2005

Why the hell did I come?

He did not have to wait long to visualize the answer. It rose to the surface and stuck to his being the morning he woke up missing Lucy. It was Alfredo's thirty-fifth birthday that morning, and for the first time, he felt afraid in his apartment. It felt cold and alien while he looked at the contents in the bedroom, facing north as if it were rejecting the sun's embrace, his worn out rug, barely visible under the load of books and clothes resting on it, and those sheets, those damned sheets in a sickly yellow color which he covered his face with. What had made him buy them? Without exception, his whole apartment spoke to him that morning, asking who the stranger was who livedthere, ignorant of the time passing and taking with it everything we love. At that moment, Alfredo decided to go to Caracas.

Trying to forget that in a few hours, he would open the door of that lonely, unfamiliar place, he thought of María Fernanda, who had got married for the third time and was living in Paris. At least he had avoided seeing her in Caracas. Then he remembered Manuel's farewell embrace, and Emilio calling him Uncle Alfredo with a happy face and Rodrigo, poor Rodrigo, taking time out of his classes to spend time with him. Warmth returned to his body as he wrote:

Hey, what the hell. I saw my panas. The friendship is intact.

He put the lid on his fountain pen and slid his seat back. With the notebook resting on his chest, safeguarding it with both hands in case a furtive thief were to creep up on him and steal it, he fell into a deep sleep in the solitary first class cabin.

CHAPTER 20

July 28, 2005

After two hours of dialing the number, Maikel heard Alfredo's voice on the other end of the line. He spoke in a desperate voice.

"Alfredo, it's Maikel. I'm here with Rodrigo." "Hey, how's it going? How's your mother?"

"That's why I'm calling, pana. She's dying. They just transferred her to a hospital in Guarenas. They're saying she has dengue, and it seems like the Cuban son of a bitch that Chávez is selling to the people as a doctor is giving her medicine that is making her bleed even more."

Maikel squeezed the telephone with all his strength, and his veins instantly popped up on his forearm and hand. They seemed about to explode due to the incredible tension of their owner, who had to tilt his right shoulder and his free hand, the left one so that the telephone did not slip away, as it was covered in sweat.

"Maikel, wait a moment, listen to me. He's probably just a nurse and not a doctor.

I doubt he would have given her that kind of medicine. Do you know what he gave her, can you remember the name? All right, you can tell me when you find out. But I'm telling you, even the worst nurse in Venezuela can diagnose dengue fever. With your Mom's sudden fever and the epidemic going on, I don't think the guy would have madea mistake. Are they sure in the hospital? Hey, listen to me, calm down and listen, please. Did you see red petechiae on your Mom's belly or chest?

"What the hell are petechiae? A rash? No, no, I wasn't with her, but the doctor at the hospital told me my Mom's case was different because she didn't have a rash."

"Tell him about the diabetes," interrupted Rodrigo, squeezing his shoulder and raising his voice.

"They also told us my Mom has diabetes and she wasn't controlling it. Do you remember I told you a few months back that she had swollen feet? That goddamned nurse did some blood tests and according to him, everything was fine."

"Maikel, you have to calm down, brother." The diabetes worried Alfredo, but he said nothing. "Whether he's a nurse or doctor, I'm sure that man did everything he could, pana. It could be that your Mom took the medicine from a neighbor or something. You know what it's like: people think that medicines are sweets. No, no, Maikel, I'm not defending Chávez, but remember what you went through with your brother in the village, where there wasn't even a first aid post. If that doctor, or whatever he is, ok… that nurse had not been there, or if this had happened to your Mom fifteen years ago when that "Inside the Neighborhood" social program[16] didn't exist,

---

[16] In 2003, Chávez created the welfare medical program *Misión Barrio Adentro*, to provide medical care in rural areas, using physicians from Cuba. Whilst the program has been praised for reducing infant mortality, critics have questioned medical competence of the Cuban physicians. In 2007, the Venezuelan Medical Federation reported that 70% of the centers were abandoned. In return for the physicians, and despite a poverty rate of at least 30% in Venezuela, Cuba will receive free or discounted oil valued at 6-8 billion dollars until 2020.

maybe she wouldn't still be here, pana. Look, the best thing is to give me the name and telephone of Anselma's doctor so I can contact him, ok? I'll try to get them to move her to the medical center when she's stable. Or even better, find the doctor and call me when you have him right there, because I want to speak to him…"

The effort to note in his head what Alfredo was telling him kept him in silence and when the instructions came to an end, the friends had nothing more to say to each other. Tears streamed down Maikel's face. He did not know what to do with the telephone, and without replacing the receiver, he left it hanging against his t-shirt, also bathed in sweat, perhaps in a gesture of defeat or perhaps to protect the device, in spite of his clumsiness, at least until it unloaded all the hope which lived inside it.

With his arm around his shoulders, Rodrigo began to shake him very slightly, as if to say: cry, but don't crack up; you have friends who love you and who are going to get your Mom out of this.

Two days later, at the wake, it was the same scene while Maikel caressed his mother's face in silence, paralyzed in a painful expression. But just when everything was set to take the body to the cemetery, and the coffin lid was closed, Maikel began hitting the coffin with his fists, in the middle, over the part that covered his mother's belly. It took three men to restrain him, while Rodrigo, alarmed by such a violent reaction, begged him to calm down. With a wild look, Maikel charged at his captors, yelling:

"This can't be, this can't be!"

CHAPTER 21

April 21, 2006

The television screen showed the names of Humphrey Bogart and Ingrid Bergman in black letters on a white background. Roberto Piruggi had no other choice but to see *Casablanca* for the umpteenth time. It was Isabel's favorite film and that day was their thirty-eighth wedding anniversary.

She refused to organize the usual party for all their friends, and instead proposed a simple meal in the privacy of their own home. Seeing that he was a little disappointed, as her husband loved playing the role of host, she told him that the offer included the famous raviolis that she made on specialoccasions.

That evening, Isabel was planning on asking him for a divorce.

That was why she sent Nonno to Herminia's place, with the story that someone should be looking after her since she had recently been widowed, and had suffered a breakdown that afternoon. In agreement with what the two women had arranged, Herminia would come across more traumatized than she actually was, not because of the loss of her husband but because of the disease that he had suffered, Alzheimer's, that had left countless hospital debts behind.

Although the dental clinic and the goings-on in the School of Dentistry kept her continually busy, Isabel was not oblivious to Roberto's absences. Over more than five weeks, she kept a mental note of the nights that her husband had stayed over at the stud farm, the endless work meetings and the evenings when, according to her, he was meeting friends to place bets and talk about horses.

It was obvious that her husband had a lover.

And without getting caught up in useless memories, without anger and without anxiety, Isabel took off the diamond ring she had proudly worn on her left hand for thirty eight years, and placed it on the table, after her husband had devoured the raviolis.

As on three previous occasions, there were no surprises this time either, not counting the force with which Roberto put the ring back on his wife's finger. With embarrassment rather than passion, he begged her not to leave him.

Isabel congratulated herself on the dramatic idea of the ring, and regretted not thinking of it the first time that Roberto had decided to get involved with one of the young architects on his team. Twenty years before, she had not known him as well and did not know that Roberto would never leave her because he was a man who considered family relationships to be sacred.

And now, in the midst of the country's chaos, and with the hatred that Chávez had stirred up for men such as her husband, Isabel felt that Roberto, although he did not realize it and however much he needed a young woman to flatter his vanity, would stick to his family now more than ever. Because for him, always so daring and audacious, the new Venezuela was uncertain and uncertainty was something he had never known.

After a few drinks and endless comments about the two foals that Roberto had turned into champions, the couple went up the elegant spiral staircase to the bedroom. And while inside her, Roberto thanked all the saints in heaven for getting him off the hook, or perhaps his wife for accepting his explanations and apologies. Isabel thought of how much she loved her husband, and of the scant way he gave it back to her.

But just like her mother, Isabel was a practical woman and there was no point in asking Roberto for emotional trust he could not give, even when they were young and he assured her of his great love for her. He was a little arrogant and fickle, in her opinion, but so energetic and so insistent that she had to turn a blind eye to everything.

Isabel always concluded her reminiscence of her dating days with another indescribable memory of the romantic film, *Casablanca*. As a young woman, she watched it many times with her mother at the Betamax, when the men of the house, her father and her three brothers would go to the ranch. It was not mother and daughter watching the movie, but two women taking a break from the simple and monotonous reality of their lives.

After a quick bath, she switched off the image of Chávez that Roberto was watching on one of endless state television channels to put on the movie where Humphrey Bogart and Ingrid Bergman revived the love that war and human ambition had made impossible in German-occupiedParis.

"What the... Who are y...?"

Salomé's final cry travelled to the second floor after a heavy, dry thud.

Roberto looked at Isabel for an instant and while he opened the bottom drawer of his bedside table to get the 38 revolver, he made signs to her to call the police and not to move from the bedroom.

He opened the door carefully until he could see the wide passageway that separated him from the big staircase, whose elegant curves descended into the main room. He covered the stretch with agility and went down the stairs, brandishing the weapon. He had hardly gone down the last step when a fast shadow lunged on him from the archway that joined the living room and the dining room. Followed by a punch in the stomach, the onslaught brought Roberto to the floor, almost paralyzed. Another shadow, much slower, came up to him and hit him again, this time in the face, making him lose consciousness.

He woke up wet, feeling that someone was slapping him and pulling him to his feet. When he opened his eyes, he saw Isabel naked on the floor, watching him full of terror, with her hands tied over her chest, and her mouth strangely contorted. When his vision became clearer, Roberto realized that they had put a ball in his wife's mouth; it was white, smaller than a tennis ball, and was fixed with adhesive tape.

"Stop right there, and don't fuck around, you old piece of shit," said the man who had slapped him.

His effort to obey was useless. He was tied to a dining chair and when he tried to move, he felt the stab of the rope digging into his hands and legs. Instinctively, he turned his head from side to side, looking for a way out, but he only saw the motionless body of Salomé on the floor at one end of the room, surrounded by a pool of blood.

He turned back toward Isabel when he heard a loud gasp. Or maybe it was a scream, drowned out by the ball and fear. It sounded like bellows emptying.

"Look, you old son of a bitch, you get three chances to answer me. If you don't tell the truth, your wife'll pay," the slightly high-pitched voice belonged to the apparent leader of the group. He pronounced the words slowly, putting his face close to Roberto's and gripping his chin with huge, strong hands.

He was the only one of the attackers who had not bothered to put a nylon stocking over his face. Very young, about twenty two, the leader exhaled pestilent breath that Roberto, with his bleeding nose, could not smell. But he could see his acne scars that deformed most of his face, and the pus of a pimple about to explode on one eyebrow, each time he wrinkled them. When he moved back a little and Roberto could see the whole of his face, he felt dizzy and had to struggle to overcome a powerful urge to vomit. The man had his eyes fixed on him, but his look, slow and lazy, was heavily intoxicated.

On his left, the youngest man was holding a wooden bat, stained with blood. He was fat and tall. He also had very short hair, almost shaved. He seemed agitated and nervous although sure of himself. He did not stop moving, as if he wanted to say something but could not find the words. The third one looked at least thirty. He was wearing cheap glasses and a very loose blue t-shirt that said "Curazao." He suddenly grabbed Isabel violently by her hair, forcing her head up so that Roberto could see with more detail the look of terror on his wife's face, who was now breathing with great difficulty. The leader of the group continued to shout at Roberto.

"OK, motherfucker. Tell me where the safe is."

Roberto tried to speak and realized that he also had a ball in his mouth. The one with the blue t-shirt let go of Isabel's hair and went to the dining room table and took a strap and a bucket of water which he tipped over his victim's naked body. Then he lashed her savagely, thrilled by sight of the blood that oozed from her thighs. Her groans were joined by Roberto's moans, who felt every lash as if it were his own body. He watched her with tears in his eyes, completely helpless.

"Oh, sorry," said the indolent leader of the pack, "Forgot that I gagged your mouth too, sorry 'bout that, chico. I'll take the tape off, but I'm tellin' ya, if I hear one word comin' out of your mouth, a single word beggin', cussin' us or whatever, my pana Gilberto here'll give your wife the second round. Got it? Yeah, I think you fuckin' got it!" This last shout was combined with a hard punch to the left side of Roberto's face.

Free of the tape and the ball, Roberto exhaled briskly. As he swallowed the excess saliva, he felt another blow, this time to his mouth and teeth, a much sharper, colder pain than the previous one. The leader had hit him with the end of a long barreled revolver which he now held in his two hands, pointed at Roberto's eyes. Leaning his head forward to the same level as Roberto, he started speaking again.

"Shit, you're very obedient. D'you see, Wilme. The old man can follow orders, chico and you said he couldn't. Hey, this dude Wilme, he was so negative about you, but he's sweet to your woman. He's not like that brute Mandinga, who hits women. No, not this guy. This guy is lovin'. Y'see? And well, looks like it's his lucky day with this bitch. Cos I bet this whore dreams of being fucked by a nice dude like Wilme."

"No! please! I'll give you anything you want." Another blow took his words away and the ball and tape kept him quiet.

"Chill out, Wilme will be gentle, he'll treat her fine, you'll see! The whore is gonna love it!"

Roberto Piruggi was sweating profusely, trying not to choke on saliva and blood that was oozing from his cut lips.

"And if she puts up a fight, I'm gonna to blow your brains away, d'you get that, whore? Open your legs after three. And give me that fuckin' ring, we can feed the whole barrio with that thing, you fuckin' rich whore. What do you say, Wilme. Shall we give it to the barrio or shall we buy us some crack and weed?"

Isabel let out no sound while the huge, sweaty beast pounded her with brisk lunges. The cackling of the three men filled the room where Nonno's stories once filled the air and children ran around. Seeing Isabel being violently raped, Roberto understood that the safe was just any other excuse to ruin them.

When his wife received the first blow from the baseball bat, he let out a deep cry that almost freed him from the tape and the ball. Then everything went black.

CHAPTER 22

April 27, 2006

Who else but me would come up with the idea of a pilgrimage to Todasana to cheer up Alfredo? We assume we can bandage and numb someone else's pain but not our own, deeper, more intense pain. A more important pain, perhaps? I haven't been able to let Carmen rest in peace in the cemetery over all these years, so why did I think that a trip to the beach would distract Alfredo from the memory of his parents? Especially of Isabel, whom he surely thought of when he was alone, when he stiffened up and looked at us blankly, without really seeing us, as if we didn't exist.

I was obsessed with the idea, it's as simple as that. The others went along with it, vaguely hoping that things would turn out how I wanted, although they were only too familiar with the quantity of absurd ideas I tend to have. But they were trying to accommodate me, thinking that maybe this time I wouldn't get it as wrong as I usually do.

It all started at the wake and afterward during the burial, when I realized that Alfredo was avoiding Manuel as if he were merely a passing acquaintance, just coming to the funeral out of duty, perhaps in case he might need some help or a small favor in the future.

Of course, Alfredo also kept his distance from poor Paolo, who sobbed relentlessly in one corner of the funeral parlor. It was sad to see the wall he put up against his brother, with whom he would always share the burden of the murders. What did he blame him for? For that visit to Caracas he postponed? For the telephone call he never made? The words he never spoke? Did Paolo not have enough of his own regret, so evident and so useless?

Alfredo could not accept that his brother would never be like the rest of us, always complaining about everything, wishing that everyone around us shared our rage. But Paolo is one of those people who goes through life without complaining, not because he is better, but because he was born absorbed, complacent yes, but absorbed in things we cannot see or that we are happy to ignore. As a boy, he was easily able to do without friends, if he had any to speak of, and dedicated his time to studying lizards for hours on end, or figuring out how a toy worked. Whenever we invited him to join in our games, he came along without any persuasion. But after a while he would leave suddenly, after losing at Monopoly or in a bicycle race or something likethat.

When Paolo began to be interested in music, Isabel rushed to enroll him at a prestigious music school in Caracas. From then on, and without me even realizing it, he disappeared from my view. Only a handful of notes which flew out of his window to land on the Piruggi's patio let me know that Paolo was alive, although shut away in his universe with only a small trumpet for company.

When I was already studying at the School of Arts and Literature and had not set foot in the Piruggi house for a long time, I saw Paolo again when he played with the Venezuelan youth orchestra once again. Isabel had called me a few days before to give me a free ticket and ask me to come along, since after the concert, we would all go out for dinner together. It was Paolo's farewell, as soon after that he was going to London to continue his studies at a music academy.

All I can say is that I felt obliged to be there, and tried to arrive as late as possible, something that I now think was a shame, as since then I have loved classical music. Also because I discovered a strange Paolo, tall and sinewy like Alfredo, although radiant each time his trumpet burst in triumphantly to dispute the melody of the violins and piano.

It only took a few minutes for me to realize that throughout his quiet adolescence, Paolo had found a game in which the marvelous trio could not take part and risk showing our clumsiness, as he did when he grabbed the balls that we passed him. I accepted this small ray of divine justice because in the restaurant, he became the same affable creature that I had known, although even more introverted if that were possible, feeling somewhat uncomfortable, as if those who had protected him so well since his childhood endangered his elusive character.

Alfredo was now set on asking his brother to stay in Caracas to help him sort out Roberto's business. Did the Piruggi family not have competent people who could arrange all the paperwork? What was Alfredo thinking? Trying to become the boss of the family? Or did the tragedy with his parents leave him feeling so alone in this world, so unbearably alone that he was hanging onto the excuse of the business that he had never been interested in, to stop his brother from returning toLondon?

Manuel must have felt the same during the wake, I thought, although Alfredo never demanded anything that Manuel could not give him. But time and distance are traitorous. It was logical for Alfredo to lecture us about organic diets and ways of living that frankly appeared ridiculous to

Manuel and me. But still, he expected us to carry on being the same. I remember the time he brought me that 'The Cure' t-shirt that he went to such efforts to get hold of. I had just lost my wife and didn't have a clue about how to go on. I was even frightened to look at Emilio, who looked so much like Carmen. However, I saw the t-shirt as an insult because it took me back to a time in my life that excluded her.

Things have also changed for Manuel, even though he still makes the same jokes.

He avoids talking about anything that sounds remotely heavy and he can still spend a whole day drinking beer in the shade of a palm tree. Now he seems a little sad and focused on other things. He has been like that since before he started at the Ministry and no one knows what is up with him. Maybe he does not even know himself and thinks he is the same, but Alfredo was definitely surprised by how little spontaneous the new Manuel is. Maybe he thought he was abandoning him in his time of troubles. But Manuel is not the type to abandon anyone.

I did not want to go any deeper into the matter, thinking that it was a passing cloud, belonging to circumstances. I thought of the old days, when to calm ourselves down all we needed was a beer in our hand and the sea in front of us, the warm blue water at Todasana beach.

Todasana itself never interested me as much as the beaches. It is typical of many small Venezuelan seaside villages, ailing and left to their miserable destiny. Even though they try to embellish themselves with a few tourist facilities, the villages are just country roads, I would say. The stretch between Todasana and the next village has plenty of curves and is paved with dubious cement, worn away by frequent rain and covered with earth from the mountains.

Like so many other villages of the north-central Coast, Todasana lives on hope, anxiously stretching out its arms to the only branch that barely joins it to Caracas. This is not the case for its beaches. To preserve their perfect wildness, their beauty would depend on getting rid of the hordes of swimmers occasionally swamping them. Because the greatest pain begins to yield when we see how well nature deals with it alone in its daily existence, no less brutal than ours.

Of course, Todasana has its limitations. It could never alleviate the pain of losing Carmen, but for days, seeing Alfredo struggle between pain and fury while Isabel and Roberto were lowered to their final resting place, I thought again about the solitude that death leaves behind, profuse and dense like a rustic landscape where the soul becomes lost and which we can never find our way out of. We fight against it in vain and with fists, learning that the only solution is to be still and to sharpen the senses until we find the raft that rescues us from the shipwreck or the wall that stops us falling into the abyss.

That was when I got the idea to save Alfredo the many blows that were awaiting him, and so I suggested the trip to Todasana, thinking that Manuel and I could be Alfredo's raft if he could recognize us in the fog. For that, it would be enough to turn back time to the jokes, the beers and above all, those Todasana waters where we would urinate away the impurities of our friendship.

We took Emilio and by about seven in the morning, we were already on the alternative road to the coast, driving around the fully collapsed viaduct between Caracas and La Guaira, which according to experts was the most important feat of engineering in Latin America after the Panama Canal.

I don't know if it once was or not, but its collapse shows that it no longer is. In my opinion, a geological error and failure to maintain the viaduct add up to a disaster. About fifteen years ago, the earth began moving near the Gorge under the bridge. The viaduct complained and people from the Engineering School backed it up, but in political spheres the cry for help went unheard. Only when Chávez came to the rescue, thinking that it was not a good idea to isolate Caracas from its port and airport, was any action taken to prevent it from crumbling further. How would our great leaders continue importing toothpicks and catching planesabroad?

Being only a seasonal road and relatively short, the alternative road was a nightmare for us to cross. We yearned for the days when 30 minutes was long enough to get to the airport and the neighboring beaches. During busy times, the hellish stretch was jam-packed with vehicles moving in both directions.

It had poured with rain in the early hours of Wednesday morning and the line was not moving. Even then, we would have felt perfectly comfortable in Manuel's new Toyota SUV if it hadn't been for Alfredo's mute silence, becoming more obvious as time went on. When we reached the main coastal area, after almost three hours on the road, we had to stop at a roadside diner to use the bathroom and eat something. And there, while Emilio nibbled on an arepa, more sleepy than hungry, I began to suspect that this Wednesday would be a wash-out.

It took us another two hours to get to Todasana. There was a collision and we had to endure the usual aggressive behavior of the drivers, which did not bother me so much because the horn blasts made up for the silence that was taking over in the Toyota. As we continued our odyssey, Emilio was fast asleep and Manuel had the good idea of putting on an old U2 concert to cover up the monosyllabic answers from Alfredo. Only when we went down the earth ramp which led to our destination, did my lungs expand.

But it was a short-lived feeling. It was only just past noon and the air was still warm under an overcast sky. We had hardly spread out the towels when Alfredo settled heavily down on one, his pensive eyes searching for the sun that was hidden behind a curtain of menacing grey. Emilio, who also seemed down, sat in the sand and began building a labyrinth. Before, he would have happily played with a ball or a Frisbee, but that day, he did not want to be separated from us. Manuel, a little disheartened by the lack of atmosphere, got undressed and ran into the water. As usual, I was the one talking about everything, without really saying much.

Among the many comments flying through my head, I struck lucky when I suggested to Alfredo that we could visit him in Chicago. Alfredo looked at me as if he finally understood Spanish.

"Hey, I've been thinking, Emilio and I could come and visit you in the States. The trip would be free if we used that trick with the tickets."

Emilio instantly raised his head, and full of candid enthusiasm for the idea of travelling to where Alfredo lived, he asked what the ticket thing was.

"It's complicated, Emilio," I told him, preparing myself for the awkward explanation. "Basically, your uncle would use my credit card in Chicago to spend at least two thousand dollars, and then he would pay me back in cash. You see? When we get to Chicago, he gives me the cash, I take that money and I sell it for double the value on the black market. Then I pay off my card and I get a profit. Then the trip works out free."

"But where's the black market? Where is it?" enquired Emilio, after mentally running through all the markets where his Abuela had taken him.

"It's nowhere," I continued, "but it's everywhere, on the streets. The money changers make the black market. They are the people who change dollars into bolivars or vice versa, bolivars into dollars. You find them because a friend tells you where they are. And you have to do it very carefully. You can't say to anyone, I'm off to buy some bolivars on the black market."

"And is that legal, Papa?"

Alfredo let out a weak chuckle that I celebrated with an even louder one.

"Well, yes and no, Emilio. Let's just say that your Papa wants to take you to Chicago. And well, the marvelous government in this country only lets him spend two thousand dollars there, so what does Papa have to do? Or rather, what does everyone that travels do? They find a creative solution to the problem. For that though, you have to break Chávez' stupid law and not think twice about corruption."

The child seemed confused by such a complicated trick, which stood in his way to going on an airplane.

"Look," added Alfredo, in an attempt to tone down the acidity of Rodrigo's comment. "Do you remember Al Capone? Well, when alcohol was illegal in Chicago, he sold it secretly, on the black market. If you visit me, I'll take you on the Al Capone tour. Then we'll go and eat a hamburger much better than the ones at McDonalds, in a new place I discovered."

As he said this to Emilio, he started twisting his hair with one hand while he tickled his ribs with the other until he heard gurgling, followed by cackles of laughter which dispersed the cloud and sleepiness of the trip.

At this point, Manuel came over and seeing us in a better mood, he wanted to join the party. He opened the cooler and took out three beers, but Alfredo had gone back to being lethargic and I, for some reason, went quiet, so Manuel spoke about how warm the water was and began reminiscing about the time all three of us had spent time there with Monica and her two cousins.

"Even you managed to get a girl that day," he said to Alfredo, laughing and offering him a beer, which Alfredo declined politely, without looking at him. But as Manuel was wishing for this moment of happiness as much or more than me, he did not give up and continued talking:

"Hey, you know what, Alfredo? We could go to Los Roques islands. A friend of mine has an amazing yacht there and I can borrow it whenever I want. This guy even has a fantastic spa on the yacht, it's huge and ..."

Alfredo cut him short. He raised his eyes, and hardly moving a single facial muscle, he said:

"I take it the money that your friend spent on his yacht is clean, right? Just like the money for your apartment and that car you just bought."

And that was when the shit hit the fan. Manuel, who is gentle at heart and usually hates confrontations, lost his cool. Instead of making peace, he chose to enter the ring, with a soft but trembling voice and with fire in his eyes. God knows why.

"As far as I know, Roberto Piruggi never turned down work at *Acción Democrática* or Chavista houses. And what about that gambling business he was involved in? Or are you telling me that those horses he collected were thrown in for free with Nonno's cheeses?"

I got up from the chair as if an invisible hand had grabbed me and put my body in the boxing ring. Alfredo was already in front of Manuel and threw a right hook at his face, but as I was the shortest of the three of us, the blow landed on my ear, giving me the impression that something had exploded inside my head. Manuel grabbed me to stop me falling and Emilio, seeing his uncles squaring up to each other and his father rubbing his battered ear, babbled something unintelligible.

Manuel was the first one to react, toning his voice down a little but without letting go of me, still grasping my forearms firmly. I now stood opposite Alfredo, too close for my liking to tell the truth, seeing as he was snorting like a humiliated bull. Feeling my caution and far from freeing me, Manuel was putting me in the firing line. I go the perverse idea that he was shielding himself behind me.

"Alfredo, I know you're feeling low, brother, but don't accuse me of things that aren't true," Manuel appealed to him, behind my throbbing ear.

"Feeling low?" he shouted, forgetting his godson's distress. "And what exactly isn't true? Look Manuel, look at what is happening around you. Look at the disaster that we have thanks to the people you mix with for you own goddamn benefit. That great son of a bitch Chávez killed the wife of your best friend and the parents of your other best friend. But you think it's all bullshit, right? You're okay and that's all that matters."

"Chávez did not kill your folks. Chávez did not kill Maikel's mother. And Chávez did not kill Carmen, who I loved like a sister," said Manuel emphatically, but not trying to provoke Alfredo. "They were killed by the goddamned irrationality of this country and the obsession that you and everyone else have to divide people into Chavistas or anti- Chavistas."

"Yes, Chávez did kill Carmen," I exploded, shaking off Manuel to put my arms around Emilio, who was now pale and was breathing agitatedly. "She died because of Chávez and I don't want to involve her in this bullshit."

"I didn't involve her. He did," protested Manuel, quite childishly.

"Yeah, right! Now it's my fault! Who encouraged the poor to destroy the rich and the middle classes? Who glorified hate in this country?"

"That's enough now," I said, trying to reconcile both of them, while I pressed Emilio's head to my chest. But Manuel went on.

"Look, Alfredo. You know I am no Chavista. And quite frankly, what do you want me to do about it? Leave my job? Be a lawyer for the poor? Or are you going to get me a job in Chicago?"

Alfredo kicked the sand in desperation to avoid throwing himself at Manuel, and said in a rage that bordered on contempt:

"That is exactly the problem. You're no Chavista. But what the fuck, there's money in it for you. So you get in with the Chavistas no matter what they do! So you think you're not a part of this mafia, buddy? You're right behind the scenes. You're not a killer, but you're in the mafia." With Al Capone still in his head, he didn't let up on his attack. "The only difference is that you wouldn't last a single round in Chicago with your Toyota and your beers and your friend's yacht. Forget Chicago. What I want to know is if you really think you are not corrupt. Look me in the face and tell me you're not a thief."

"So what? Where do you think the Chavistas came from, outer space? The Chavistas are the very same ones from the *Acción Democrática*, the MAS, the COPEI lot and the hoods. They're the ones that paid for the new swimming pool at the Country Club and all your trips to Europe…"

"That's enough" I cried, feeling as though I would go out of my mind. "Manuel, this is over. Take us home."

I must have sounded desperate, because they both looked at me, and as if by mutual agreement, they each took one handle of the cooler and started up the hill to the car. Emilio and I followed behind them, our heads hanging low. When we reached the parking spot, Alfredo and Manuel started joking with Emilio while one shook the sand from his feet and the other arranged his cap and opened the back door of the Toyota for him. But they did not look at each other or utter a word. It was like that all the way back to Caracas.

When we were on the road, I thought of the hatred that I had seen in Alfredo's eyes when he tried to hit Manuel and that I would never be able to erase it from my memory. I also thought how absurd it was to make assumptions about other people's pain and of our naïve desire to bring back old times, which at that moment seemed so distant and alien, as if the past had never belonged to us. None of it interested me, nor the present we were living and which I could have thrown out of the car window as if it were an empty beercan.

CHAPTER 23

May 3, 2006

"Herminia, stop insisting. You know it's crazy to go to the airport at this time of night and I wouldn't want anything to happen to Rodrigo on my account. And the truth is I don't want anyone to take me."

Alfredo embraced her before she started to cry. She couldn't help but shed another tear. "Do me a favor," he said, softening his voice. "Go to bed. I promise I'll call you from Miami."

After he had given her a fourth goodbye kiss and his blessing, Herminia started up the stairs slowly. She looked slightly hunched and seeing her leaning on the handrail, Alfredo had the urge to tell her that they should come with him, but what would she and Nonno do in Chicago in the cold, with so much traffic and crowds of people rushing from one place to the next? At least in Caracas, they would have their domino games in the 'old hags club,' which was what Nonno called Herminia's friends and cousin, who she had taken under her wing. Alfredo thought somewhat sadly that at least his parents' death had led to Nonno finally moving in withHerminia.

It was almost four in the morning. There was still half an hour before the cab arrived and Alfredo felt the urge to pick up his suitcase and go into the garden to breathe in a bit of fresh air. He had not slept well for several days and he felt nervous just thinking of what lay ahead of him: a three-hour drive, another three hours crossing the bureaucratic jungle of Maiquetía airport, then the three-hour flight to Miami with a two and a half hour wait for his connecting flight. If everything went smoothly, he would be opening the door of his apartment in Chicago at nine thirty at night. What bullshit! Other people travelled from New York to the Middle East in half that time. That goddamned road, this goddamned country, swore Alfredo to himself, going up the steps two by two, as if by hurrying to get his baggage, he could escape from Caracas more quickly.

Herminia's house was like a cage. Like all the villas in the east, its doors and windows were protected by bars but also, an ingenious wrought iron lattice stretched from the house's walls to the top of the high walls that surrounded it, forming a roof over the back and side garden and most of the beautiful terrace at the back of the house. Some climbing plants rested on it, their thickness creating delightful pockets, shielded from the sun. The thickest wall that separated the house from the street was interrupted by two adjoining iron doors, one for the garage and the other leading to the street. The last, through a passageway of steps, led to a landing, an iron gate and the main door, made of solid oak. A little stone path that led to the service door, also made of iron, went around the wall.

Despite the huge iron structure, Alfredo activated the alarm system as he opened the back door and leaned his head out furtively, due to the minute possibility that someone could have got through the railings. After closing it, he slid the key under the door, opened the gate and shut it again when he went through, but this time he put thekey at the back of a hanging flower pot, where Herminia would retrieve it when she wokeup.

It was a cool night and the moon was full. Alfredo went to sit on the little wall between the steps and the garage. From there he would be able to see the cab arrive. He was concerned about Nonno, now gloomy and plagued with new obsessions due to his old age.

Thousands of frogs raised the swell of their song and two or three dogs strung their barks together in a useless discussion. Then there was silence, peppered here and there with a lone frog and the erotic cry of a cat.

The cab passed by without stopping and Alfredo jumped up to open the outside bar. With great relief, he saw the cab reverse. It was a 1976 Dodge Dart and for a few seconds it lit up his soul, even though rust was eating away the light blue bodywork.

What a gem, he thought, as he closed the railing and sneaked the key into a pot full of bird of paradise flowers.

A short, well-built woman got out of the car, opened the trunk and approached him, smiling placidly.

"May I?" she asked as she stooped down to lift his suitcase.

"Please, I'll do it. Leave it to me, it's quite heavy," replied Alfredo, surprised to see that the cab firm had sent a woman.

"Don't worry, I'm used to it," insisted the woman, lifting the suitcase effortlessly and placing it in the trunk. Then she hurried to open the back door opposite the driver and turned to her customer in the same calm way.

"How are you, Sir? Where you going, to International Departures?

Alfredo thought he was dreaming. The cab driver had used "Usted," the polite form twice, instead of the usual informal "tu" and "mi amor" that the people of Caracas loved.

For that reason, when he sat down, he took in her small eyes, too close together, her large forehead and her long hair, tied up in a low ponytail, at the base of her occipital bone, thought Alfredo, always so precise with medical terminology. She must have dyed her hair some time ago, as a halo of dark hair framed her face, contrasting starkly with the corn yellow that started at her crown. An impeccable white t-shirt which was too baggy covered her torso and in contrast, her blue jeans clung to the lower part of her body, showing her very few curves.

"I guess you're going overseas on business, right?" she asked again in a singing voice.

"No, actually I've lived in the States for a few years now."

"Ah, I see. I bet you came to visit your Mom then. It must be hard for her having you so far away. You have to visit your Mom a lot. After all, you only have one!"

Alfredo laughed, pleased to see that after five minutes of exile in a parallel dimension, his cab driver had returned to old Caracas ways, dropping the "Sir," and chitchatting, trying to find out about his life. And in fact, he had not even finished placing his laptop bag on the floor and opening the window when, after struggling with the stiff steering wheel for a few seconds, a torrent of questions rained down on him, about his wife, children and job. Stretching out until he touched the front seat with his knees, Alfredo predicted that coming next were the complaints about the political situation.

But the cabdriver was quiet, thinking it was quite strange for a man of his appearance to not be married. Of course, everyone had their own taste and could pair up with who they wished, especially over there in the north where most women were tough; it was a country very different from Venezuela. Quite violent with all those bombings, children shooting their classmates, gangs running around everywhere like crazy. What a shame! Such nice shops and so many buildings. But anyway, as the passenger seemed like a nice guy, the cab driver told him he should have kids with a woman who also wanted them, as having kids is the best. She had two sons and two daughters that she had brought up alone, with a lot of hard work. Her eldest son was working as a mechanic in a Caracas barrio and repaired the Dodge Dart whenever it broke down.

Alfredo continued listening, with his mind fixed on every villa, and corner, every tree and wall along the highway. Out of everything around him, the Ávila mountain jumped out like a magnet to him.

He turned around completely to look at it through the back window. Its huge opaque shadow, outlined by the shining darkness of the sky made it look arrogant, but in the light of day, El Ávila always looked more impressive, Alfredo thought. There lived many lizards that he had learned to dissect and dozens of insects that he kept in formaldehyde for several years. With Manuel and Rodrigo, he had explored steep precipices, clearings and paths there, which he had come to know like the corners of his own home. As a boy, he had never thought twice about the tragic destiny of this beautiful mountain, while now he tried not to think about what it would inevitably become. Alfredo was sure that in the not-too-distant future, thousands of little shacks would set up home there and then El Ávila would cease to be the same, turning into a concrete lump full of rubbish, crowning the disastrous urbanity of the Caracas Valley.

With such thoughts, and maybe due to his persistent insomnia, his eyes filled with water, blurring his vision of the summit, the only part of El Ávila still visible through the tops of the buildings and the downhill journey of the car. He was sure he would never see it again…

That's enough, he told himself, tired of so much sadness, convinced that the only way to overcome it was to live in the present moment, according to the self-development books he sometimes read. In this spirit, he straightened his head and looking ahead, his gaze met the little figure hanging from the rear-view mirror.

Smiling and frolicking, with its snubbed nose and two holes for nostrils, a red beret and open arms, Hugo Chávez stared at him with big, open eyes.

He made an effort to control his urge to pull it down and rip it to pieces, and when he managed to regain his senses, he asked the woman abruptly:

"Don't you mind that people know that you are Chavista, Madam?"

"Amigo," answered Francisca, going back to formal speech, but not flinching at the man's impertinent tone, "I was brought up in a dangerous barrio, like the ones they have over there where you live. That's why I'm not afraid of anything. Time's up for the opposition and they know it. Now we're the ones calling the shots."

"But señora, it's been proven that the Chavistas are the violent ones, just look at…"

As the car veered to the right, the wheels suddenly hit the bottom of a huge pothole and Hugo's little body sprang around while Alfredo grabbed the front seat in vain to minimize the inertia that pushed him up.

"No way," said the cabdriver, ignoring the slight mishap and the groans of the car. "Those lies are from the TV channels, amigo. Just so you know, I'm the one who always got kicked around. But my president's taught me to value myself. Love myself. We've never had a president like Chávez. He's the best. The best!" And saying this, the cabbie looked at the little doll which was now swinging around, and gave a big sigh.[17]

---

[17] Several of the comments made by the fictitious character Francisca Márquez were partially taken from the official English transcript from

"You stupid idiot! Don't you see they are manipulating you!" Alfredo was about to yell at her, totally infuriated and feeling like getting out of the taxi. But he did not have time to order another cab, so he half-closed his eyes, concentrating on his breathing. He was just about to tame his anger, on the point of clearing his mind, when his eyes wandered and met the gaze of the doll again. A new wave of fury took hold of him and he succumbed to the temptation of having the last word.

"Madam, can I just say that…"

"My name's Francisca, Francisca Márquez, here to serve God, Chávez and you."

"Francisca," continued Alfredo in a preaching tone. "There are a lot of deceived people out there. Chávez pretends to be there for the people, because he wants power. But the results are hidden, Francisca Márquez, hidden. Everything here is going to hell: industry, education, culture…"

"No, hijo, I've seen the results with my own eyes. I'm only a cabdriver in the mornings, but I work in cooperatives and I do voluntary work in the barrio. We have a soup kitchen and we feed the people who need it. The government pays me…

"Not enough though, if you still have to work as a cab-driver," thought Alfredo.

Alfredo returned to the attack with the same heavy tone, trying with all his might to avoid the doll, so that he would not lose his concentration.

"Francisca, I congratulate you for your work. And I totally agree with you. There's never been any respect for the poor in this country. But look. See how most people are against

---

the documentary *The Hugo Chávez Show*, televized by the public American TV channel in 2008. The person being interviewed was Mrs. Francia Urbina, a Chávez supporter from a poorbarrio.

Chávez. The proof is the coup against him. And because the opposition went from being polite to naïve, the man came back to power."

"No, sir!" Francisca rushed to say, trying to correct her passenger's mistake. "He came back for us. We were all there that day, like… how do I put it, for the cause. We left our doors open 'cos we knew no thieves or looters would come. We were all rooting for our father, our leader. We were all together. The cripple, the old man, the youngster, the blind man, all the mothers, everyone. We all went to the presidential palace and demanded to see him. The people put him back there and the people will keep him there."

"But you know, Francisca Márquez, Chávez controls everything. This is a dictatorship. Remember Bolívar's words, *"Flee from the country where one man holds all the power: it is a country of slaves."* To his regret, Alfredo pronounced the sentence with a wooden voice, like the voiceover in a detergent advert.

"Look, sir," she continued, switching randomly from formal to informal speech, "If he's the only one with power, then he's the only one. But remember, amigo, he's not alone. The people are with him. And the dreams… I think the dreams will be reality, the dreams of every Venezuelan. That's why I love our president so much, because he's given me hope and meaning. I don't care what people say, like my boy Julián."

"The one that repairs your car?" asked Alfredo.

"Yes, him," she replied. "He's always on my case. Why am I wearing red all the time? Y'know, because I'm red through and through. Why do I spend all day cooking for other people? Why do I have Hugo's picture hanging up at home? So, what's the problem? He's such a handsome guy. Can't you see? A real man!"

Francisca let out a cackle and moved her right arm toward her passenger to give him an enthusiastic little slap on his knee, but she couldn't reach, as Alfredo had squeezed his knees together, guessing what she'd do. She turned to the side, stretching out her arm as much as she could in another blind attempt, which landed on Alfredo's left thigh. The slap was so strong and fast that Alfredo leaned forward with the sting. For a few seconds, they faced each other. His face was astounded and hers was lit up by twinkling mischievous eyes and the fluorescent turquoise of hereyelids.

The spontaneous happiness of Francisca pulled down the wall that the little dancing Hugo had put up around Alfredo who, overwhelmed by the woman's naivety, imagined the day, not too far away, that her brightly colored eyes would see the cruelest nightmare between the cracks of her social dream. But Alfredo refused to give in, perhaps due to his stubborn nature or his hatred for Chávez. Or perhaps with the desire to warn her off, so that Francisca would not fall too hard. Or perhaps it was a hotchpotch of many different reasons that made him speakagain.

"Well, Francisca, then tell me. How do you explain the terrorism? This country is a hot-bed of terrorists."

But for the first time in ages, Alfredo's voice came out weakly, without sadness and without rage.

CHAPTER 24

July 1, 2006

Manuel awoke that morning with the same emptiness in his stomach that had kept him from sleeping for more than two hours at a time during the night. Each time he dropped off to sleep, distressing new images gnawed away at his mind: men hiding in a stable, children playing innocently in a trench as war tanks approached, a dead horse on the banks of a wide, solitary river.

With his feet on the floor, he sat for a long while, massaging his temples. He could not remember more than the vortex of images, their echoes and beams of light. The image of the horse was the only one that was fixed, like a painting; its stomach was swollen and its eyes were set on the upper part of a huge rock, which was being battered by the angry swell.

"There's nothing sadder than a dead horse," thought Manuel and immediately smirked at the stupidity of this idea since he had never even seen a dead horse. He continued with this flow of thought to make himself feel better: how can you compare a horse's life with a person's or even a group of children's?

The self-criticism disappeared as quickly as the image of the beautiful cinnamon- colored horse popped into his head. Manuel would have been about thirteen years old when he saw him come out of Roberto Piruggi's stable. The stud farm foreman, a robust middle-aged man named José Benítez was taking him out onto the patio when something fell down somewhere and the crash made the horse rear up underneath the beam of the stable, just as the sun invaded its shade. Tangled in the rays of light, the horse seemed like a burning torch, resisting the foreman's effort to control the rebellious flames.

Seeing the young boy enthralled by the horse, Roberto felt himself overwhelmed by the affection and compassion he had always felt for Manuel, and against his own better judgment, he shouted to José to bring the animal over. Now calmed down, but still reluctant, the horse came towards them, shaking away the flies with a whip of his tail, as Manuel's heart throbbed like it never had before for any muchachita at school. Face to face with the boy, the colt heard the greeting that the men exchanged while out of the corner of his black eye, he noticed the suspicious look that Roberto threw him. With the other eye, he saw the entranced smile of the visitor.

With a new impulse, as obedient as the first was to pity, Roberto asked Manuel if he wanted to go out on him. Seeing his childish alarm, he reassured the boy with a smile, adding that Boulette's stubbornness did not extend to children. On the contrary, he only took light loads, and if at any moment the weight were too much, he would simply put down his four hooves and would refuse to move an inch more.

They had named him Boulette in the hope that he would come shooting out of the starting gates like black bullets shot out of rifles, small and round during the days of Independence. Although as fast as greased lightning, Boulette was a difficult colt, as Roberto explained to Manuel, saying the word "difficult" slowly and accusingly, as if the animal could understand as long as Roberto was sparing with the syllables. Contrary to his parents, the champions Chateaubriand and Salaparuta, who had won several trophies in Caracas, Boulette would never compete, and so the expense could not be justified to "Los Turpiales," the horse breeding ranch that Roberto considered his most prized possession.

It was not just weight that the colt rejected, continued Roberto with his doleful sermon, but everything that should come naturally to him at this young age: he refused to run if it was too hot; if it was raining and not so much a shower as a weak drizzle, he would flare up at the person taking him out; and if he didn't get an apple or carrot or any other such treat with his breakfast, he would whinny wildly. And to top it all, he would go crazy when he was having his blinkers fitted.

"But you can take him for a ride," concluded Roberto, completely dismayed by the weight of his own words. "God only knows what's going on in his twisted mind, but Boulette likes riding with children. Don't be scared. José will go with you." Having said that, he went straight to the door of the main house, where the farm manager was waiting for him.

At that moment, Boulette began to neigh in a quiet and pitiful way, sounding to Manuel more like equine mockery than a cry, as each whinny was interspersed with two or three snorts, and a turn of his head from side to side. The sequence, repeated several times by the horse, was brilliantly orchestrated and its ironic tone seemed to resonate with the painful musings contained in the words of his troubled master.

As Roberto went into the house, the colt calmed down as if by magic and stopped to wait with saintly patience until Manuel came over to stroke him. Manuel let the horse muzzle his right shoulder with his moist and playful snout. Tired of the schmoozing, José lifted the boy onto the saddle as if he were a feather, putting the reins in his hands without giving him a chance to protest. Then he walked them toward the yard, and such was his trust in the horse or so great was his annoyance at being left as babysitter that he did not turn even once until they reached the entrance of the field.

"Only tighten the reins when you want him to stop," he told Manuel before closing the gate and telling him to wait a moment while he asked Dorotilda, the ranch's cook, if she wanted to go to the village with him that afternoon.

Manuel's soul shrunk and without letting go of the reins, he grabbed the horse's saddle and mane. He wished he had another pair of hands to stick like a leech onto Boulette, who at this precise moment stopped dead and stood rooted to the ground for a long time. Deciding that it would be very cowardly of him to slide off the saddle and run away, Manuel gradually began to straighten his back. When he was finally able to raise his head and look ahead, he forgot his tragic situation for long enough to watch with surprised eyes as at that very moment, a magnificent heron crossed the sky right above them, heading towards the infinite horizon.

A short whinny from Boulette told him to get ready for action and straight away, the animal advanced a few steps before stopping stock still again. Horse and rider stayed that way for a long time until Manuel finally sat up properly on the saddle and Boulette made a text-book step that his student thanked him for, stuttering and trembling while cursing José for having disappeared.

With unusual ease, Manuel asked the foreman that same afternoon to put him on Boulette again and open up the field. "Don't worry about me, José. You don't have to come with us," he added without blinking, surprised by the unusual display of bravery that was pouring out of his heart, without him being to stop it.

Once in the yard, the horse began to obey the language of the reins. Each time the rider let off some slack, Boulette increased his speed slowly and on two occasions, he offered the child the opportunity of a light trot. Growing in confidence, Manuel thought that riding Boulette was like riding his bicycle, although he was well aware that the horse was the one in control.

They managed a small gallop on the fourth day, when Boulette was able to feel enough constant pressure from Manuel's legs on his flanks. At this moment, Boulette's mane rippled and the child felt the breeze caress his cheeks. He was never able to explain to himself, let alone to Alfredo when they were having lunch together at the big house, the intense emotion he felt at that moment.

"It's as if he could read my mind, pana. I swear to you, he knows what I'm thinking..."

Alfredo ignored this blinding comment to tell Manuel that a foal had just been born in the Mendieta stud farm, about twelve miles away, and that the following morning, they would be going by jeep to see it. For a moment, Manuel wanted to go with them but realized that the outing would cost him his two-hour morning session with Boulette.

For a week and a half, he made all kinds of excuses to not go with his friends to find slugs or catch alived piranhas, which Alfredo enjoyed throwing into the swimming pool, hoping that someone visiting his father would decide to shake off the heat of the day. Manuel also did not join them on the trip organized by José to find howler monkeys, whose cries at sundown, according to Alfredo, sounded like the voices of wandering souls.

Alfredo and Vicente were really hurt by the attitude of Manuel, who tried everything to placate his friends when the three of them met to chat. But no explanation was possible. Manuel would never find a way of explaining to Alfredo that as soon as José placed him on the animal's body, he felt a jolt of electricity. His thin child's legs, weak from little exercise, took on a life of their own when in contact with the horse. It was as if they detached themselves from their owner and feel the slightest muscular contraction of Boulette, who would acknowledge him with a slight snort, pulling back his ears and looking toward the gate they would go through alone, to explore the never- ending expanse of prairie.

Not long after sunrise, Boulette would take him over to the colts that had already begun training for the races. Then they would visit the islands of trees where hundreds of parrots chattered and finally the semi-dried-up pool at the back, where wild donkeys took great pleasure in burying their hooves, lapping up the last of the moisture from the mud.

The expanse of prairie beyond the last fence, was a sight that Boulette always lingered at, as if he wanted to determine its size as well as the starting point of the small groups of veins, which crossed cautiously into the distance, fleeing from the nakedness of the plain and the people who lived there. Or perhaps the horse's thoughts were spatially superimposed onto the long plain made up of lights, smells and movements that humans would never be able to feel. Even less Manuel, a mere child, happy at looking at the beautiful landscape and feeling accepted by the horse, with the only condition of bringing him a carrot every morning. He had never been asked for so little to be shown such wonder in return.

"There goes the maiden in search of her prince," Alfredo and Vicente would chant at him during their early breakfast, in a mocking tone which Manuel took obligingly, imagining that he was back at the stables helping the men to feed and groom the horses, especially Boulette, whose beautiful mane he would comb, standing on an old stool. He would carefully untangle the reddish strands of hair and talk in his ear. Then he would turn to José in his brave, bossy child's voice to see if he would let him take the horse out for a while when it was not so hot.

Those ten days sped by for everyone, but unlike his friends, Manuel did not show much enthusiasm about going back to Caracas. He had to control his emotions when he hugged Boulette and when he finally left him, he stuck his hands into the pockets of his worn-out blue jeans and tightened his fists hard, as if he was trying to hide the world that his new friend had brought to him, far away from his mother's chitchat and the demands of school. From that moment on, Manuel knew that he didn't want to live with the worries of adults or the tricks that his mother used at the Mayor's office. His ideal, as clear as the blue sky of that last morning at "Los Turpiales," was to have a corner at the foot of the plain and a horse like Boulette.

Back in Caracas, he managed to persuade his mother to let him return to "Los Turpiales" in June, as soon as he had sat his last exam. Roberto had promised to take them all, including Rodrigo, who had not been there during that unforgettable Easter week as his father had sat him down in front of his math book every single day, with the exception of Easter Sunday.

Manuel's happiness ended abruptly when Alfredo told him that his father was thinking of sending Boulette to the farm of a friend of his, after breeding him. "Anyway," he added, without realizing how his words were crushing his friend's dreams, "he's only good for riding with children, and only when he's in a good mood. But I'm sure they'll look after him well," he added warmly, sensing Manuel's sadness. "Really, pana, the only thing that animal does is drive my dad crazy.

There are much better and more intelligent horses out there. You should see the foal that was just born..."

Manuel pushed these memories to one side and went to the bathroom. While his feet enjoyed the freshness of the tiles, he adjusted the two shower faucets and waited for a curtain of steam to form. Then he stood under the stream of water and let the pressure fall on his neck. He kept his mind empty for a long time and concentrated on the fine splashes of water that began to slowly cover the shower curtain until they joined other droplets. Manuel thought of the futility of the union of bubbles, whose bloody trickles would soon disappear into the black waters of the city.

As he was drying himself, his built-in alarm took him to the last voice he had heard the previous night and he knew he was now ready to recall even the finest details of it.

"Manuel, forget about it, chico. There's absolutely nothing you can do for your friend. The order came from above."

It was Vilma Montilla on the line. He had called her just before going to bed. In an attempt to end the pointless discussion they were having, she had already set the tone herself with her high-pitched, grating voice, making any retort impossible. Her words fluttered around Manuel's gut all night long like a black butterfly.

"Christ, Vilma, don't you see that they are attacking the stud farm," he told her anxiously. "This morning the foreman called to tell me. What do you expect my friend Alfredo to do when his parents were murdered? On top of that, he can't leave his job in Chicago. What? Slow down... no, I already told you that his brother is not interested in any of it. But old Piruggi left everything organized and there are plenty of horses ready to compete. I don't know. Maybe we could put forward a horse breeding plan to the government..."

"Manuel, please understand the country is not interested in racehorses, only in beans. What is the problem anyway? The government only wants to plant on one piece of land to see if the beans will take, and then..."

"Are you kidding me, Vilma? What planet are you on? You know what'll happen; they'll take the land away from them and blackmail them, charging a thousand different fees. Then they'll value the ranch for peanuts which they don't have the slightest intention of paying. And in the end, they won't plant a single damnbean."

Anger had begun to show in Manuel's voice, not only because of Vilma's persistent negativity, which showed her own helplessness, but also because he had expected much more from her. Impatient to hang up the telephone, as she didn't like Manuel's tone of voice one bit, Vilma repeated her chorus once again:

"There's nothing we can do. I've spoken to everyone. Do you understand? To everyone. The norm is to push through the Land Law. Redistribute unused land to the people, to the peasants."[18]

"Did you tell them about Piruggi's project to create jobs? That alone would produce a good five hundred..."

"Manuel, I'm telling you for the last time. The order came from above."

One month earlier, Rodrigo had called him to say the Piruggi stud farm had received an order from the National Land Institute and that Alfredo was still in shock about his parents and did not plan on returning to Caracas.

Manuel had to sit down when he heard the unexpected news. Although he had refused to set foot on "Los Turpiales"

---

[18] *La Ley de tierras* (Land Law) was put into practice in 2001.

since that time with Boulette, he could still hear the squawking of the birds that crossed the prairie sky in the early hours of the morning. It was an incredible place, open like a welcoming hand, clean and serene. He could not imagine the stables and the stud farm disappearing, or that the magnificent horses would become fodder to Chávez's civil servants for the greedy masses that would settle there at some point.

He tried in vain to contact Alfredo, who still was not answering the phone.

Hopelessly, he approached the Chavistas he knew and who could have done him the huge favor of putting the notification from the Land Institute into the shredding machines.

With no more cards left to play, he decided to persist with Vilma, who was away on one of her trips and who had hardly given him the time of day when he had called to explain the problem.

The evening she returned, Manuel met her at the airport, took her home and then to bed. There he begged her again and again, between caresses and a secret or two, without mentioning Boulette, to save his friend's horse ranch. When two weeks had passed and she did not seem to be lifting a finger to help him out, Manuel transformed his pleas into humiliation, asking Vilma to do it for him, for what they had between them both, so that he could win back his childhood friend.

When he hung up the telephone, the feeling of betrayal added to the attack on his male pride made him feel powerless. He went to sleep, more alone than ever, with the illusion that he had created to endure Vilma smashed into tiny pieces.

When he finished getting dressed, he went up to the huge window in his bedroom with his cell phone in his hand. A flock of little chachalacas flew by, just under the penthouse level, showing Manuel the back of their wings. They were seeking shelter in a gigantic rubber tree, growing in the upper part of Valle Arriba. As they disappeared into the tree, Manuel used his cell phone.

"Please leave your message," said Alfredo's voice, sparingly.

If Alfredo could negotiate a little, he thought impatiently, if he could reach an agreement with the Chavistas, giving them a good cut or if he took the matter to court, maybe something could be done. But at the moment, Alfredo was not even answering the phone. Manuel knew through Rodrigo that he was hopeless at everything at that time, including the friendship they had had since they were boys and that in the last years had suffered all kinds of misfortunes.

"Shit, Alfredo!" he said in one of his messages, finally getting annoyed. "We have to be more practical about this. I'm doing everything I can, but you have to come and defend your business. Answer the damned phone!"

He dialed the number again.

"Come on, brother. Come over. We'll take it to court. We'll go to the press. We'll take it wherever you want. Let's put up a good fight!"

That was when he heard the comforting and unexpected hustle and bustle of Rosa in the kitchen and he crossed the labyrinth of barely furnished rooms that separated him from her.

"What are you doing here, Rosa? I thought you weren't coming down from La Victoria until this afternoon?"

"Yes, hijo, but these last three days were so difficult with my cousin having those awful fits. I couldn't bear it any more. But don't you worry about that. Wait till you see this juice I'm making you with this papaya I bought on the highway," said Rosa, cutting the green curved fruit in two.

Manuel dropped to the little table in the kitchen and began to watch the perfect synchronization of Rosa's movements back and forth, blending the fruit, kneading arepas and preparing the frying pan for the ham and eggs. He liked this woman, incredibly energetic for her almost seventy years, who lived in the servant's room with no other ambition other than to feed him, look after the apartment and bicker with him every morning.

With the juice ready, and the oil heating up in the pan, Rosa went straight to the small TV set, sitting on top of a rickety kitchen cupboard and switched it on.

"Please, Rosa. Can you turn the volume down?"

"No, Manuel, hijo. Let me watch my television," Rosa answered, unmoved, stirring the eggs in the pan and checking on the arepas in the oven. "Anyway, today it's María Felix in Doña Bárbara."

Doña Bárbara: "*What you mean with this?" Did we not agree that you would never stand in my way?*"

Lorenzo Bartero: "*It's not about me, it's about our daughter, Marisela…*"

Doña Bárbara: "*Our daughter? Is there actually anything in the world that we can call mine and yours?*"

Lorenzo Bartero: "*Everything that was once mine is yours…*"

The old black and white film took hold of Manuel completely as soon as he deduced that María Félix was the stone-faced woman that mistreated men.

Santos Luzardo: "*I have demanded the appearance of these people before the authorities…*"

Colonel: "*Did you demand or beg? Mr. Mujica, lay the law down plainly…*"

Doña Bárbara: "*Don't worry, Colonel, Doctor Luzardo is right. Don Guillermo is obliged to fence off his property…*"

Colonel: "*If you are sure about that, my lady, then that's how it will be…*"

Although he had never read the novel about the process of civilization in rural Venezuela in the early days and the battle with a woman who represented barbarity and resentment, Manuel remembered very well the huge cheat sheet that Roberto had passed him the day before the final literature exam. It was on a long roll of paper, with so much information written in tiny letters, that he preferred to take the book and memorize a few themes: barbarity, fences representing civilization, Santos Luzardo as the educated man from the city, witchcraft and Marisela. The literature teacher had insisted on the importance of fences, and Manuel tried to understand it, but at fifteen years of age, it all seemed so strange. Roberto Piruggi's horse ranch always seemed well fenced off to him.

But back then in the twenties, the Santos Luzardo character from the novel had gone from Caracas to the plains, with the intention of claiming his inheritance, a half abandoned cattle ranch. Being a lawyer, he firmly believed that the cattle breeding would be greatly improved if all ranches were forced to define their territory with fences, according to the land deeds.

Even as a boy, he found the solution very simple. But now, reminded by a stupid film he had found dumb as a boy, he understood the ironic question asked by Mr. Mujica, judicial clerk in Apure in a different light. Luzardo repeats the question in a quiet, hoarse voice:

Santos Luzardo: "*The Law of the Plains?*"

Mr. Mujica: "*Do you know what people call it around here? The Law of Doña Bárbara, because they say that she paid for it to be made according to her wishes.*"

Doña Bárbara was the María Félix that became rich, stealing cattle and hectares of land from her neighbors, killing those opposed to her. Exotically beautiful, she was a woman full of hatred and with good reason to be that way. But instead of being afraid of her, the hero of the novel, Santos Luzardo, who looked so much like the photo of the newly-wed Roberto Piruggi, was disgusted by her and her lack of moderation.

Santos Luzardo: "*I wanted to speak to you...*"

Doña Bárbara: "*I can already guess what you want to say... that I abandoned my daughter Marisela to a miserable life when I ruined Lorenzo Bartero... I also went hungry and had only rags to wear! Brutal men had their fill with me...*

Manuel followed the plot until the end while eating very slowly, hardly touching the juice that Rosa had served him. It's just another cheap soap opera, he thought, as he watched the final scene, when Doña Bárbara was lost forever in the shadows. Whose idea was it to cast that actress in the role of Doña Bárbara? And Santos Luzardo, where did this little lawyer come from who thought he was superman? It would have been more realistic to put Chávez in the role of Don Bárbaro and Vilma as the Sorcerer, Doña Bárbara's side-kick who sows the seeds of death wherever he goes. Of course, Luzardo would have to get beaten by his own, so civilized fences. Because in this country, where everything is a barbarity and the government takes your land, there is no happy ending. And they should put me in a new version of this film as the whore of barbarity. A whore with a penthouse in Valle Arriba, according to Alfredo.

"Manuelito mi amor, you're going to be late. You're in a daze. Are you all right?"

"Aha," he said, swallowing the scrambled eggs that had fallen asleep in his mouth.

CHAPTER 25

May 12, 2007

At six thirty, as he started the engine of his Mercedes, Alfredo thought that it was a good morning to hate everyone.

He was running twenty minutes late getting to the hospital, as usual when the roads were frozen. But he could do nothing about it. Alfredo was defenseless against the cold. He could never get used to the blizzards or to the tires sliding on iced potholes, or to central heating, constantly drying his respiratory tract, or to tight spaces. As he adjusted his seatbelt, Alfredo recognized that he would never get used to the Illinois winter, its long nights and the languid sun of its short days.

As he came out of the garage of his house, he turned right into Cherry Hill and immediately saw the sign for the 294 freeway that went around Chicago. Alfredo drove onto the freeway, although for a brief moment he considered going east, where the very long freeway would lead him to the blue sea of Florida. What was he doing in this grey city, full of immigrants, sick of hard work and factory smoke? Most of them could only speak Spanish and did not even have medical insurance. Alfredo was capable of recognizing their ills as soon as he entered the emergency room of the University of Chicago Hospitals: men with broken bones, muscular sprains and sciatica, women with hemorrhages, and everyone, including children, suffering from a long list of diseases which became chronic when left untreated. However, despite the ailments that Chicago doled out to them, these people seemed better off there than in the south of Río Grande.

Not always though, Alfredo remembered, thinking of Alejandro. A brain tumor had taken him in six months. He was 29 and ran a team at the landscaping company, Greenscape. His brothers and wife lied to him, telling him the chemotherapy would cure him. As he had no medical insurance, every injection cost his family 500 dollars, sold in an abominable downtown oncology consultation.

His brothers took him to the emergency room every time he suffered a wave of convulsions, and when he became stable, they kept him on the third floor. Hours later, Dr. Perkins, the head of Neurology, would go to surgery to ask Alfredo, whom he considered a direct and clear man, to explain to the family once more, in simple terms and with plenty of detail that the hospital did not deal with terminal cases. That was what hospices were for.

But Alfredo did not speak to them of hospices because they could never accept the idea of telling Alejandro the truth. They could not bear to be separated from him and not be the ones to prepare his food and feed him. All Alfredo did was buy lots of Coca- Colas and bring them up to Alejandro's room. Here he handed them out, first giving one to the sick man, who took it with great relish, thinking it was a beer. Then he would sit in one of the chairs and tell jokes. Alejandro's brothers would be his counterpart, and after a little while, the room seemed like a party. Everyone ended up hugging each other, including the sick man, as if they really had all been drinking copious amounts of beer.

Abraham had called him to tell him that Alejandro had died. He also said that they had a financial problem and they couldn't pay for the funeral services.

Alfredo accelerated the Mercedes for a good stretch on the freeway as he remembered the sallow face of the funeral agent, who asked the brothers to pay him in cash. He went there immediately. Refraining from his desire to grab him by the lapels of his sleek, dark suit, Alfredo took out his credit cards and paid for the coffin, the wake and the mass. But two days later, when he went back to the funeral parlor, he could not bring himself to look at the body. So used to seeing death, he was unable to go to the room where Alejandro was on show. He stayed in the reception area for three hours and stoically endured a thousand apologies from the funeral director about the money.

"Look at this," Alfredo had told Rodrigo in the Vallés Funeral home in Caracas, two months before Alejandro had died. "The only things left of my folks are these two cases. I called the best mortician in the whole of Caracas and not even he wanted to show them to me. That's how bad those animals left them!"

In the Rosehill Funeral home in Chicago, Alejandro's body lay with his hands crossed over his chest. Between his thick working fingers, someone had placed a rosary and a holy card showing the Virgin of Guadalupe. Lots of photos of the dead man were resting on the hinged edge of the coffin. Taking advantage of the distraction of the prayers and the widow's inconsolable sobs, the eldest child among the mourners quietly began to touch the cushioned base of the display case, putting his little 10-year old hand just below Alejandro's shoulder. Down there, he had discovered a biting cold, like in a freezer and he encouraged the other children to touch it as he was sure that his uncle, serenely pale and asleep in his wooden box would not mind. On the contrary, he had been a man who loved parties, dancing and games, so he would be delighted to have his mischievous black-eyed nephew messing around next to him.

In the reception room, a group of women came and went, placing flasks of coffee and trays of donuts on a row of small tables. After the prayers and mass, the adults milled around, while the younger ones ran about everywhere under the unwelcoming glare of a member of staff. Some who saw the young doctor noticed his calm state and the long hours that he spent in the room, sitting down with his head bowed. For each of those hours, there was also someone offering him coffee, which he always refused. Someone wanted to bring him some beers from the liquor store but the little doctor asked him please not to go to any trouble.

Although everyone knew how much he had done for Alejandro, they did not understand why he refused to approach the coffin that he had paid for with his own credit card. But Alfredo couldn't see the perplexity in their sallow faces. On the contrary, he thought that some more than others rebuked him with their caresses, kisses and long gazes which, like the impeccable grey suit and the marine blue tie, they bestowed upon the corpse so that it would be clean and profoundly loved in God's presence. On the other hand, he was so intimidated by death, that he took the advice of the mortician. Isabel and Roberto's coffins stayed sealed, turning their back on life to those who gathered at the Vallés funeral home to pay their last respects. A common life, no better or worse than anyone else's, but so delicate and fragile, wretched and in a terrible state, fearful of being abandoned to death and depriving them of the lastcontact.

If he could have turned back time, Alfredo would have hammered Isabel's coffin open, and embraced her lifeless body, with nothing to offer medical science but evidence of all the horrors for every mourner to see. He would have held her right there, not ceremoniously or for the benefit of those who might have been looking, but to cling on to something. A vague perfume, an island of softness that death in its hastiness had neglected to take away.

"Alfredo, your father and I have been here a week now. We've hardly seen you.

Why don't you take a couple of days off? We could go somewhere and spend a bit of time together," Isabel Piruggi told him on phone from the Hilton in Chicago.

"Christ, Mama. How many times do I have to tell you? This isn't Venezuela. I have a lot of work to do."

That's what he told his parents on exactly the same day he signed Alejandro into hospital for the first time. That evening, he went for dinner with them and the next day, he took them to the airport. He never saw them again. Three months later, in the Vallés funeral home, Alfredo burst into sobs as he told Rodrigo about his farewell, in which he pulled away from his mother's embrace because he only had two weeks to prepare a presentation he was giving at the medical school. It was his first step to success. He was about to patent a computerized system for brain surgery which he had been working on for years.

There was a traffic jam on the freeway. There was only another five miles to the exit that led to the hospital and a weak, icy drizzle slid down the Mercedes' windshield. He was going to arrive even later than he thought, and that exasperated him.

Since the death of his parents, dejection and nostalgia had frequently taken hold of Alfredo. But in the last few weeks, sadness had given way to irritability. The neurology nurses avoided him and even Dr. Perkins had suggested he take a vacation.

Alfredo thought again of the blue Florida Sea, but he was sure that even there, nearer to Venezuela, he would not be cured of the anger he was carrying with him. When he was alone, his thoughts were stuck in Caracas, on the wild beasts that had murdered his parents, and who had got away unpunished. According to the police, those men could be hiding in any barrio, or could have fled the city. Not even the money offered to the detectives, or the few contacts he had in the Ministry of Home Affairs and Justice had got him anywhere. Alfredo was a tangled mess of helplessness. He would have liked to kill the man who had separated him from his mother with his bare hands. As for Chávez, he wished he could wipe him off the face of the earth. There were so many things he wished he coulddo!

He mechanically glanced at the clock on the dashboard. It was already seven fifteen and he realized that the show, *Talk of the Town* had begun. It was as important to him as eating breakfast for some, and he hated to miss this program.

He switched on the radio just as the host said the word "Venezuela," lengthening the "u," as if his throat had turned into a funnel where the vowel had slipped down forcibly. Alfredo deduced that the brief report was about the persistent rise in oil prices around the world and was leading up to the topic of the day: Venezuela, the oil country whose president Hugo Chávez was anything but conventional.

The special guest on the show was a journalist and expert on South American politics whose most recent book, *Chávez, The President* had been featured in the New York Book Review and was already on sale in bookshops throughout the States. Much of the content of the book came from a couple of interviews that the author had done with the Venezuelan leader in Caracas.[19]

---

[19] The following dialogue was partially taken, and then modified from the official transcripts of the show, *"Talk of the Nation,"* aired on February 18, 2008 by the National Public Radio of the USA. This show is aired five times a week and consists of guest interviews –in this case Bart

"Author: *I've tried to show both points of view in an objective way... Thanks to Chávez, the Venezuelan state is distributing the country's oil wealth to the people. At the moment, the poorest barrios in urban areas have schools with ambitious educational programs; they also have medical centers run mainly by Cuban doctors. Traditionally, doctors in Venezuela prefer private practice and there are relatively few who work for the state.*"

When it came to the telephone calls from the audience, a listener called in, who after a few digressions, finally came up with the phrase that he thought summarized the problem in Venezuela: There is no democracy. And if it was not created, it was enough to remember that a few months before, without permission, Chávez had put his own judges in the Supreme Court after dismissing the previous ones. In gratitude, perhaps after their swearing-in ceremony, more than one judge had publicly declared their commitment to the Chavista course of action.

More than once, Alfredo dialed 1-800-TALK but the line was engaged. Now it was a professor in political science from some university whose name Alfredo did not catch, who was talking on the subject of democracy again with a lucid reminder of the closing down of a private television station, Radio Caracas Televisión (RCTV) with the excuse that it had supported the coup against Chávez, even though seventy percent of the population opposed the move. The professor wondered to what point Chávez was prepared to follow in the footsteps of Fidel Castro.

"*...We mustn't forget that Radio Caracas Televisión was involved in the 2002 coup. They tried to take over power,*" replied the writer at the academic's comment.

Jones, author of the book *Hugo!* The program also involves the participation of listeners who can call into the show.

At a constant speed as if on automatic pilot, the Mercedes entered onto the local highway that passed The University of Chicago. Alfredo was surprised at the scant traffic on the road, and he eagerly prepared mentally what he would say when he was given the word. For a moment, he tried to picture the face of this journalist who he thought was just one of Chávez' footmen. He was obviously one of those pseudo-socialists who loved the poor but who cannot endure their suffering and so keeps them at a distance. Or maybe he was just an idiot.

As all these thoughts were flying through his mind, he carried on calling the program. He reacted as he heard a voice on the line.

It was a pre-recorded message: "Unfortunately, we have run out of time and can't take any more comments on today's show. However, we'd like to invite you to send your comments to our website. Please remember that *The Talk of the Town* has been created for people to express their opinions."

He was about to hang up the phone with a quick, irritated gesture, but then an idea came into his head. Not many people seemed to be affected by what was going on, but he cared. At that moment, it mattered more than ever what Chávez was doing or not doing. Taking himself by surprise, he heard himself hatching an audacious plan to claim revenge on the man that had caused him so much pain. He did not feel helpless any longer.

He dialed Rodrigo's number but only got another answering machine. When Alfredo started to leave him a message, the telephone slipped out of his hand and landed next to his right foot, which was on the accelerator pedal. He bent down to pick it up and at that moment his speed, the ice and a small involuntary movement on the steering wheel sent the Mercedes flying across two lanes of traffic to the hard shoulder.

Alfredo corrected the steering and lifted his foot off the accelerator, managing to stop two hundred yards from where he had changedcourse.

The cars behind him braked sharply as Alfredo's car swung around in a curve over the highway, and passing by the wayward Mercedes, now under control, the furious drivers looked at him in consternation.

It took at least five minutes for Alfredo's hands to stop shaking. Parked safely on the hard shoulder, and now able to breathe properly, a sob rose to his throat, followed by another and yet another until Alfredo found himself drenched in tears. A little boy again, wishing that his mother would come to save him from the darkness.

CHAPTER 26

April 3, 2007

Carmen opened her eyes after a nod of the head pulled her out of slumber. In front of her, she saw Rodrigo, watching her spellbound, and she wanted to go to the warmth that his eyes radiated. But she could only smile at him as Emilio lay asleep with his head on her chest. As her husband stayed with his eyes fixed on her, she tried to free her hand around the baby's bottom. Cautiously free, she held her hand to her lips to blow him a kiss. He smiled starry-eyed, still in a trance, recalling Giovanni Battista Salvi's most beautiful painting, in which the Virgin's lap protects her sweet sleeping son. It was her, this magnificent Madonna, possessing Carmen in Rodrigo's vision, the only indestructible wall in the world, pleasant times frozen in the oil painting, sheltering the man on his return from martyrdom and death.

His joy faded quickly, giving way to the greatest terror: Carmen's look, tainted with the infinite love of the virgin, began to darken until it became fossilized. And her mouth, still carrying traces of the dedicated smile to her husband, became stiff and half open, like a fish, frozen in its last and painful gasp. From his hollow cavity, as if coming from a loudspeaker, came the voice of a famous television presenter: *"De Gouveia, one of the seven gunmen...what has happened here is a tragedy that reflects the social violence existing in Venezuela today."*

"I'm getting off here. Let me out, please," said the woman nervously, holding a baby in her arms and trying to cross the compact and sweaty crowd, squeezed together at the back doors of the carriage.

The train braked abruptly, making Rodrigo forget for a moment the nightmare of the speaker that had been plaguing him for five years. The young mother had lost her balance and as she was flung headfirst onto the shoulders of a large man standing in front of her, she compressed her baby against her chest, who feeling suddenly squashed and shaken, let out a vibrant cry. But the man did not seem to notice the incident, since he was wearing earphones and was reading a magazine, his large volume leaning on the vertical bar, next to the carriage door.

Without thinking twice, Rodrigo got up from his seat adjacent to the bar, to hold the woman up and thumped the large man on the shoulder. The man was surprised and apologetic, and moved as much as he could to let the dark girl with large, frightened eyes get off the subway train.

She looked like Carmen as well, thought Rodrigo, getting a quick feminine smile that he would never see again. In the last five years, countless women had looked like her. Sometimes, he did not even have to see their faces to recognize the resemblance; it was enough to look at their hair, their shoulders and their hurried gait. On some occasions, however, the presence of Carmen seemed totally ghostlike: a shadow that disappeared down the steps of a subway station or her singsong voice in the whirlwind of voices, buzzing around in shops or in Parque del Este. With each of these mistaken sightings, Rodrigo felt that Carmen was sending him signs from the other world to help her return to him. But only on a few occasions had he felt her as near as on that morning, when he was waiting with Emilio at Altamira subway station.

As the train waited on the platform, he felt her by his side, so near that for a moment he thought he could feel her breath and smell the shampoo she used to wash her hair every day. The strong impression, combined with the recurring nightmare that had awoken him again that morning, filled his eyes with tears.

When the train resumed its journey, Rodrigo glanced at Emilio who was reading *The Last Mohican* without realizing that his father was not sitting next to him anymore and that the seat was miraculously empty. They're getting off at Chacaíto station, concluded Rodrigo when he saw that several passengers were moving toward the door and he hurried to reclaim his seat.

After taking out his bag which he had left under the seat, and placing it in his lap, he passed his hand around his son's head, patting down the rebellious hair on his crow, always swirling around when his hair grew.

"Tomorrow I'll take you to the barbers for a haircut, Spiderman," he whispered in his ear. To answer, Emilio grabbed his father's idle hand whose strokes were distracting him from his reading and placed it on his backpack, patting it gently as if to tell him not to interrupt again.

His son's gesture made him laugh for the first time that day. Satisfied on seeing his serious kid face for a few seconds, Rodrigo thought that Emilio was growing well. Since he was a boy, he had learnt to replace the absence of his mother and the long hours his father spent at work by reading adventure books and soccer manuals. On Sundays, when Rodrigo was completely free from classes at college, from private tutoring and his attempts to write essays which would never be published, father and son went to church, to the cemetery and then to an intercollegiate league soccer game. To break up the monotony, some Sundays they went to the beach really early or went for a walk on the Ávila mountain and then went for lunch at the grandparents'.

If on a rare occasion, Rodrigo went to a party or a get-to-gether to have a bit of fun and see old friends and colleagues, he was always consumed by guilt. That was when he was grateful to his parents and sister for their enthusiastic help in bringing up Emilio, who despite his young age was not a handful, per-haps because he took after hisfather.

His grades were excellent, his character was pleasant and his skill on the soccer pitch was a gift from God. Emilio sur-vived the hurricane of losing his mother at five years of age as if he were an oak tree with magic roots. That was what his father thought, while in comparison he felt like a dry leaf, forced by the wind to float adrift, condemned to fall to the ground sooner or later due to its own dead weight.

The memory of the dream came back to him as he opened his bag and saw the red t-shirt that he had reluctantly put among his papers that morning. His supervisor had forced him and every other public worker in the country to use it in support of the Chavista movement. No t-shirt, no job. Once again he saw the pool of blood that he had inadvertently put his hands into when he had reached for Carmen's pale face. Maikel did not want to let go of her. He didn't want to give her body to Rodrigo and when the ambulance arrived, he clung on to it, her strange pose folding even more and lulling into a deathly sleep.

How many times in the last five years had he woken up, sweating and crying out in terror, hearing the shots of Joao De Gouveia in Plaza Altamira against the protestors, whose only crime was to challenge Chávez with banners and vigils. They com-pletely took over the square, Rodrigo told himself, overwhelmed by sadness once again, but they were no obstacle to anyone. And his Carmen, a little glum in the last days, went around offering coffee to those brave citizens, as she called them, helping them to write slogans or to give passersby a chat or two which had very little to do with the ones she prepared in her student days.

They had protested in the square for a year, a whole year in which Rodrigo had watched Carmen from the apartment, placing her flask of coffee on a folding table which wobbled dangerously and inviting the people around her to warm up their stomachs.

He saw her every day from the balcony, although Sundays were special because it made Rodrigo happy to see her smiling out there, caught up in the noise of the skates, the shouts of the children and the pacifying swell of tires that passed through Francisco de Miranda avenue in the afternoon.

Every day, even when it was raining, Rodrigo went out on the balcony to search for her among the people. From there, he heard the shots that evening, just after his parents and sister had gone to the movies, making him run downstairs from the second floor of the building, not stopping to think that Emilio was left alone, asleep in front of the TV in the living room.

According to old Raimundo, the owner of the magazine stand in their street, in front of the square, she was the fourth and final victim of De Gouveia, the gunman who probably never ended up in a court and who was surely now serving an imaginary sentence.[20] Rodrigo could not remember much

---

[20] Days after the tragedy, a video was released showing De Gouveia and chavista leader Freddy Bernal, then a mayor of the Libertador municipality in Caracas. This led people to believe that the assassin had been hired by the Chavistas, who responded claiming without proof that it was the opposition leadership who had hired De Gouveia in order to create chaos andconfusion.

about the condolences he received from the School of Arts and Literature, where Carmen was finishing her doctorate in Linguistics, or from the Dean of the university or from the Salesian high school, where she had worked for a few years. He also remembered very little about what had been written in the newspapers and on the news, who interpreted the deaths in the square as being a result of the antagonism of the last few years. "Antagonism?" wondered Rodrigo stubbornly, realizing that he hated that word as much as he hated De Gouveia.

Many other things had started to bother him since that evening at seven thirty, when Carmen collapsed in Altamira square. And that was logical, he reasoned, as she had suffered many tragedies in her short life, but even so, sometimes he was shocked by his own reactions and by the anger that was sometimes sparked by a courteous gesture of his students, the comments of Charito, his neighbor, about how intelligent and mature Emilio was and even the Sunday siesta his father would take, snoring as if life was wonderful.

But he did understand why it bothered him that Altamira square had won back a name that had not been used for a long time in Caracas. Not everyone, including his parents was set on calling it Francia square. And although the trend had started in the newspapers, perhaps with the idea of appealing to the dialogue and democratic values embodied by this army dissident that began to use the square as a forum, Rodrigo thought that since the shooting, everyone, including his father, was keen on calling it Francia square because somehow, it had to be said that it would never be the same square. For him, it was no consolation but rather a curse on his own life. How would any man feel, due to his economic difficulties and family commitments, living a few yards away from the place where his wife had been murdered?

Carmen was the only one who would have understood the reproachful way Rodrigo beat up his soul in his darker moments. She also had to pass through that bitter tunnel when in 1998, her parents and sisters were buried in layers of mud that inundated La Guaira. She would tell him how naïve she had been, how unforgivably careless to leave them there, trusting that the rainstorms would pass without destroying the barrio where her family lived, paradoxically also called Carmen. And now Rodrigo thought of his own blindness, in the fear of seeing things as they were, as it was very naïve or stupid to pretend that the Altamira protests would come to an end without a high price.

The subway stopped at Venezuela square station and Rodrigo closed his bag, thinking of the red t-shirt they had given him yesterday in the school office. They had asked him to join the Chavista countermarch and stay until the end. There was nothing to do, he told himself in a whisper[21].

With such conviction, he touched Emilio's arm to signal to him to get off the train and he immediately swung around to look out of his window at the swarming mass on the platform, tense and ready to pounce the moment the doors opened. But between the greasy marks, the glass reflected his own image, dressed in a t-shirt and red beret. Behind that appeared Carmen, looking at him with ghostly wide-open eyes and saying to him: *The same people who killed me are dressing you up as a red doll so that you go out to march with a little flag in your hand.*

"Come on, Emilio. Hurry up, or we'll be late for school."

---

[21] In Caracas, marches against Hugo Chávez are common. The largest reached over half a million people. The Chavistas commonly organize countermarches when the opposition schedules a march. According to many, public employees are forced to participate in them.

The boy put his book away and after stepping onto the platform, made his way to the stairs without waiting for his father, who lagged behind for a few moments, pensive. When Rodrigo finally quickened his step and reached Emilio's side, he put his arm around his shoulder and told him he would pick him up at the usual time.

"But yesterday didn't you say that Abuela was coming to get me?"

Rodrigo replied that that was yesterday and they both got in line to stamp their tickets.

Going up the stairs, Rodrigo noticed the beams of brilliant sunlight filtering through the subway entrance and the infinitive particles of dust that floated like snowflakes. He stopped again, taking Emilio to a corner, out of the way of the flow of passengers. Now he thought he could see things clearly, as he groped in his bag to find his cell phone. When he got it, he pressed several buttons until Alfredo's name appeared on the screen, then he started to write. The letters in the message started appearing one by one: A-l-f-r-e-d-o, a-b-o-u-t y-o-u-r p-r-o-p-o-s-a-l. H-a-v-e d-e-c-i-d-e-d I-'-m- i-n. w-i-l-l s-p-e-a-k w-i-t-h-M.

As he closed his cell phone, he looked at the boy distractedly and took the wrinkled red t-shirt to throw it in the trash. He went down a few steps to do it. Then he watched his son waiting for him above, at the end of the tunnel of light, and went quickly back up, leaving behind him, trapped in the electronic screen on the platform, sculptured women running along the beach in their bikinis.

CHAPTER 27

September 5, 2007

The drum of the lock gave way with a light pressure from the key. As if it were waiting for this slight touch, the door opened instantly in front of Maikel. Once inside, he noticed the pleasant smell of freshly made coffee and the muscles of his face relaxed.

Following the magical aroma, he followed the passageway to the right, leading to the kitchen, where he found Rodrigo's legs, dressed in shorts and his feet in beach sandals. The rest of his figure was hidden behind a huge refrigerator.

It was a double refrigerator, incredibly tall with a stainless steel veneer. On the left, stretched a long kitchen counter made of black granite, completely empty and split in the middle by a quadrangular shape space where the shining kitchen sink sat. At the end of the counter, on the opposite side of the fridge were the stove and a hood towering over it. The cabinets, following the line of the counter, were also interrupted in the middle by a large window, naked and defenseless against the stream of sunlight which had begun to spread over the whitened stone floor.

"Hey," said Rodrigo, hearing Maikel's steps. "Do you want some guava? They look fresh; the woman who looks after the apartment probably left them."

"Just coffee," stated Maikel, spreading the newspaper over the unusual pink- colored marble table, situated opposite the kitchen furniture and on the right of the door.

Two laptops were resting on the marble, one next to the other like twin sisters, but Maikel hardly looked at them. His eyes were tired. He had been exploring the area around the bank and at some point, he had lost his sunglasses. He had spent several hours coming and going, checking the new map of the area, exchanging opinions and discussing where to place the security agents. And the stinging glare of the morning refused to give him a rest, just when he had not slept for threenights.

He pulled out one of the chairs that surrounded the table and collapsed into it, closing his eyes. On opening them, he saw a Munch lithograph hanging near the table. In recent years, due to the nature of his work, he had seen countless luxuries in Chavista homes and he had become immune to the excessive marble, springy rugs and paintings from relatively well-known artists who shared the wall with cheap posters. But this kitchen, large and as clean as a laboratory, he saw from another perspective. Its layout was comfortable, its execution was impeccable and its owner represented the anti- Chavista face of opulence. Even so, far from being impressed, Maikel regarded everything with the same contempt that until now, he had reserved for Chavista homes. Could they be the two faces of the beast that gnawed away at his insides?

In the middle of the large room, an island with four stools ran parallel to the adjacent furniture, in the same black granite, with a walnut base. On top of it, suspended from the ceiling with four chains, was a steel quadrant just as impeccable as the refrigerator, the sink and the oven. From it was hanging a battalion of copper pots that looked brand new. Seeing them, Maikel remembered the old cauldron which had been used to cook stews in his childhood, and the huge iron pan his mother had used for frying. He glanced at the free space in the middle of the room and calculated that there was enough space for at least twenty folding beds. For many years, he had shared such a bed with his younger brother, Juan in the coastal Afro-Venezuelan village of Cúpira. Juan had never taken a single step, since he was born with spina bifida and had not been treated intime.

Rodrigo had come up to him in silence, absorbed in the dilemma of going to the supermarket or taking Maikel for some arepas for breakfast. He brought coffee and a plate of guava which he placed in front of Maikel.

"They're delicious, pana," he told him in a jovial whisper, delighted that the role of perfect housewife had given him some time-out from his doubts and exhaustion of the last few days.

Without taking any notice of the guavas, Maikel's eyes followed Rodrigo, and watching him return to the counter, he thought the Gallego seemed like a kid. He wondered if he would have the guts for what lay ahead. Well, maybe he would not need them, since he, Maikel had the worst part and he knew he had what it took; he was more than sure that he would not let this school teacher, or anyone else for that matter play in this game where he had been collecting the aces one by one.

Maikel was the right hand man of Florencio Álvarez, the most important Chavista leader in Nueva Esparta. He had met him during his days as a hooded protester at university and thanks to the absolute trust that Álvarez gave him, he managed to get put in charge of logistics for the opening ceremony of Banco del Tesoro that Chávez was due to attend on September 9. Maikel was planning on ruining the party with the assassination of the national leader.

He sipped his coffee and without paying much attention to Rodrigo, who had started a lecture in favor of Venezuelan desserts, he went over to the laptop and opened it. Rodrigo immediately went quiet and sat down in front of one of them. Maikel had already started typing on the other. After a minute, Maikel looked expectantly at Rodrigo, who looked back at him, agreeing with a slightsmile.

The following appeared on both screens: A column on the left of the internet browser showed the subtitle in vertical letters, "*private chat room Los intrépidos*" followed by the names Rodrigo and Maikel, both with a green button at their side, and one for Alfredo, whose button was red. At the beginning of the page was the date: September 5, 2007. On the right of the page was a bigger column with the following words: *We are currently recording IP addresses of all users*. Underneath: *Joined: Maikel has joined this chat room*. And underneath that: *Joined: Rodrigo has joined this chat room*.

They both paused with their eyes still fixed on their respective screens. For security reasons, they considered this ritual rich in paraphernalia very important and they took it very seriously. The whole picture was a caricature since Maikel's face had lost all traces of tiredness and his eyes did not seem to be bothering him. Rodrigo seemed even more jovial than five minutes before, as if connecting to the computer had taken place in his mind. They were now two boys trapped by adrenaline, fuelled by imminent danger and Hollywood influences. But although they were amateurs, what they were acting out was no cowboy and Indians fantasy. Alfredo was joining them to put the finishing touches to a plan, audacious in its simplicity and scale of its objective, and which he had masterminded. He was also the owner of the penthouse which was the venue for their meeting and where Rodrigo was staying.

Alfredo's button turned green and in the right hand column appeared: *Joined*: Alfredo *has joined this chat.* Immediately, the dark blue words began to flow while the only sound was the tapping of keys and the last hurried sips of Maikel finishing his coffee.

—Alfredo: What else?

—Rodrigo: What's up, Alfredo?

—Maikel: What's new, chamo? Look, *Rosa María* is all ready. It has the same operating system as the one we tested a month ago, but three times bigger. Of course, I can even test it on the day, no problem. The tricky bit is planting it. I've found out as much as possible about security, but well… I think they're filming inside. Like I said, I don't want to take any risks. Trying to put a short-range bomb under a table is fucking difficult. So I decided on a bomb in a book. I'll take it with me in the morning. I'll hide it there somewhere and as the detonator has a delay of three minutes, I'll activate it when Chávez is nearby. Whatever, like I said, whoever is inside dies… that's it. No worries.

—Alfredo: Ok. Remember, Maikel, history will say we did the right thing. This is the only way. We're not cowards, just realistic. I've already opened a separate bank account for you. I'll mail the debit card to your postal box this week. Now, let's go over the plan:

In the morning, you go to help with the last minute preparations with Chávez's people, as you already arranged with them. I'm asking you again, for Christ's sake. Are you sure no onesuspects?

You take the bomb in the morning. Or have you decided to take it withyou later?

—Maikel: Believe me, they don't suspect a thing.

—Maikel: I'm going to take it with me. Those guys totally fucking trust me, no problem. If they catch me, they catch me. Who knows? Those fucking gunmen from Puente Llaguno shot a load of innocent people on film. Chávez turned them into heroes[22].

—Alfredo: 3. Rodrigo will have the motorcycle ready in the opposite street... If you make it to the bike in one piece, you've cracked it, Maikel. Ah, and don't forget to call Rodrigo when you hear the explosion so that he knows it worked. Rodrigo, then you call me too.

—Alfredo: 4. From there, Maikel, you go to the room that's rented in barrio Bella Vista. You've checked the way twice already, right? In the barrio, you shave off your moustache, you dye your hair, you change, you take the car and you get the hell out to the beach. I've already given instructions to the captain of the boat. I paid him well but he knows nothing. By the way, it's not in his interest to say a *word,* because he's got his own racket in the Caribbean. All he needs to know is that you're a rich friend of mine who's buying the boat, and you live in Grenada. This guy is made up, because he had to go there anyway to deal with some stuff, which I know *nothing* about, of course.

Passports are all ready. Then you go to Aruba. You wait till the next day to fly to Amsterdam. The main thing is to get out of Venezuelan water.

—Alfredo: Rodrigo, you fly the day before. You go Porlamar-Caracas, Caracas- Madrid. Maikel will call you from Amsterdam to confirm about JC. It's a Spanish truck firm which takes fruit to the rest of Europe. They'll take Maikel as an extra

---

[22] On April 11th 2002, during the coup against Chávez, a video captured a group of Chavistas firing from the Puente Llaguno bridge at a march against the president with the participation of over 600,000 people. 19 people were killed. The aggressors were never jailed and President Chávez called them heroes.

driver, and if it's a hassle, they'll take him in the back of the truck to Spain. By the way, I'll send the money and everything, and the tickets. Don't forget the list I sent you. Don't leave anything behind, tickets, your real passports and checks, the cards…

—Rodrigo: I already told you. I'm not repeating myself. I'm not going without Maikel.

—Maikel: Alfredo, I've had this bullshit from Rodrigo for 3 days now. I agree with you. He shouldn't stay here. He's not helping, in fact, he's in the way.

—Alfredo: Rodrigo, don't be so stubborn.

—Rodrigo: No. I made it clear from the beginning. We're together in this. I'm not leaving Maikel. I'll wait for him in the Bella Vista bar. El Corsario. It's a small hole, full of whores from morning on. I'll wait for him there and we go together to the boat. I think it looks better to the captain and coastal guard if we see one. Maybe it's worth paying some whores and taking them to the port. Maikel will be very nervous. Someone who can think clearly needs to be there.

—Alfredo: Rodrigo, the tricky bit for Maikel is getting to the barrio. The rest is easy. Don't be stupid. You're being a pain in the ass.

—Maikel: Told you.

The conversation went on for another half an hour. The keys sounded like a tropical downpour on an aluminum roof. It was impossible to convince the Gallego. Maikel felt completely frustrated by his attitude, but he refrained from making any more comments.

CHAPTER 28

From: piruggia@uchicago.edu
Subject: Re: Tickets
Date: September 6, 2007 8:50:29 PM CDT
To: cervantes2008@gmail.com

Rodrigo,

Everything is ready. Call the travel agency at the number I gave you and ask for Claudia. She has everything.

Like I said pana, I don't know why you're being so stubborn. Leave Maikel, he'll manage on his own. He agrees too, there's no point you waiting. It's better if you leave the day before. Waiting in a bar is something you'd do in Galicia.

Anything you think of, or if you have a problem getting the passport or whatever, call me straight away. I wasn't sure so I bought you another ticket to Mexico on the internet just in case. You could fly to Monterrey if needed, with a stopover in the capital. Then you get a car. I've paid the money into the account. You have the number, right?

Brother, I love you 100%. Good luck,
Alfredo

CHAPTER 29

September 9, 2007

The strong gust of wind that had awoken on the afternoon of September 8 suddenly died down very early the next day, after sweeping away cans, beer bottles, empty boxes, cigarette ends, chip packets, papers and a canopy or two from Igualdad street in Porlamar.

Scores of locals were preparing to welcome Hugo Chávez, who had arrived from Caracas to give his backing to Banco del Tesoro and to greet the people from Margarita Island. This banking institution was destined to award different kinds of credits to families in need. The bank had been criticized for taking over important tasks from Banco Central de Venezuela, such as the administration of treasury accounts, giving total control of the national treasury to the executive powers. Private banks were alarmed as at least 25% of their deposits were transferred to the new institution to belong to the government. Chávez's agenda boiled down to cutting a ribbon and recording a presidential greeting.[23]

Chávez would not be spending more time than necessary in Porlamar, the main city of Margarita Island, but this still

---

[23] The first Banco del Tesoro was opened in 2005

meant the mobilization of his inner circle from Caracas, a security team consisting of personal bodyguards. Agents from the secret service and armed forces had also just landed at Santiago Mariño airport.

Rodrigo and Maikel knew about the visit thanks to Maikel who, infiltrated into the extreme Chavista branch in the state of Nueva Esparta, had extracted valuable information from a one-night stand, during breakfast in bed in a five-star hotel, after an inebriated night of 15-year old Scotch and bodily fluids. Luna María, owner of a deep voice which served her to an advantage in her political leadership, confided the secret to him in the same way that she had given him her whole body; all of it, naked and draped in risk and complicity.

It was barely seven o'clock this bright morning. The security ropes had not been put in place yet and the floorboards in the bank were being removed. Impeded by the oblique thrashing of the first September tornado, workers had stayed at home the day before, threatened by rain that never came. Everything had to be done today, because even the placards signs tied to lampposts with wire showed the antipatriotic effects of the wind.

Maikel and Rodrigo, former Chavistas and former classmates at the School of Arts and Literature, were in a diner near the apartment where they had spent the night. The inept ventilators insisted on playing their irritating dirge, like a violin played by a young boy in his first lesson. The tables were held up by aluminum legs, many supported by improvisations of empty cigarette packets, napkins and matchboxes. Crusty salt deposits and the remains of an inefficient wipe with a sponge covered the top of the cheap formica.

With his long, bony hands, Maikel took the beef arepa that he had just been served. Rodrigo just ordered a coffee since on arriving at the diner, he knew his stomach could not withstand any solid food. An hour before, his optimism had impelled him to tell Maikel that an arduous day lay ahead of them and that breakfast would be the last thing they shared under such conditions. Later, everything would run smoothly: tomorrow, the day after or perhaps in a month, when things had calmed down, the future they deserved would appear. However, Rodrigo's optimism started to dissolve as soon as they left the apartment. He was already in complete distress when the owner of the diner, with messy hair and wearing espadrilles came over to their outside table on the uneven concrete of the terrace, to take his only clients' order.

Maikel ate with huge bites, with his back bent and his shoulders hunched forwards, as if he feared that someone would pull his hidden prey from his large hands. As he ate, his mouth produced a rhythmical smacking which stopped as soon as the right side of his jaw started grinding the food down. At this moment, a vein became visible on the right of his forehead, just above his ear. The muscles of his temple and cheek throbbed in unison, as if they were part of a huge heart irrigated exclusively by the untamed, prominent vein.

Rodrigo sipped his coffee slowly, trying to distract his gaze with the beach landscape painted on the wall, the mandarins arranged on the counter and the crooked chair he was sitting on, but it was all useless. The vein that climbed up from Maikel's throat up over his ear seemed to have him hypnotized.

After the last bite, Maikel wiped his glistening mouth with a paper napkin and got up with a decisive air. Rodrigo imitated him out of inertia, but once standing he did not know what to do, and he gave him a hesitant hug. Then he put his hand in his pocket to look for his wallet. While opening it, he told himself that he had no reservations and that the dice was already cast. But waves of panic and the voice of good sense coursed through his mind like flashes of an automatic camera that shot off by themselves, without pausing, totally out of control.

As they separated, Rodrigo's forced smile acted like a detonator on Maikel's nervous system.

"What the fuck, you faggot!" he said, trying to hide the anger that Rodrigo's attitude stirred in him.

"Chill, if everything goes to plan, I'll see you at two o'clock, Gallego. Don't blub now. I'll see you then, I'm sure, pana."

Maikel made a half turn and began to move very slowly, with a thug's swagger that had earned him so much respect as a hooded protester. Then he walked quickly around the bend to where his car was parked, followed by Rodrigo's gaze.

CHAPTER 30

September 9, 2007

Maikel Salgado was no ordinary man. At moments like these, his face showed the marks of the world in which he had grown up: a sick brother who he cared for most of the day, two step-fathers who used him as their favorite punching bag for not being humble enough, and a mother who spent her time dodging blows from her current alcoholic partner at the time, bearing his children and giving him almost all the salary she earned as a cook.

Maikel's mother was an extremely reserved woman although capable of vehemence if she was given the opportunity to express it, and was devoted to her children as well as to the men she paired up with. It was she who had taught him the affection that on rare occasions Maikel showed towards a few friends, also his attachment to his siblings, for whom he would have given his life.

More than his mother's attitude and words, Maikel's intuition told him that he was her favorite, although in her meek-ness, she demanded a lot of him, because after all Maikel was the eldest. Every night, no matter how tired she was, she went to the room he shared with Juan, the sick child, to tuck them in and bless them. If the rest of the family were already asleep,

Anselma would rock Maikel, telling him fantastical stories, full of heroes who found treasure after destroying bands of criminals and who challenged the devil himself to a singing duel. At the age of ten, during the period of the hardest beatings, Maikel would wake up in the morning, wishing for night to come soon.

He got into university thanks to one of those sporadic father figures who appeared when they moved from the village of Cúpira to a miserable Caracas barrio in the Petare area, in search of elusive urban riches. Rotundo Manrique was under the impression that it was highly educational to tie Maikel to the foul-smelling toilet bowl, brimming with dark water, until he had learnt his daily lessons. One afternoon, full of rage and cheap anisette, he put a cigarette out on Maikel's chest for refusing to learn his nine times table.

"I'm fucking out of here, bitch. I can't stand your crap anymore or those four losers you call your children." That was how Rotundo announced his departure when he finally left the damp gloomy hovel, with cracked walls and an improvised roof riddled with leaks. Maikel saw the look of repulsion that his last stepfather aimed at him and Juan, before he disappeared forever into the Petare night.

Out of pride, to prove wrong the ghostly memory that terrorized him so much, Maikel decided that studying was the only way out of his misery. In this environment, where 14-year old kids were already learning to smoke, sniff glue and hold a pistol, he ended up the exception, a strange creature.

In the Universidad Central, he became friends with Carmen, an intelligent, somewhat shy girl, who on becoming Rodrigo's girlfriend shattered the only romantic dream that Maikel had harbored in his life. Rodrigo was not a bad guy, on the contrary, he quickly accepted the fondness that Carmen had for Maikel and after a while of sharing books, lunches and conversations with the pair, Maikel accepted that he was not immune to Rodrigo's ingenuity or to the affection he showed him.

Through them, he also met Alfredo and Manuel, characters from another world that he could only imagine or watch on soap operas as a child. It was a world of holidays and mansions with swimming pools and gigantic gardens, full of flowers, guavas and mango trees. Alfredo and Manuel had welcomed him with open arms and now they were his accomplices.

On the morning of September 9, with a bomb hidden inside a book, Maikel smiled as he imagined the reactions of his work colleagues and the people of Margarita island to the explosion: dozens of people, their faces frozen with fear and astonishment, fleeing in a stampede through the tunnels of his mind, while a huge screen began to grow to excessive proportions in the cold, dark background of the collective panic. It was the screen of a computer connected to theinternet:

Megaresistence.com …the people's hero, the key man of our times.

He laughed at the thought that if he failed and was captured, Chávez would call him the leader of an attempted coup, a betrayer and a pro-Yankee while the opposition, anxious to match up to his insults, would suggest here and there that the attack was nothing more than an conspiracy hatched by the president and carried out by one of his most evil puppets.

He was not afraid. His days as a hooded protester had hardened the calluses that he had cultivated during his childhood. Grasping the book tightly, he walked into the branch of the bank and glanced around in search of his bosses, recently arrived from Caracas. The large blue bag that he had bought a week before was perfect because it matched his best polyester pants and it would help to camouflage the book, which at that moment was tucked under his left arm.

With an agile step his attentive eyes, he searched until he found the security coordinator.

"Salgado," said the latter to Maikel, impatiently. "Go have a look at the communication systems. Then go and calm down the producer. One of the cameramen got sick yesterday and this morning they managed to get another one with a Hollywood complex. He's fucking up the lights and other stuff. Make sure he's just some jerk and not a professional hit man."

As he made his way toward the cameras, Maikel began to give instructions through a walkie-talkie he was carrying in his right hand. With his left, he gently pressed the book, protecting it from the people hurrying back and forth. He prayed that there were no literary buffs among the guests.

It took him more than ten minutes to skirt around the swarms of activity and approach the producer of *"Hello Mr. President,"* a TV chat show in which Hugo Chávez appeared every Sunday.

Maikel managed to introduce himself and asked the producer two questions in his ear. The producer replied with brief answers, interspersed with instructions to his team and suspicious looks at the new cameraman, who at that moment was complaining about the microphones with melodramatic gestures.

Maikel was not worried about the location's security. He knew that some of the waiters, on standby to serve drinks on the left hand side of the bank, and two TV technicians were intelligence agents. Anyway, the real problem for them was not inside the bank, but the stretch that the president would cover from the armored vehicle to the entrance.

The five counters were situated on the right hand side. Behind their windows were some desks and a door which led to the back section of the bank, where the safe bank manager's office was probably located. On the other side, a bar and two tables with bottles and crystal temporarily occupied the space of the large flower pot, which would occupy the entrance of the bank the following Monday. The flower pot, now resting right in the corner of the bank, next to the bar, was a plastic container wedged perfectly into a rectangular structure made with light wooden planks and metallic spikes. Its new and original design, combined with the radiant greenery of the healthy palm plant, presented a contrast to the old cement pots, dry earth and dying plants that usually stood in banks up and down the country, perhaps to warn clients that everything in life was transitory, even banks.

On the left wall, where the bar and the flower pot were lined up, emerged a black formica counter where the bank's customers would fill out forms for withdrawals, transfers and deposits, from the following Monday onwards. For more complicated transactions, they would have to go to the back of the bank, to two black formica and metal desks facing the door of the bank. Today there was only one, totally empty except for two microphones, which were being adjusted.

Most of the space that the other desk would occupy next Monday was now invaded by the elegant window box. Camera number 2 was filming laterally to define the president's face between the somber desk and the exuberant tropical greenery. The lamps, cameras and the chair where the director of "*Hello Mr. President*" would sit formed a wall which isolated the improvised stage from theguests.

"He's already here. The President is here!"

The preparations for the broadcast lasted almost two hours. Maikel had time to check communications again, chat about boxing, have coffee and see close-up, mixing with guests, that robust man who he had admired in times gone by and who he now loathed. The more he watched him, the more vividly he conjured up the faces of Carmen and his mother in his memory. They would both have approved of what he was doing.

At some point, he noticed that the make-up artist had entered the counter area to go to the bank manager's office, where Chávez had taken refuge with his bodyguards. The tiny make-up artist received a sonorous cackle when the door opened.

Maikel knew that in twenty minutes, the biggest function in Venezuela's contemporary history would begin. Before sitting at the immaculate desk, the President and the director would go into the street, where they would film him cutting the ribbon. After them would come the guests, complacent, smiling and half inebriated. Holding the walkie-talkie to his mouth and pretending to have a conversation with someone, Maikel went up to the plant pot like a detective searching for clues. Before slipping the book into the dense vegetation, one last glance at the bar area convinced him that the few agents still left in the bank were entertaining each other, chatting.

As he left, he crossed the street slowly, kicked an empty beer can and stopped opposite the bank, looking around, as if he were looking for traces of conspiracy. His pulse had started to accelerate uncontrollably. He pulled out the light blue handkerchief from his polyester plants to dry his face, now damp and shining due to the heat and fear. Then he put his hand in the right hand pocket of his new jacket and pressed the detonator without bothering to check the little red light on the device which was flickering. In three minutes, everything would change forever.

CHAPTER 31

September 9, 2007

Maikel went up to the motorcycle that was waiting for him less than 100 yards from the bank. It was a Kawasaki Ninja 250 which Rodrigo had left for him, opposite a small park.

He greeted the last security officer with a friendly gesture, and the man, short and slim, and who looked like a cattle herder, returned his wave with hardly a second glance. As he reached the bike, he looked around him to be sure no one was following him.

Maikel's hands were still trembling. He was impatient to get away.

He took the keys that Rodrigo had given him out of his pocket and unlocked the front wheel and black helmet that he put on before starting the engine.

If he had stayed there two minutes longer, perhaps he would have seen the two men from Chávez's personal security team that were following him, probably out of instinct, thinking that Maikel might be on to something and had decided to investigate on his own account to gain credit. Afraid of being second rate, they desperately wanted to be ahead of every tiny detail, including what was going on in the deserted streets around the bank. The very idea that Chávez could humiliate them in public for incompetence, as he did with his ministers on public television, even led them to keep watch on the island's security team.

When they saw him starting the motorcycle, they looked at each other, wondering why Salgado had abandoned the opening ceremony and was riding a motorcycle,whereas they had seen him arrive by cab earlier that morning. They could not recall anything about a motorcycle in the report they had read about thisagent.

"Martínez reporting to base. Do you read me? Over." "Yep, Martínez, what's up?"

"Listen, Camacho, we're a hundred and twenty yards from the bank. The head of operative security, I think his name's Salgado, has just left the bank suspiciously. He's in a hurry and now he's leaving the square on a green motorcycle which doesn't appear on his report. He's heading north. Over."

"I got you, Martínez. Follow him for a while, although it's probably nothing.

Everything's fine here. Over."

"By the way, Camacho, if Garcia's men are taking over to-night, we're thinking of going to the beach. We have a double key, Pampero rum and three Margaritan girls, brother. You're invited. Over and out."

Two minutes and forty seconds after Maikel activated the detonator, the agents were dreaming of a night by the beach that would free them from the tension and high temperatures of the day. They were going northwards and had already caught sight of Maikel.

"So, Martínez," said López from the back of the car. "You know, we're known for being the unbeaten domino champs even outside of Caracas. But I think we'll have to be careful when we're moving the piec…"

Maikel heard an explosion and checked his watch to see if the bomb had gone off on time. The blast seemed too weak or maybe that was just his impression. For a moment, he had to remember that he was wearing a helmet and his feet were on the motorcycle pedals. He laughed at his own fears. If only he had his feet on the ground and had felt the last vibrations of the device that had finished with Chávez.

"Shit, López, that was an explosion, chico! Base, base! Do you read me? Over.

Step on the gas, blind man, this smells of fish and Salgado is the fisherman. Base, base, I repeat, base! Do you copy? Over."

The blast which went off less than a mile away liberated the dreams that Maikel had been carrying in his heart for so long. Euphoria building up in him, he sped up the motorcycle to feel the breeze blowing intensely on his face, as if only the strong friction of the wind could confirm the reality of what had happened. He should have called Rodrigo to tell him the bomb had been a success, but in his emotional state, he completely forgot. He breathed deeply, inhaling the salt from the sea, already nearby and tried to calm himself to focus on the last stage of the plan: he had to leave the motorcycle one block from the building and go up to the apartment rented on the internet through a phony import company; then he would dye his hair blonde and change clothes. The van would then come, he would meet Rodrigo and a little later, the motor boat would take him to Aruba. From there, he would fly to Spain. Finally, he would end up sitting on a café terrace in Madrid somewhere with scores of glasses full of sangría to toast with Rodrigo. He did not go through the plan, rather he visualized it, he imagined it with such deep ecstasy that he even managed to touch the minute pieces of fruit lingering in his mouth with the tip of his tongue after the first swig.

Maikel had already crossed the border of the poor, cruel world which he had been born into. Now he only looked ahead, without realizing that the screeching of tires he heard were not only his.

While he accelerated to a suicidal speed, he mentally visited his brother Juan in hospital, exactly the day he was let out, after the operation on his spine had been a thorough success. Maikel imagined Juan smiling, walking towards him with just a pair of crutches. He also saw himself giving a lecture to a group of students, young men and women that looked like Carmen and the few noble classmates he had known in the School of Arts and Literature. They listened to him intently, interrupting when they had questions. He replied to them patiently, reading them excerpts of novels by Guillermo Meneses, Arturo Uslar Pietri, Miguel Otero Silva…Surrounded by friends and family, he also danced a bachata with a dark-haired girl in a fuchsia pink suit, wearing a yellow rose in her hair. The girl looked at him with twinkling eyes which promised him infinite pleasures.

Finally, with the last push on the accelerator, he enjoyed the company of many friends, all sitting in his living room with a beer in their hands, listening to him describe the best hit of Omar Vizquel, number 23 of the Caracas baseball team. Maikel had exchanged greetings with him on the two occasions that he had worked as a security guard at the university stadium.

He stopped the bike so suddenly that he almost went flying into the gaunt man resting on the steps of the small shop called "El Tigre." The man hardly moved enough to lift his bare feet to the side to make way for the young man who had just jumped off the motorcycle and was heading west. Maikel began to walk, covering his eyes with his right hand as the sun was already dazzlingly bright. Then everything came crashing down.

"Stop right there, Salgado. Stop, chico, or I'll blast you away! This is the President's personal security guard."

The warning shot that flew into the air was for Maikel like a ton weight falling on his shoulders. His legs buckled and his eyes, about to stream due to the sun's reflection, stopped him from seeing the outlines that defined the street, the cars parked to the left and the building he was heading to. Everything turned strangely white and hazy, even the sun, which was no longer yellow or round like a plate. Still, he made an extreme effort to ask his heart to stop beating wildly. After all, they had no evidence againsthim.

This moment of lucidity was swept away by a wave of panic that did not belong to Maikel, but to the body holding him up, and that now broke into a run, without asking his permission. This time a clean bullet into his abdomen stopped him in his tracks. He felt a blaze of fire rise up his spine until it reached his brain.

Leaning on his elbow and his left forearm, he tried to get up but he could not feel his legs anymore. He fell on his back to see the deep blue Margarita island sky, convinced that Chávez was dead. In this position he began to dream again.

CHAPTER 32

September 9, 2007

Rodrigo's index finger was busy playing with the only cube of ice floating in his glass. Although it was quite small, it was not melting as fast as the other three, now gone. Its unexplainable endurance left it alone at the mercy of the dirty, trembling finger that pushed it to the depths of the yellowing Cuba Libre.

Sometimes the game was different and instead of pushing it to the bottom, the finger trapped the slippery cube against the side of the glass. Engrossed, Rodrigo left his task as jailor to concentrate on the surface of the liquid, which instantly registered the tidal wave caused by the techno merengue.

Just like the solitary ice cube, the ups and downs of this song the jukebox had played three times in less than an hour were also prisoners. Sometimes Rodrigo tried to follow the piano lament, crushed by the unbearable percussion dominating the tune and finally let its judgment drop: Shit! There was no democracy in this merengue! And if it was a question of prisoners, at least the melting ice cube would destroy the chemical balance of the Cuba Libre with its own demise. Even drunkards would be able to tell. But no one there noticed the melodic prison, no one.

Proof enough was a glance at the few couples who were dancing at this time of day, defying the asphyxiating heat of the bar. In the half-darkness, the women shook their flesh mechanically, with their thoughts fixed on the bolivars they would earn that afternoon while the men surrounded them, their minds befuddled by liquor and lust.

It was enough to turn around and watch them, although this was only to distract Rodrigo from his anguish. But Rodrigo didn't try, fearing that the view would make him run into the street, looking for light and oxygen. With his elbows leaning on the bar, he listened patiently to the same techno merengue and he prayed to heaven for the boleros to start. Then maybe that would calm down the passing arms, shoulders and hands that kept rubbing him as if he were a piece of furniture, or the loud shouts by his ear, exchanging money for cheap liquor.

Immune to the attacks, Rodrigo checked his cell phone for the hundredth time. His left hand hid it protectively between his legs, totally ignorant of the prisoner game that his right hand was playing. Maikel had agreed to call him when the bomb went off and meet him around two in the afternoon. Now it was past four, and there was no sign of life from him. Full of anxiety and although it was not in the plan, he began to drink rum as if it were water. Should he call Alfredo? Or perhaps fly back to Caracas? He didn't know what to do. As he played with the ice cube, he realized that not one of them had considered the horrible possibility that was slowly dawning on him, his mind becoming hazier andhazier.

Four o'clock in the afternoon and Maikel has not called or appeared in this bullshit bar, so small and hot that a handful of people were enough to inundate it with humid sweat, reeking of dirty clothes and patchouli. Now, with his eyes fixed on the trembling surface of the rum, he envisioned being left terribly alone as well as the consequences of this childish plan, incredibly foolish, even for the most stupid of coup leaders. If only Maikel would appear...

Rigid, trying to concentrate and exerting his weak pulse on the only ice cube left swimming in the rum, Rodrigo felt a light wandering hand rest on his shoulder. Patchouli filled the air and the unexpected caress freed the ice cube that Rodrigo was holding prisoner. Suddenly, he was overcome by the effects of the long hours he had been awake, the futile wait and every single shout, push and shove he had endured in that barstool at the disgusting bar's dirty black counter.

Without thinking and without even looking into the eyes of the ill-timed person, a reflex that came from the deepest part of his guts or from his overloaded brain made Rodrigo push the human lump with all the strength his drunkenness allowed him, like a bull at the end of a fight, wounded and desperate.

CHAPTER 33

September 10, 2007

"Alfredo, it's Manuel. Please, pick up the phone, chamo. They've killed Maikel, pana. He's dead!" As he spoke, the desperation grew in his voice as he heard no answer from his friend on the other end of the line.

"You won't believe it, but Maikel planted a bomb to kill Chávez in a bank in Margarita. Looks like the bomb failed and people were injured. But no one died. They killed Maikel in some barrio, I don't know, Bella Vista I think it's called. The police shot him as he was running away. I can't find Rodrigo anywhere. What if he's caught up in this mess? His mother told me he went to Maracay. What's he doing in Maracay? I'm begging you, pana, call me back."

From time to time, Alfredo rested his head on the steering wheel of the Mercedes and sometimes held it backwards, leaning back completely in his seat, but always with the same worried face. He had listened to the third repetitive message from Manuel and he couldn't make up his mind whether to call him or not.

Alfredo left the engine of the Mercedes running, even though he had been in the University of Chicago hospital parking lot for a long while. Very early in the morning, he had started to call Rodrigo with a throwaway phone so that no one could trace his call.

On CNN, they had also said that it was likely that Maikel had acted alone. But he could not risk it, especially as Rodrigo was still missing. What if they had taken him captive and were now interrogating him?

He probably did not follow the instructions and went to the bank after Maikel.

What the hell, Rodrigo, what a stubborn man!

It was one of those fall mornings capable of turning the University of Chicago into a beautiful place. The sun caressed the numerous ochres and oranges of the fallen leaves and the ones that still hung on the trees would soon join their brothers. When that happened, several city trucks would come to take them away and pulverize the huge autumnal carpet that blocked the passage. Then there would only be cold winter in Chicago.

Alfredo thought he should look for a job further to the south or perhaps on the Pacific coast. Anything would be better than enduring the winds that blew from the great lakes, attacking his core. That was what he had to do...if Rodrigo was safe or managed to keep quiet.

Vehicles had already begun to fill the parking lot, too small for the growing number of visitors the hospital received lately. In less than half an hour, all the spaces would be full and the drivers would have to park on the edge of the sidewalk, risking a fine. From the comfortable seat of the Mercedes, Alfredo watched the procession of men and women entering the main door of the building. Some were wearing white overalls and carried thermos flasks, others were in groups, some with children, others alone and pensive.

Almost all of them, even those more engrossed in their worries, looked with curiosity at the man in the Mercedes when they reached the hospital door. The engine was still running, contaminating the morning air of this beautiful fall day. Alfredo looked at them too, scrutinizing their behavior as if they were laboratory rats. He detected the same furtive look in all of them. That brief moment of curiosity in which they turned to look at him, their attention pulling them quickly back to their own problems and obligations. Alfredo thought that even if he had been dressed as a clown, he would not be able to attract their interest any more than now. Despite the rejection that he experienced from these people's mechanical attitude, he would have given his life to be one of them, to have their minds occupied by a pending job, a sick child or an old mother dying in hospital. Anything would have been better than the weight that had begun to burden his shoulders in the early hours of the morning. Maikel was already dead and there was no way to turn back the clock.

He grabbed his cell phone again but sat staring at it in a daze, as if he had seen it for the first time. "Alfredo, being the eldest is a big responsibility, because the youngest ones will follow you. Remember that." Those were the words of Nonno the first time he looked at Alfredo severely, disapproving of his behavior for having locked one of his little cousins in the garage of his house.

Four second cousins had come from the west of Venezuela to visit them one weekend. One girl and three boys. The youngest, Ricardo, was an unbearable child who had brought a new computer game with him, and refused to share. Alfredo tried to convince him many times that the others should have a turn. He would have left him alone, but the child got angry and started hitting his sister, the only one apart from Paolo who was not interested in the new video game.

Alfredo wanted to teach him a lesson. So he ended up locking him in the garage, very dark and humid, full of dusty boxes, and let him scream there for a while, until Nonno went to see what was going on. When he got out, Ricardo started showing signs of the first of many asthma attacks.

Alfredo tried to explain to Nonno what had happened, but he refused to listen. "You are the eldest, practically a man," he said, angrily to Alfredo, not yet eleven years old. "I want you to think hard about what you are going to tell me. Did you lock him up because he behaved badly or because he made you angry? Have a good think about what you're going to say, Alfredo."

According to the doctors, the asthma attacks that Ricardo started suffering since that day were caused by an endless number of allergies and of course, no one thought of blaming Alfredo and the incident was soon forgotten. But very early that morning, he heard Nonno's voice again, as clearly as he had when he was eleven. And now the image of Maikel's face smiling at him in their favorite restaurant would not leave him.

Alfredo spent all morning sitting in the Mercedes, with the engine running and with his hospital pager beeping constantly. Although he tried several times, he could not bring himself to call Manuel.

Newsflash! A bomb exploded this morning at the headquarters of Banco del Tesoro in Porlamar where President Chávez was attending the bank's opening ceremony. Several people were injured, including a camera operator from the national Venezuelan television channel who was adjusting the spotlights close to where the bomb went off.

The person responsible for the attack was shot dead after police located him in Bella Vista. The man in question, 38-year old Maikel Salgado, worked for the government on Margarita Island. It is believed that Salgado acted alone using a defective homemade bomb that failed to fully detonate. Officials and agents who worked with Salgado have confirmed that he had experience withexplosives.

The green fly had been gone from his sight for a while and light penetrating through the barred skylight announced to Rodrigo that it was already morning. The radio message was stuck in his head like one of those progressive rock songs in which the singer repeats a psychedelic phrase again and again until it is interrupted by musical instruments.

"The liquor worn off now, treasure?"

Rodrigo finally got up. As he did so, he did not dare meet the eyes of the prison guard but as he stretched his pants which had stuck to his buttocks and the back of his thighs, he saw the man's face out of the corner of his eye and thought he looked more bored than interested in his prisoner.

"Don't you think you're too old for fightin' in bars?" The police officer spoke at a hundred miles an hour but moved at ten, typical Margarita Island style. "C'mon, get outta here and go home to sleep. And don't let me see you around here again so goddamned loaded, d'ya hear? And especially not hitting a lady."

"No, Sir. Absolutely not," replied Rodrigo, who felt ashamed as he remembered that he had pushed a woman. "I didn't know what I was doing, it was a stupid reaction. But look, she wasn't a lady, she was a prostitute."

"Shut up, chico and get outta here!"

Rodrigo obeyed and immediately left the cell. But he could not leave the jail until he found out what had really happened to Hugo Chávez and when he reached the room, he slipped out the question as nonchalantly as he could.

"Could you tell me what they said on the radio?

"Here we go. Don't leave without signing here," said the officer, taking no notice of Rodrigo and looking for the form underneath his newspaper.

"Look, sir. What they said on the radio. What happened with Chávez?" "Jeez, get outta here. Don't jerk around with me, chico!"

Without insisting, Rodrigo spun around in the direction of the exit. But when he opened the door of the room where the policeman was sitting again, listening to a folk tune, the doubt and anxiety of the last few hours emerged with more strength and his legs began to tremble. A narrow and badly-lit passageway opened up before him and Rodrigo thought that someone would be waiting at the end of the tunnel, someone who knew about his conspiracy, a Bolivarian intelligence agent or perhaps one of Chávez' personal security guards would arrest and torture him. He was sure of it.

Nevertheless, he began to walk. As the soles of his shoes were covered in the sticky mess from the cell where he had spent the last twenty-four hours, each step made a smacking sound which scandalously announced his presence in the deserted corridor, as poorly lit as the cells. Rodrigo fixed his eyes on the polished cement and the dirty green walls, not daring to lift his head, distracting his thoughts with weak and hopeful arguments. Who would suspect a drunkard of being an accomplice in the bombing?

At the end of the claustrophobic passageway, he came to the last of the light bulbs and five small steps which led him to the exit of the police station. When he finally faced the double door of eroded metal, he saw a sign which said, "Block number 3." Just before opening it, he wondered if he would ever see his son Emilio again, realizing that he had not thought about him since he had decided to follow Alfredo's plan.

When he opened the door, he closed his eyes, expecting the policeman's morbid joke to end. They would be there, dressed in dark civilian suits, or in green uniforms with red berets, or a mob of henchmen ready to stone him. But all that was waiting for him was the warm, clean morning air and the intense Margarita sunlight. There was nothing or no one else. Not even the shadow of a stray dog could be seen along the street which seemed to end in a plot of wasteland, full of trash and rusted cars. He inhaled deeply several times until he felt the air filling his stiff muscles with energy and clearing his mind. He started to walk aimlessly, turning around every so often and quickeninghis step, staying close to the doors that he passed, checking the ones that were open, and thinking that such a blessing could not be real.

After walking for less than an hour, and sure that no one was following him, he found a patch of green grass on the crossroads of two deserted streets. There he saw the calabash tree which seemed to beckon to him, happily showing off its huge string of future maracas. No tree had ever seemed so alive to him. He let himself fall to the ground, under its shade, just when a gust of wind shook its head and the maracas of the calabash quivered. Lying on his back totally exhausted, he heard chatter and raising his eyes, he saw three gray-breasted parakeets playing at the top of the tree.

An instant later and without understanding why, he stood up and started running down the street, looking for the town center. While he ran, tears began to fill his eyes. He continued running, crying and wiping the tears with the back of his hands until the lack of oxygen obliged him to stop. Then he started desperately thinking of a plan: Call Alfredo? Hide? Get out of the country? Explain to Manuel what he had done and hug Emilio, hold him for hours and whole days.

With the thought of Emilio in his mind, he began to walk again and as he sped up again, he realized he did not care anymore about the answer to the question he had asked the policeman. He was frightened and expected the worst, but the reply was no longer of interest to him.

Epilogue
(2008)

August 3, 2008

I

Speech by Hugo Chávez during his television program, *"Hello Mr. President,"* episode 316.[24]

"You remember that railway tunnel, eh, Caracas-Tuy, where they took me to knock down the last stone, to demolish a wall? They told me: No, you can knock it down in five minutes... and do you know the worst thing? No one knew it at the time, but now I'm telling you and I'm laughing: I had colic at the time, I mean, compadre, I had the runs!

*I'm a human being just like any of you, and sometimes people forget that, right?...*I get up on that machine, and I start getting cold sweats, and I whack it, BAM, I didn't hit it in the right place, and I was sweating, and squeezing down there, you know? And that sweating. My God! Again and again. I was almost shitting myself, y'know?

---

[24] Partially and literally taken from the official video archive of the program *"Hello, Mr President,"* episode 316, published on the television program's website: http://alopresidente.gob.ve

I get down, walking really tightly... we were in the middle of the tunnel, and you can imagine, being in that state. On live television! I pass through all the people to see where I can go, to see if I can find a bush or a field around there somewhere, and what I see in front of me is like, a hundred journalists! I was trying to stay focused, thinking, with that helmet on, good God, earth swallow me up! And I said to them, ladies and gentlemen, I've finished, let me pass and something or other... And I see a bus, I get on the bus, I left security behind, no way the security's coming, compadre! And I tell the driver, buddy, just get out of here, and I'll get out somewhere, I don't know... And the cameras were coming after me, compadre; sure, the innocent cameras, they don't know about the drama I'm going through... Then I got there, ahhhhh, what a relief."

II

In the cemetery in the east of Caracas, the sun warmed up the white tombstone surrounded by red roses and daisies. Surprised to see so many flowers, the little girl stopped, letting her mother walk on alone the short way to her father's grave.

She had been trying to work it out for several weeks, and seeing the bed of flowers she resolved to succeed in her mission to read the epithet. Once more she began to join together the words written on the gravestone and finally she could read:

CARMEN: you will know the verses brought to me by loneliness.

The line was from *Platero and I,* the book that Carmen and Rodrigo read together in the botanical gardens during their happiest days. The little girl did not understand the phrase although she thought that a little old lady called Carmen must be resting there, whose many grandchildren had brought her flowers that morning. Satisfied with herself and her discovery, she cheerfully started running to her grandfather's grave.

III

In downtown Caracas, under the reddish lighting of a fetid bar, the small TV set showed Hugo Chávez in the middle of his speech. Rotundo Manrique was cackling with laughter at his leader's wisecracks when suddenly, probably due to an unconscious association, the image of Maikel as a baby in his bitch of a mother's arms came to him. The memory of his angry, defiant little eyes stifled the laughter in his throat.

Mumbling crude comments between swigs of sugar cane liquor, he remembered the countless beatings he had given his stepson back then. Rotundo always knew that nothing good would come out of that boy.

Maikel Salgado's remains lay next to those of his mother, in the rocky earth of a solitary cemetery not far from his birthplace.

IV

Three days later

Manuel was working in his new office, located in the city of Mérida, when he saw on his computer screen that he had just received a new email. Out of tireless habit of reading everything he received, he clicked on the little envelope-shaped icon and the message appeared on the screen. It was Francisco, one of the few people from the Ministry who still remembered him. Manuel smiled as he read the title of the message: "Chávez' continuous diarrhea."

After going online and looking at what Chávez had said the day before on *"Hello Mr. President,"* Manuel slid back his chair and put his feet up on the desk. It was a good place there, looking at the side of the Pico Bolívar mountain and watching the pigeons that stopped on his window sill. There were about five of them that would watch him intently, as the previous weekend he had made the mistake of throwing them a handful of corn. Since then, they had been spying on him around the clock.

He wanted to lower his legs and go back to work, but he felt lethargic and had a few more minutes rest while he thought of Vilma and the marvelous distance that now separated them. Things had been going well in Mérida and he hardly missed life in Caracas. Only Rodrigo had him worried for a while, until he realized that as a good Gallego, he would soon wake up. Rosa had also concerned him, but he managed to drag her with him to the mini kitchen of the small apartment where they both lived in Mérida and he still squabbled with her every morning, as he had when they lived in Caracas.

Rosa had given in to Manuel's demands because her own children seemed to have disappeared off the face of the earth and because Manuel had promised her a plasma TV so that she could carry on watching her Mexican films.

Before returning to the document he was working on, he mailed Rodrigo, sending him the link to Chávez' latest speech. And then he sat still, watching the pigeons at the window, and touching his belly.

He wondered if there were some stables somewhere or a small stud farm where he could get a horse, or rather, a stubborn cinnamon-colored horse which would not complain about carrying a load twenty-five years heavier…

V

… As I said before, I would love to work for you. Revising texts and correcting proofs for your editorial is no effort, it's a dream I have always had, above all here in Bogotá, where I intend to settle

down with my son. You already know what it's like in Caracas and anyway, we love Colombia... Or Spain, or Mexico, or anywhere that is not Venezuela, thought Rodrigo, who was planning what he would say in the interview. If he did not get that job, he would go to work at the gas station belonging to his cousin, Juan José Presas, who lived in a village near Oviedo in Spain.

At that moment, his cell phone beeped, announcing a new email.

"Gallego, don't miss this. Believe me; you haven't seen it all with Chávez. http://www.youtube.com/watch?v=2NPWhqw7jCI"

After looking up the website, Rodrigo began to write to Alfredo with incredible manual skill. He still refused to forget his friend in Chicago, who he had not heard from since Maikel's death.

VI

Alfredo checked his emails after another hectic day at the hospital. When he saw that Rodrigo had written to him, he opened the mail and skimmed through it, hurriedly. "...Well, I've already told you enough and now I have to go, but I'm forwarding you this video that Manuel sent me. You have to see it."

With an impassive expression, Alfredo glanced at the maple trees on the other side of the window. Dusk was falling and the lamp posts threw their white light on the beautiful trees planted around the main entrance of the building.

Alfredo squashed the hamburger wrapper and the box from the fries he had just eaten into a ball which he aimed at the wastepaper basket a couple of yards away.

Then he moved the cursor to the *delete message* box and clicked the mouse.

Acknowledgements

Our thanks go to all those who took on our project as if it were their own, helping us to collect data and take photos of places we wanted to describe.

We would also like to thank the many people who did not let us give up. Thanks to you,

High Treason exists as a narrative and as testimony to many years of essential discovery.

Eternal thanks to all of you.

The authors

About the Authors

Amelia Mondragón (Spain, 1953) is a Literature professor at Howard University (Washington DC). She grew up in Vene-zuela, where she completed her undergraduate studies at The Universidad Central de Venezuela. She earned her doctorate in Latin American literature at the University of Maryland (1986). She has written several critical essays on Central Amer-ican literature and contemporary Hispanic poetry. She has also edited the book *Aesthetic Changes and New Cultural Projects in Central America* (1993). She currently lives in Hyattsville, Maryland. She enjoys swimming and yoga, as well as nature.

Alberto Ambard divides his time between writing and prac-ticing maxillofacial prosthodontics. His short stories have ap-peared in various anthologies. His novel *Dogma, A Red Door And A Birthday* will soon be published by Adelaide Books. In his native Venezuela, he received the José Félix Ribas Medal for his achievements in collegiate and international karate. A de-scendant of French, American, Spanish and Venezuelan fami-lies, he has lived in Caracas, a remote Afro-Caribbean coastal town, the Amazon, Birmingham, AL, and Chicago. Currently, he lives in Portland, OR with his wife and children. You can find him at wwwalbertoambard.com